D0272400

SPECIAL MESSAGE TO READERS

This book is published under the auspices of

THE ULVERSCROFT FOUNDATION

(registered charity No. 264873 UK)

Established in 1972 to provide funds for research, diagnosis and treatment of eye diseases. Examples of contributions made are: —

A Children's Assessment Unit at Moorfield's Hospital, London.

•

Twin operating theatres at the Western Ophthalmic Hospital, London.

•

A Chair of Ophthalmology at the Royal Australian College of Ophthalmologists.

•

The Ulverscroft Children's Eye Unit at the Great Ormond Street Hospital For Sick Children, London.

You can help further the work of the Foundation by making a donation or leaving a legacy. Every contribution, no matter how small, is received with gratitude. Please write for details to:

THE ULVERSCROFT FOUNDATION,
The Green, Bradgate Road, Anstey,
Leicester LE7 7FU, England.
Telephone: (0116) 236 4325

In Australia write to:

THE ULVERSCROFT FOUNDATION,
c/o The Royal Australian and New Zealand College of Ophthalmologists,
94-98 Chalmers Street, Surry Hills,
N.S.W. 2010, Australia

Francis Cottam was born in Southport, Merseyside, in 1957. A full-time journalist, he has lived and worked in London for the last twenty years. His first novel, *The Fire Fighter*, published in 2001, was shortlisted for the W H Smith Literature Award.

HAMER'S WAR

A courageous and dedicated German soldier, Martin Hamer has never questioned the cause for which he fights — until he is seconded to a labour camp in occupied Poland to recover from a war wound. There, Hamer finds himself confronting the evil and horrors of Nazism for the first time. He also finds himself falling in love. As his growing relationship with the enigmatic Julia Smollen, an inmate of the camp, causes mounting tension among prisoners and guards alike, a startling revelation will force him to reassess his troubled past. Hamer will be faced with a heartbreaking choice — and a chance of redemption. A chance which would mean forsaking his rank, reputation and homeland. Is he brave enough to take it?

FRANCIS COTTAM

HAMER'S WAR

Complete and Unabridged

CHARNWOOD
Leicester

First published in Great Britain in 2003 by
Simon & Schuster UK Limited, London

First Charnwood Edition
published 2004
by arrangement with
Simon & Schuster UK Limited, London

This book is a work of fiction. Names, characters, places and incidents are either a product of the author's imagination or are used fictitiously. Any resemblance to actual people, living or dead, is entirely coincidental.

British Library CIP Data

Cottam, Francis, *1957* –
Hamer's war.—Large print ed.—
Charnwood library series
1. Germany. Heer—Officers—Fiction
2. World War, *1939 – 1945*—Prisoners and prisons, German—Fiction
3. Love stories
4. Large type books
I. Title
823.9′2 [F]

ISBN 1–84395–389–7

Published by
F. A. Thorpe (Publishing)
Anstey, Leicestershire

Set by Words & Graphics Ltd.
Anstey, Leicestershire
Printed and bound in Great Britain by
T. J. International Ltd., Padstow, Cornwall

This book is printed on acid-free paper

For my mother

The medal presentation now, in Hamer's memory, was impressionistic and distant. He remembered the hot lights and the tall, elegant woman orchestrating the cameras as the event was filmed. The barked citation. Banners stiff with ritual and the weight of incense from sconces scorching the walls in ceremony. The Führer had been moist-eyed, his breath rank, his touch the briefest squeeze of Hamer's shoulder, after the palsied, double-fisted handshake. And Hamer had been dragged into his orbit, felt the power of the man's presence like gravity, turbid, weighing on him with twice, three times what it should. Exhilaration followed in the passing of the Führer and, with it, a brief passage of exultant pride.

There were backslaps from fellow officers and handshakes from men in long leather coats with grins turned to rictus by the fortunes of the war. Slipping from Hitler's orbit now, Hamer could take in little of his own spectacle. The film lights dazzled him and made him sweat. He was accustomed to the cold, after all. There were toasts celebrated with champagne glasses filled with some thick cordial of which the Führer no doubt approved. Its sweetness, after the battle rations of the Eastern Front, forced Hamer almost to gag.

Amid this, Martin Hamer thought of his dead

wife, Lillian. And of the pleasure she would have taken in the moment. For a while he watched himself amid the pomp and congratulation the way a posthumous hero might; through the unfeeling eyes of a corpse. Despite trying, he could discover in himself no way to enjoy the occasion. Battle to him was chaos. He had achieved no distance from its waste and barbarism. Without question, without pause, he would do it again. He loved the Fatherland. But he felt, at the ceremony, like spitting the corrupt concoction in his glass into the face of the woman transforming the reward for an episode of frantic courage into an interlude of movie propaganda.

Prior to the medal presentation, they had given him morphine and treated his wound. Sitting with his cordial, he became aware that he was bleeding again through the fresh dressing. His blood had thinned with persistent cold and undernourishment on the long retreat from the Donets to the banks of the Dnepr and the counter-attack launched with the frozen waters of the river at their backs. The counter-attack, the battle and the ensuing chase and killing had exhausted Martin Hamer. His wound had cost him strength and blood. The blood left in his body would not coagulate. Now, in the Reich Chancellery, under glittering chandeliers, he could feel the life leaking out of him and splashing in droplets that made a puddle on the marble floor. Darkness loomed through the bright lights, and Hamer thought he was passing out. But it was just the film lights. The tall woman had seen the stain spreading like spilled wine across the field grey of his dress uniform and ceased the attention of her cameras.

Medical orderlies appeared through the heat and the crush, and they took him through long corridors to a room with a cot where he was spoon-fed soup and given pills to swallow and told, not unkindly, to sleep. Many of the men decorated in the medal ceremonies must be wounded, Hamer thought, for them to have medics so close to hand. He was still embarrassed about leaving his blood for others to mop from the Reich Chancellery floor. Last, an orderly took with gentle fingers the medal from around his neck and placed it on top of a locker next to the cot. Hamer slept, the pain of his wound an insistent throb through morphine with every sleeping breath. He dreamed of a courtyard piled with new coffins. Brass fittings embellished the yellow wood under dancing snowflakes.

The officer sent to wake him first ordered coffee and then tried to make small talk. He seemed never to have experienced combat. His fingernails were manicured and his eyes innocent of killing. He asked about the battle. He looked longingly at the medal on its crisp new ribbon on the locker by the bed. Then he told Hamer about Poland and the camp. A chance to recover your strength, he said. Vital work. But work a man can accomplish while his wounds mend. You don't have the strength to return to the rigours of the campaign in the east, the officer told Hamer. Perhaps in three months, when spring is here.

Now, however, your orders take you to a General Government camp outside the city of Poznań.

Hamer tried to protest.

'The decision is made. The Führer himself has taken an interest. Reconcile yourself.'

* * *

Dr Ariel Buckner's quarters were lit. Lamplight bled through a shutter in his window. Closer to, a song played on his gramophone. It sounded mournful, subdued; Hamer recognized it as Mahler, from the Kindertotenlieder song cycle. Hamer shook his head, baffled at the strength it would require in a man to discipline art out of grief; concoct music for public performance out of private desolation. Attempting to steal by Buckner's door, he smiled to himself in the darkness. Buckner would probably reason that the song cycle written after the death of the composer's child was created not out of an artist's grief but out of greed; for profit. Or would he? Buckner didn't have to listen to Mahler. There were plenty of other composers. The fact that he was doing so was surely a simple acknowledgement of Mahler's punished talent.

Hamer didn't escape the doctor's vigilant need for attention.

'I scent a hero,' Buckner said, dragging open his door, which caught and scraped because its timber was young and had swollen, unseasoned, with damp in its frame.

Cast in Buckner's spread of yellow light,

Hamer tried to look as though he welcomed the approach. He was aware of his own growing reputation for aloofness, had sufficient of an officer's instinct to recognize the danger of that. And he possessed sufficient instinct for self-preservation and sanity to know that he could not survive his internment here entirely alone.

'Doctor,' he said.

'Ariel. Please.'

'Martin, then.'

'Come, Martin. I have questions. And schnapps. Questions and schnapps in equal measure for the Reich hero of Kharkov.' The slapping hand was heavy and avuncular on Hamer's back. The doctor's quarters smelled slightly of ether. Heat cooked the air, heady in waves from a cast-iron stove. The two men sat in leather chairs placed to either side of a chess table. Buckner's drinks, generous, shared space with carved ivory chesspieces. It looked to Hamer as though the doctor had most recently played himself. He couldn't really win that way. On the other hand, he never risked total defeat.

'You don't like it here, Martin.' It was not a question. Hamer shifted slightly and sipped schnapps. 'You don't approve?'

The question seemed to Hamer dangerously vague. 'I'm a soldier.'

'We're all soldiers.'

'I'd rather fight my battles at the front.'

The music had stopped.

'I'm surprised you listen to Mahler,' Hamer said.

Buckner laughed. 'Because he was a Jew? I'm surprised you, a soldier, recognize Mahler.'

'My father liked music.'

'You don't?'

Hamer shrugged. 'Popular song.'

'The stuff the party has banned?'

'I'm not ignorant,' Hamer said, avoiding the question.

'I'm sure,' Buckner said, letting him. 'So. The war in the east. Which composer?'

Hamer thought for a moment. 'Beethoven.'

Buckner's emphatic nod signalled the soundness of the choice. 'Which work?'

'A symphony, of course. I think the Ninth. Only the Ninth has the grandeur, the sweep.'

'A very German symphony.'

'We're fighting Germany's war.'

'You can't go back,' the doctor said. 'You might be killed. Probably you would be killed.' He said this forlornly. 'God knows the mortality rate is high enough.' He tapped his glass. 'The Reich needs live heroes. Some of them, anyway.'

'Am I a hero?'

Buckner pursed his lips. His expressions are pantomimic, Hamer thought; probably the consequence, or even the requirement, of some fashionable pre-war medical practice. Hamer imagined a place more salon than surgery, coffee and cake, cream and chocolate heavy amid the polished mahogany and velvet drapes. He had endured hours of agonized waiting in just such a place with his wife. Those places were redundant to him now.

'The men here tend not to believe in heroics.'

Hamer laughed. 'Yet they sing the Horst Wessel song.'

'And why shouldn't they?'

'I knew Wessel. Had the peculiar misfortune to encounter the man.'

Buckner nodded and tapped his glass again. 'Not a hero, Wessel, then.'

'A bully. A thief and a pimp. None of which comes as news to you, doctor.'

'Not a politician, are you, Martin?' Again, words shaped as a question delivered instead a verdict.

'A soldier. As I told you.'

Buckner's eyes were blue and alert, youthful in an ageing face. 'It isn't that they believe in Horst Wessel. It's that they approve of the myth. They see Horst in themselves and themselves in their martyr. They're of the party. Abandoned by events, here in the General Government, they fall back on fond memories of street battles.'

Hamer nodded. 'Jew-baiting.'

'Jews,' Buckner said. 'Communists.'

'Victories,' Hamer said.

'In battles fought when the party was young and they mattered to it. They remember the marches in Berlin and Nuremberg behind their blood banners. They need the legend of Wessel.'

'Well, they're welcome to it.'

'Precisely what they don't need is you.'

Hamer drained his glass. The doctor refilled it. The man was generous with his schnapps. There was a pause in the conversation. Hamer's instinct was to leave, but he could not imagine where he would wish to go.

Ariel Buckner bit the end off a cigar and wet the torn tobacco between his lips before lighting the tip. He smoked and then watched the smoke rise from his cigar. At its tip, tobacco burned and turned to grey ash. Buckner hawked and spat into a chamber-pot placed for the purpose on the floor beside his chair. 'What are they like to fight? The Russians?'

Hamer laughed. 'Pray that you never find out.'

'Is it true they attack with a war cry?'

Hamer nodded, his eyes on space.

'Describe it to me,' the doctor said.

'An attack?'

'The sound, Martin.'

'Savage,' Hamer said. 'Bestial. They're animals, after all.'

'Quite,' Buckner said, nodding. He spat again.

'Before the war, Herr Doctor, was your practice in Berlin?'

Buckner smiled and shook his head, his eyes on the gathering ash at the tip of his cigar.

Hamer remembered then the Mahler. 'Vienna? Did you practise there?'

'Before this conflict, I did not prostitute what skills I possess pandering to the hypochondria of the comfortably off,' Buckner said. He looked Hamer in the eye. 'I ran a government-funded clinic. In Düsseldorf. It was our mission there to stretch the boundaries of medical science. I flatter myself that on occasion we achieved this.'

Hamer's glass was empty. He didn't notice.

'Now take off that tunic and let me look at your wound. I saw you wince as you sat. We don't want the Reich hero of Kharkov dying of septicaemia,' the doctor said. And he smiled . . .

Later, lying between starched sheets in darkness and silence, Hamer remembered what it had sounded like when the Russians had attacked.

⋆ ⋆ ⋆

His father had liked poetry as ardently as music. His favourites had been the English Lake Poets, and one year, when Martin was a boy, they had spent a six-week holiday touring England, climbing and walking. Martin's own passion then had been not poetry but football. England were to play Germany in a friendly match at the Old Trafford ground in Manchester during their stay, and Martin's father took him to the match as a special treat. After ten minutes, from open play, the England captain scored. A marvellous goal. It seemed to Martin that silence welled for a moment, like a vast wave on the brink of breaking, in the packed stadium. And then came the low, rumbling roar of celebration. The crowd waved scarfs and shook rattles and jumped with their arms held aloft. But it was that gleeful roar that Martin remembered, as it numbed the air and thrilled through his bones and thrummed through the concrete under his feet.

And it was this sound, this gleeful roar of celebration, that he heard again, as a man, when the Russians attacked. You could not see them, against the snow, with their wrapped rifles, in their white camouflage. But you could hear them, all right. A man could hear the attacking

Russians even broken, crouched in a frozen dugout with his hands pressed over his ears as he soiled himself, screaming for the sound, and the horror it sanctioned, to cease.

* * *

Hamer lay and listened to the low moan of the wind through the fence wire and the watchtowers and the wooden buildings of the camp. The wind across the plains of Poland was a chilly and insistent thing that was mostly, to Hamer, significant as a sound. The shrieking wind that scoured the winter steppes had been a relentless, killing element that had always signified danger and destruction. It froze fuel in the panzers at night through their tarpaulins and burned exposed skin black. Hamer had seen the wind of Arctic Russia shatter rifle barrels and render the limbs of the dead as brittle as ice within minutes of life surrendering them. In Poland, the wind chilled and shivered men. It brought damp to burrow aches into the bone. It bred a mood of nagging dissent among the guards and carried the sobs of the women inmates at night, confined in their huts. The persistent night keening of the wind across the Polish wastes signalled desolation, not death.

But Hamer thought now about death. And he grieved, as at night he always grieved, the loss of Lillian, his lovely, dead wife.

* * *

He was making his routine clockwise inspection tour of the perimeter at eight the following morning when he passed Hans Rolfe as Sergeant Rolfe walked two short-leashed Doberman dogs in the opposite direction. Rolfe met his eyes for a brief glance as he struggled to control the pace of the slavering animals under his command. Muscle rippled under the short coats of the dogs in wan sunlight. Rolfe's boots skittered to find purchase on the packed ground as he tried to use his weight to sheet-anchor the ravening animals. Rolfe was sweating and breathing heavily and, as he passed, Hamer smelled beer sour on the sergeant's breath from the evening before. Rolfe had a fine singing voice and enjoyed putting it nightly to patriotic use.

Hamer was about ten paces further on when he heard the woman scream. He had seen her hanging laundry on a washing line as he walked equidistant between where she worked and the perimeter fence. She screamed again as he ran the short distance back towards what was happening. The dog still tethered by Rolfe strained against its leash and let out hoarse barks in its fervour to join the attack. The other shook its head and heaved with the lower part of the woman's arm between its jaws. She screamed again. As Hamer gripped the flews of the attacking dog between the fingers of both hands and tried to tear its jaws apart, he saw that the woman had wrapped some damp piece of prison drab around her arm before the dog's assault. There was blood, but she might keep the limb. Hamer used a thumb to try to gouge the

Doberman's eye. The animal shook its head, and he heard tendons tear in the woman's upper arm and she screamed again. Hamer let go of the dog, took a step back, pulled his pistol from its holster and, jamming the barrel hard behind the attacking dog's ear, pulled the trigger twice. Brain and fragments of pelt and bone splashed, streaking the ground. The dead dog slumped on top of its mess, and the woman jerked her arm free and fled. Hamer held his pistol in a hand still tacky with saliva and blood from the torn flews of the Doberman. From his rear, he heard the voice of the doctor. Ariel Buckner said, 'You shot my dog.'

'You'll treat the woman?'

'You shouldn't have shot my dog.'

Hamer turned. His pistol was still in his hand. He ejected a spent shell from the chamber and it landed on the ground. He was aware of sentries watching them, leisurely, from the nearest observation tower. He was aware of the eyes of inmates, unseen, hidden witnesses to what was happening. The doctor looked at the pistol. 'Since the hero of Kharkov request it,' he said, 'I'll treat the woman.'

'Thank you.' Hamer turned back towards Rolfe. The dog still on its leash, defeated by the presence of death, whimpered and mewled for its lost companion at the sergeant's feet. Rolfe was smiling.

'Why did you do that?'

'I didn't do anything, sir. The dog slipped its leash. They're strong as fuck, and I'm not their usual handler.'

'Where is their usual handler?'

'Sleeping one off,' Rolfe said, still smiling.

Hamer took a handkerchief from the pocket of his britches and wiped the stickiness off his pistol. He holstered the weapon and used the handkerchief to wipe clean his hands. 'I'm putting the dog's usual handler on a charge. You can tell him to come and see me as soon as he sobers up. I want a written report from you describing exactly how you lost control of an animal you were supposed to be exercising. It will be on my desk by noon.'

'With respect, sir,' Rolfe said, 'you shouldn't have killed the doctor's dog.'

Hamer nodded, thinking that respect was not a quality prominent in the delivery of the sergeant's words.

* * *

The commandant of their camp was a former career politician from Heidelberg. After three weeks of his secondment there, Hamer had still not been introduced to Wilhelm Crupp. Buckner had explained that Crupp was much in demand in Poznań, raising revenue for the General Government, hosting dinners, liaising with influential people, preparing a situation that would seduce civilian Germans into their duty to colonize the land in the east, theirs as their Aryan birthright, without the need for coercive resettlement. In Crupp's absence, Hamer was by rank the second in command. But the choice was nominal. Hamer admitted to no experience of any but a field command. With the doctor, he shared equally the task of governing their carelessly constructed domain of wood and wire and oppression.

In Crupp's predictable absence, they were holding the inquest into the death of Buckner's dog in Buckner's quarters. Hamer's military theory was rusty, but he was sure it had been the Prussian tactician Clausewitz who had stressed the need always to choose the ground for the fight. Buckner held the high strategic ground. The look on his face said as much. He sat behind his desk. He had in front of him Rolfe's written testimony. Both men had read its flat, dishonest prose. Buckner closed this inadequate file and pushed its pages away from immediate reach.

'I'm not going to waste your time or insult your intelligence discussing the good sergeant's version of events. She's part of our Joy Division. One of our prostitutes. I'm sure her ripe Romany looks were not lost on you.'

'I didn't notice her appearance.'

'Yes,' Bruckner said tiredly, 'you did. Or you would not have expended energy and ammunition saving her.'

Hamer thought about this. 'So what's the real story?'

Buckner took a cigar from the teak humidor on his desk and lit it with a match. 'Rolfe is one of life's enthusiasts. He approaches those things he enjoys with vigour. Sometimes too much vigour.'

'He rapes the women?'

Buckner shrugged. 'Rape is not really an appropriate term in these times. In these circumstances.'

'Rape is rape.'

'And I'm sure the Russian Front has made you an authority on the subject. It's an emotive word, Hamer. Personally I think it a waste of time to discuss moral imperatives when we're talking about a slave.'

'A slave who cost you your dog.'

Buckner pointed the tip of his cigar. 'You, Hamer, cost me my dog.'

'We can agree about one thing. Rolfe set the dog on her. Why?'

Buckner smoked. Smoke concealed his features for a moment. He spoke when it began to dissipate. 'She was hanging washing outside the laundry. That's sixty feet or so from the south watchtower. A sentry, Landau, was descending the ladder to visit the latrine and take a piss when Rolfe approached the laundry with the dogs. The woman had a clothes peg in her mouth. Landau has extremely good eyesight, even distracted by a full bladder. It's why we have him spend so much time in the towers. He's probably the best rifle shot in the camp. At least, he was prior to your arrival.'

'And what did Landau see?'

'He saw the prostitute take the clothes peg from her mouth, grip it in one fist and use her thumb to push the peg down until only an inch of it or so was visible. This gesture was intended for Rolfe. Then she smiled at him. And then, Landau says, the sergeant let slip the dog.'

There was a silence between the men.

'What do you think, Martin?'

'I'm not a betting man. If I were, I wouldn't wager Hans Rolfe is hung like a horse.'

'You'd have caused less of a stir here, frankly, if you'd shot the woman.'

'What Rolfe did was undisciplined.'

'You lack perspective, Martin. Rolfe could have shot the woman. Could shoot her now. She might justify the cost of a bullet. She did not justify the life of such a dog. You know the way this war is being fought. During your duty in the east, did you see a single Russian prisoner?'

'I'd heard the stories. Rumours of execution squads, following our progress.'

Buckner laughed. 'Squads would have been entirely inadequate. We dispatched execution divisions.'

'When we were forced to retreat, I saw the burial pits. Different methods, Herr Doctor, producing the same effect. They force-march our captured soldiers, stripped of their greatcoats and boots, until the men die of exhaustion and cold. We make them dig their graves and finish them with a nine-millimetre bullet. I believe the phrase used to describe this phenomenon is 'total war'.'

'And the woman?'

'I don't give a shit about the woman. I think what she did took appalling courage. I acted out of instinct. She must be a fanatic of some kind. But it's Rolfe needs watching.'

The doctor nodded. 'I agree it's foremost a disciplinary matter. I've told Landau if he repeats to anyone else what he's told to me he'll be using his sharpshooting skills on the Russian Front. I've curfewed Hans Rolfe for a week.'

There was another silence.

'And that's it?'

'Like you, I'm not a betting man,' Buckner said. 'But I would bet my soul she'll be dead by morning.'

Hamer rose to leave.

'It isn't the first time she's been attacked by a dog,' Buckner said.

'You talked to her?'

'No. I treated her. A torn ligament. Surface abrasions. Severe bruising. I don't converse with them. But she knew what to do. She wrapped the arm with one of the rags she was there to peg out and she showed the arm to the dog. I believe she's had cause to do it before.'

* * *

It was raining hard when Hamer left the cigar fug of Buckner's quarters. Rain had opened rivulets on the packed earth. It was odd for him, after weeks of aimlessness, to walk with purpose towards a plotted destination. The ground was treacherous, turning to mud and ruin, squelching under his boots. But he knew where he was going.

He hadn't really lied to Buckner about his impressions concerning the woman. He had seen shorn hair the colour and length of corn stubble. He'd registered the glitter of pain in green eyes shaped like those of a cat. Full lips had been pulled back from her teeth in pain. Beyond these snatches he could not now compose her face in his memory. But her smell had assaulted him. Her smell was a compound of female sweat and fresh menstrual blood and grease and cistern water from the soapless washing of the rags she wore. He had not had a woman fill his senses with such shocking potency for years. The last time had been with Lillian, in the final, frenzied couplings of their trying for a child. He had desisted from the rape of Russian widows and their daughters. He had stood next to the desiccated beauty filming in the Reich Chancellery and been aware of leather and perfume. She hadn't roused in him anything other than a sort of wary repugnance.

* * *

They were in the stables. They were playing cards on a farrier's bench while the horses slept under blankets on their feet in their stalls and rain thrummed on the roof like a drumbeat. Hamer kicked the stool Rolfe sat on out from under him and the sergeant sprawled to his feet. His balance was good. He was two or three inches taller than Hamer and outweighed him by fifty pounds. Fat was welded to his muscle. He looked like he could fight. Five to one, Hamer thought. Not good odds if they elect to back their card-playing, anthem-carrying comrade. He didn't think they would. And he didn't give a shit, either way. Some men saw this when they encountered Martin

Hamer and reacted accordingly. Rolfe did not.

'The toy soldier,' he said. He dropped his hand of cards on the shit- and straw-strewn paddock floor and pulled a knife from a sheath on his belt. 'The pin-up.' He slashed at Hamer, missed, but kept his balance on spread feet. He grinned and licked his lips. The sergeant was up for this. 'The paint-by-numbers hero,' he said. He hawked and spat, the phlegm and sputum spattering on the chest of Hamer's tunic. 'I'll slaughter and fucking pickle you, boy.'

Hamer took Rolfe's legs with a sweeping kick and stamped, hard, twice on the knife hand. The knife was released, but the sergeant was up fast. He threw a right hook. Hamer blocked the punch with his left forearm and felt the stitches mending his wound tear with the weight of the blow. He drove the heel of his right hand twice up into Rolfe's nose. Bone cracked and blood began to gush. Hamer held the sergeant's head by the hair in the clench of both fists and pulled it down, driving his right knee again and again into the sergeant's face until the man dropped. Only then did Hamer look around. It appeared he and the sergeant now had the stables to themselves.

'My preferred weapon is a rifle,' he said, cocooning the sergeant's head in his hands, on his knees. His wound had opened. He could feel fresh blood seep under the dressing. 'But they are never deterred by rifle fire.' His chest hurt like a bastard. 'So you use grenades. And then you take out your pistol and hope to fuck it doesn't jam. Then they're on you, and it's the bayonet, or the knife. There comes the moment when you lose the knife. It sticks, jammed between the ribs of the man intent on killing you, its hilt so slick with blood you can no longer grip the thing to pull it out. That's when you start to use your teeth, Rolfe. That's when you start to use your thumbs to gouge and try to blind a man.'

Rolfe, conscious, said nothing. He breathed heavily. Wind wickered rain off the roof and walls of the stables, and the horses whinnied, uneasy, scenting the stink of fear.

'I've bitten out a man's throat, in battle, sergeant,' Hamer said. 'I tasted the tar from his last cigarette on my tongue as I spat a piece of his windpipe on to the snow. Don't ever call me a toy fucking soldier.'

Rolfe groaned.

'And leave the woman alone. Harm her and I swear to Christ I'll castrate you.'

* * *

Martin Hamer was fourteen years old when they came to his father's land. They arrived unannounced, two Americans with a deputation of French. Neither of the American visitors spoke German. The French deputation refused to. The voluble American carried a volume of Baedeker printed before the war. He was a large man from the city of Boston and wore a frock coat and spats. He spoke in phrases gleaned from the Baedeker which Martin had to try to translate for his father. It was more guesswork, in truth, than translation. The man from Boston read poorly and spoke worse. Gesticulation and curses, Martin surmised, provided his natural language.

Martin was frankly afraid of the second American. He was tall and thin and from a city called Baltimore. He favoured wax collars and bow ties with chequered suits, and he carried a cornball pipe and affected a straw boater that Martin thought the most sinister headwear he had ever seen on a living human being. He wore a moustache stained with chewing tobacco, and his teeth showed even and greenish on those frequent occasions when he grinned in response to one of his American colleague's wisecracking American remarks.

His father treated them all as honoured guests. Nightly he plundered what was left of their cellar for some vintage suitably auspicious for the foreigners here to plot and haggle over his eviction from land his family had owned for four centuries. Martin did not truly know how much his father understood of what was happening. His father had fought himself to exhaustion and come home silent in his nation's defeat. Then one night, late, as their visitors drank in their conservatory brandy bottled before the death of Metternich, Martin chanced upon his father, gazing at the framed title document to their domain, where the old parchment hung in their library. And he realized that his father understood everything. Martin looked first into his father's tormented eyes and then hugged him. And he knew then, gripping as tight as he dared his father's diminished frame, that this ordeal was killing him.

They liked the conservatory. Martin's father had built it for his mother out of blond wood when the century was still new. Now the Americans sat, bathed in sunlight through glass, at its card tables doing their daily calculations. The Baltimore man chewed tobacco and used a Meissen vase as a spittoon. The man in the spats hauled a portable gramophone from the trunk of their Ford and they listened to recordings taken in greaseproof sleeves from a box. The recordings sounded riotous to Martin, a chaos of sound without sense or meaning.

'Devil music,' the Baltimore man said to him, catching his eye with a grin, flicking his tongue between green teeth, winking.

Years later, Martin broke a vow and returned. He did it at Lillian's insistence. She said it was the only way he would lay the ghost. The estate had entirely gone. Black scars of opencast mining obliterated the land. The woods where he had shot snipe with his father, where his father had taught Martin Hamer to shoot, was a shunting yard. Wagons filled with coal slack gathered rust stains in the rain. Smoke rose from sheds in the distance, smudges of whitewash under corrugated roofs. Lillian tried to smile at him as rain pattered on her umbrella. Martin went to the approximate spot where he had found his father, half his father's head blown off, his favourite gun held almost benignly across his chest. He had found him in a stand of silver birches. He had carried his father's body back to the house, the burden so light between his own strong arms that it broke his heart to think of it.

No ghosts were laid in the rain that day with Lillian. But Martin Hamer did make some promises to himself.

* * *

'You've no one, have you, Hamer?' The doctor continued to sew. It was another of his interrogative judgements. Buckner's enquiry invited no reply. The doctor pulled the suture taut, the needle pinched between thick fingers, and Hamer flinched. 'A whiff of ether would help.'

Hamer shook his head.

'It's why you are so dangerous,' the doctor said. 'Nobody to sorrow over you. No one to grieve. It's the danger of leaving a widow and orphans that makes a man cautious, Martin. You are the opposite of cautious. You are a danger to yourself.'

'I'm sure Rolfe gets plenty of backhanders from the farmers he supplies with camp labour when the fields need digging or the harvest gathered. I'm sure he gets a premium back on every blanket we weave here when it's sold. He was probably bribed by whichever timber merchant fooled the camp into buying immature wood for the construction of the outbuildings. I've never met an NCO who didn't secretly think he ran things. What I will not have is anarchy in matters of camp discipline.'

Buckner snipped off the suture and dabbed

iodine at the ragged seam below Hamer's left shoulder. Hamer looked at the stitches in the steel reflection of Buckner's surgical mirror. 'It's neat work.'

'Thank you.'

Hamer got to his feet and began to button his shirt.

'You were never married, Martin?'

Hamer smiled. 'Because I don't approve of rape, you mean? I'm not queer, doctor. I was married. My wife died just before the outbreak of war. An automobile accident. There was something wrong apparently with the steering column of our car. The car went into a ravine.'

'I'm sorry. My God. And no children?'

'I can't have them. I'm infertile, doctor.' Hamer smiled again, without mirth. 'I'm the last of my bloodline. You've told me you're not a betting man. But you could wager with certainty I won't be leaving any medals to my proud daughter or son.'

* * *

They met when he was twenty-one and she a year older. They met three years before the world they lived in was transformed. A mutual friend introduced them at a garden party, saying that since they were both skiers they should have something in common to talk about. Lillian was flushed with summer and wine. She had been reading Hemingway, she explained to Martin. She had been most impressed by Brett Ashley and Lady Brett's relentless consumption of alcohol. Not a happy woman, though, Martin said, seeing her look of surprise that he had read the book too. Drink had made Lillian hopelessly transparent in a way her new-found heroine would have thought absurd. Martin smiled. Let's find some shade and sit down and discuss this further, he said. Lillian nodded in agreement and fifteen minutes later was asleep under a lawn parasol with the weight of her hair spread across his shoulder, one brassiere strap brilliantly white and tantalizing on the rise and fall of her breasts through a gap between the buttons of her blouse.

They skied and cycled and swam together and argued over books and music and the choice of film they would queue to see. They never talked about politics. Politics was a dead, exhausted subject in Germany. The Communists and the National Socialists fought their street battles, armies of thugs transported from town to town in fleets of lorries, their hatred fuelled by beer and rumour, to beat and to bomb each other through turbulent nights. But all of that seemed far away from the urgent things in the life led by Martin and Lillian. Hamer had less time for ideology than for history. He did not see the undeclared civil war being waged across his country as the way to heal Germany. Killing fellow Germans would surely not repair a nation neighbouring powers had looted and debased. For Lillian, it was even simpler. Art was what mattered. Berlin was stagnant, moribund, sinking into sleaze and self-parody. Berlin was finished. Paris and New York were the twin cultural capitals of her world. She worked as a fashion buyer for a large department store. She spoke French and English fluently enough to read André Gide and Scott Fitzgerald in their mother tongues. Martin still had cadet status in a Weimar army that was duty bound and solemnly sworn to political neutrality. His barracks was one of those where any sympathy for the factions remained clandestine. The anarchists were mad and would implode. The reds were a containable menace, not a force entirely spent, but in apparent decline. The Brown Shirts were thugs who couldn't get the smell of cowshit off their boots. The storm would abate.

And Lillian laughed at Martin. Ever since his father's death, he had felt compelled to overreach himself. The parade ground and the climbing wall and the strategy seminar and the wrestling mat were his competitive arenas. There he would not be defeated. But Lillian still laughed at him. It happened once on a rest day from a skiing trip in the Alps. They took the train to the Eiger station. They picnicked on the meadow under the north face of the mountain. It was Martin's choice of location. He didn't tell Lillian why. As she plucked tiny blooms from the flower-strewn meadow and chatted about nothing, he stared through army binoculars at the looming enormity of the Eiger's north wall.

You're looking at that mountain like a man picking a fight, she said. That's because I'm going to climb it, he said, taking the binoculars away from his face, looking at her. And Lillian threw her head back and laughed out loud, rocking with laughter, until Martin started laughing too, the pair of them in an embrace on the sweet earth, too weak with mirth to disentangle themselves from one another.

That night, after a shared supper of lamb stew and white wine chilled in glacial snow, she crept into his room as he read by candlelight. She knew the book, had lent it to him at supper.

'What do you think?' she whispered.

'That Gatsby will come to a tragic end,' Martin said, whispered. 'He has a fatal innocence about him.'

Lillian laughed. 'It takes a fatal innocent to know one,' she said. She blew out the candle flame and stretched to open the curtains of the small window under the eaves at the foot of his bed. The night was black and clear. Above this high part of the world, the stars were close, bright and incalculable. Lillian shrugged her nightdress to the floor. Starlight dabbed ivory highlights on the gold of her skin in the darkness. He held out his arms to her and she slipped between the sheets.

The next day they took a funicular and then climbed, carrying their skis over their shoulders, to a peak above a smooth, dizzying slope that descended to the tree line thousands of feet beneath them. The conifers far below, powdered by fresh snowfalls, looked like the painted foliage of intricate children's toys. Lillian buckled her bindings and then stood, wiping her snow goggles on her sleeve and breathing plumes of frozen air. Her lips had reddened with altitude and the effort of their climb and looked as ripe and moist, under her pale eyes and paler skin, as forbidden fruit. Martin pulled a glove off with his teeth, reached across and fingered the thick ringlets of hair that fell to either side of her face under her cap. He kissed her.

'I love you,' he said.

'You do, don't you, poor boy,' she said, her voice thick in her throat and her lips against his neck. She looked up at him and her eyes were wet. 'So I suppose I'd better try to make you happy.'

They telemarked down the mountain in long, parallel turns, small avalanches following them in the furrows ploughed by their skis in the fresh snow, Martin part-wishing that their sweeping descent through the clean wind to the toy trees could go on thrilling through them for ever.

They didn't have for ever. It would be seven years until the evening Lillian's car slid and skittered into an abyss beside a rain-washed road.

* * *

On the morning of the battle, Hamer assembled his men and took stock of the force he would be able to deploy. So many men had died during the retreat that weaponry, at least, should not have been a problem. But it was, of course. Weakened by hunger and the pace of their forced march, some of the soldiers had thrown down their rifles. To do so confounded instinct, Martin thought. For a soldier to discard his weapon willingly was a denial of who he was. Worse, he betrayed his comrades. He was liable to be court-martialled. Offenders were commonly and summarily shot. But this army had been through horrors that no soldier could be trained to endure. They had suffered and gone on suffering to the point where their own survival seemed a sort of mockery. They endured only to endure worse than that which had not yet killed them. A rifle weighed heavily on the shoulder of a man harried over the frozen steppe with bundled rags on his feet to replace the worn-out boots he'd boiled and eaten. As Hamer had the sergeant take the roll call, he saw the faces of the men telling him as much. But even though he saw the weary weight of suffering on their faces that morning, he did not see defeat. He saw hatred and anger and a hunger for retribution.

The river was behind them. It had frozen, and the thaw was months away. But a river seldom wholly freezes and, like most rivers, in the strength of its deeper channels the Dnepr was no exception to this stubborn rule of nature. Between plates of heaving ice, the current ran grey and turbid in a porridgy slush. Tanks would disappear in it. To cross the river, they would have to improvise pontoon bridges and leave their armour behind. Could they really litter the river's bank with abandoned panzers and tigers for an exultant enemy to claim? Their fording of the river would be a desperate scramble over what trees their pioneer corps could fell to improvise a makeshift bridge of boughs lashed to the ballast of empty diesel drums. They would flee no further. They were Germans. They were the soldiers of the Reich. Now was their moment to determine destiny.

Hamer had lost four more men in the night. One had frozen to death with his fingers wrapped around the stolen bottle of schnapps that had delivered cold and oblivion to him as he lay in his sleep. One had simply disappeared. A third had put his pistol barrel in his mouth and blown a bullet through the top of his head. It was Breitner's death, though, that Hamer took the hardest. Soldiers become inured to death in war. And Hamer had seen a great deal of death. But Breitner had been a sixteen-year-old volunteer at the start of the campaign. He was a boy from a village outside Leipzig who wrote at least once a week to his mother. Hamer could not recall ever having heard him utter a swearword. Breitner had lost toes to frostbite and survived a sniper bullet that passed close enough to his skull to shave one of his ear lobes off. He'd walked oblivious through a Soviet minefield. He'd disabled a T-34 with a single grenade. And now he had perished in his sleeping bag, his big-framed body finally succumbing to starvation and cold. Hamer would burn Breitner's body. They couldn't bury their dead in the permafrost. Fuel was too precious a commodity commonly to use for pyres. But Hamer was damned if he was going to leave the boy's body lying uncommemorated on the snow. Searching his uniform for Breitner's few pitiful keepsakes, Hamer composed in his mind those comforting lies he would write to the boy's mother should he himself survive the battle to come.

The deaths meant that all the men under Hamer's command that morning would at least carry a rifle into combat. Ammunition was scarce. 'But we have enough bullets,' he told his boys, 'if you just remember to shoot sufficiently straight.' The old joke raised a ragged grin through the ranks.

Two nights earlier he'd been called to the field commander's tent and told of the planned counter-offensive.

'I don't think it will surprise them greatly,' Hamer said. 'With the river at our backs, it isn't as if we've got anywhere else to go.'

'It will surprise them,' the commander insisted. 'They think we're in complete disarray, morale shattered, all order and discipline gone.' He took a silver cigarette case from his hip pocket, depressed the catch and extracted a cigarette. He screwed this carefully into a short holder made of yellow tortoiseshell and then lifted a lighted candle from the table where it illuminated his maps. He lit the cigarette with the flame of the candle and inhaled heavily. Hamer, watching, listening to a short lull in the boom of artillery fire that always sounded from the east, could only marvel at the precise steadiness of his commander's hands.

'They think they're pursuing a rabble into extinction, Martin,' the commander said. 'Well, they're in for a shock.'

As the commander talked intelligently about the subtle but crucial distinction between soldiers who were battle-weary and soldiers battle-hardened, Hamer silently thanked God, not for the first time, that he was led by an army and not by a party man. That was more than mere good fortune, of course. Party men seldom strayed intentionally to the front.

The following night, the commander gathered his officers together in his tent and read them Field Marshal von Manstein's precise orders concerning the timing and deployment of the counter-offensive. The men knew this was von Manstein's initiative and not Hitler's. Von Manstein was the conqueror of Sebastopol, and the men recognized his skill and daring in the detail of the battle strategy. Perhaps too late, the Führer was finally listening to a man capable of orchestrating victory for their army. As a gale gathered and boomed about the stiff canvas sheltering them, Hamer looked at his fellow officers in the light cast by the brazier keeping them warm and the storm lanterns suspended above their heads. Their field uniforms were little more than belted rags kept together by ingenuity and the persistence of the darning needle. Their faces were wind-blackened, those of the luckier officers, those still in possession of snow goggles, panda-eyed. To a man they were thin, unkempt, ragged, feral. And despite their best efforts to wash when possible, and shave, they stank. God, how they heaved to high heaven, these chosen sons of the Reich. On a parade ground their appearance would have provoked laughter and outrage. But they were not yet beaten men. Hamer had faith in his fellow officers. He had faith in his commander. He had faith in Manstein's judgement that the Russians had finally overstretched themselves in pursuit. Their tactics, while desperate, were battle-proven. Only the coming test of his own courage caused doubt to burn its corrosive path into Martin Hamer's soul.

An hour before the battle he built a trestle out of the wood of empty ammunition cases and poured a careful litre of petrol over Breitner's raised corpse. He lit the pyre and measured thirty paces upwind of the burning body at a slow march through snow. Then he turned and saluted a brother in arms unaware, unashamed, of the tears freezing in the Russian morning on his wind-burned face.

⋆ ⋆ ⋆

They shared a boat, on the Wannsee, with Heidi and Karl. The water was limpid under Martin's dipping oars. The sky was a pure, unsullied blue. High summer in Berlin. It would have been perfect, Martin thought, were it not for the mosquitoes and their spiteful thirst. At the front of the boat, Heidi trailed a hand in the tepid water and wore a dreamy expression. Perhaps the insects were only biting him. They were looking for a picnic spot. Lillian had packed the picnic food between folds of cool linen in their woven picnic basket. Rhine wine chilled in the cold box full of ice Martin had hauled aboard the boat.

It was Heidi who had first introduced them. Karl, who worked with Lillian, was her returned favour. Karl designed domestic interiors that would accommodate the kitchens and bathrooms and furnishings sold by the store in which Lillian worked. Lillian advised Karl on trends in fabric design. Karl earned a lot of money in commission. He worked long hours and frequently bemoaned his lack of female company. Listening to Karl, resisting the urge to scratch mosquito bites into wounds, Martin Hamer couldn't but wonder at the quality of the favour done by Lillian for her friend.

'I still don't see how you can judge,' Karl said. Said again. 'If you haven't seen the man — '

'For God's sake, Karl,' Lillian said. 'I'm not doubting he has a talent for public oratory. I'm sure he's a very entertaining speaker. I've heard him on the wireless, and he sounds extraordinary. I'm not taking issue with his delivery. It's the message being delivered. He provides his audience with a shopping list of scapegoats to blame for the plight of the country. Pointing the finger is all very well. Providing solutions is rather more difficult.'

'And it doesn't win ovations,' Martin said. 'Not in the way that stirring hatred can.'

'Martin's right,' Heidi said to Karl, a hand above her eyes to shield them from the glare of the sun. 'I mean, have you even met a Jew?'

Karl's eyes were very blue in the reflected sunlight off the still water as he thought about the question. 'No, I haven't. They have a reputation in business for paying promptly and in cash, as Heidi will tell you.'

'I can tell you no such thing,' Heidi said. 'I'm

a bank teller. It isn't my job to chase debt.' She smiled. 'Anyway, let's talk about important matters. Have you proposed yet, Martin?'

Lillian laughed. 'Martin has a mountain to climb.'

'In earning your hand? Yes, I suppose he does,' Heidi said.

'No. He has a real mountain to climb. And we can't get married until he's climbed it, can we, darling?'

'Why ever not?'

'In case he falls off,' Lillian said, ruffling Martin's hair, patting his cheeks as he coloured, defenceless, his hands occupied with the oars. 'And I'm left a tragic widow.'

'Well,' Heidi said, 'that's practical, I suppose. But do hurry up and climb it, Martin. I love a good wedding.'

'Wedding or funeral,' Martin said, 'you'll definitely be invited, Heidi.' He dodged a blow from Lillian.

'It isn't the Jews in particular,' Karl said. 'But their loyalties are to their creed and to one another, you see. That's his point. It isn't the Jews in particular. It's anyone whose loyalty is not to the Fatherland first and last.'

They were silent for a moment. Water lapped at the varnished planks of the boat. An aeroplane with an aluminium fuselage burned with reflected sunlight in the sky as it passed overhead.

'My father had a sergeant called Blumenthal,' Martin said. Lillian looked at him sharply. Martin never mentioned his father. 'He won an

Iron Cross during the Ludendorff Offensive. I don't think Blumenthal's loyalties could have been all that divided.'

'He's the coming man,' Karl said. 'See if he isn't. He's the man to put the country back on its feet.'

'Well,' Heidi said, 'somebody needs to.'

Martin Hamer rowed their boat through limpid water. There were a lot of boats on the Wannsee that day. A mosquito bite throbbed angrily on his neck. Accordion music, a sugary waltz, sounded from a bandstand on the bank. He thought about his father, remembered the weight of his father's body as he carried him through the morning woods, through the chatter of birds in the high branches, through bracken and ferns, his trousers from the knees down and shoes sodden with dew and his heart so heavy in his chest that he could barely breathe between the sobs grief hauled out of him. He had never met Blumenthal, his father's decorated sergeant. Martin Hamer didn't think he had ever met a Jew in his life.

* * *

Hamer was making good progress. He tried to convince himself he was not, excitement and overconfidence both being sentiments on a mountain that tended to precede disaster. He was climbing methodically but with certainty and at pace. He attributed this in part to his equipment. He had been able to buy the best clothing and the best kit. He was clad in English climbing boots and clothing stitched from waterproofed English gaberdine. His ropes had been woven in Italy. A waterproof watch was strapped, ticking steadily, to his wrist. His climbing goggles had been manufactured by the German lens specialists, Zeiss. He carried an ice axe fashioned from Swedish steel. Equipment failure seemed the last thing likely to undermine Martin Hamer's attempt on the Eiger's forbidding north face.

What did seem more likely was history. And the sheer level of climbing difficulty its 6,000-foot near-vertical wall imposed on the ambitions of any mountaineer. Then there was what the very few in the climbing brotherhood aware of it considered to be the true madness at the heart of Hamer's attempt. He was endeavouring to scale the north wall solo. Most experienced Alpinists would have judged his attempt little more than a ritual suicide bid. But he had a reason he considered to be a compelling one for climbing solo. He was very aware of the potential for disaster. He had not wanted, out of pride or folly, to condemn another man. So he would succeed or fail alone.

He'd studied the sky at dawn, packing his food and water and bivouac bag into his rucksack. He'd tracked the contours of the route one final time, rehearsing his ascent through his binoculars. He had eaten the breakfast prepared by the woman who kept the inn at the edge of the meadow a short walk from the railway station and a few hundred yards from where the mountain began its abrupt vertical rise. He'd paid his bill and asked her to alert the local guides if he had not returned in seventy-two hours. There was no rescue service on the Eiger; the mountain's dangers were considered too great for such a provision. It was impractical. If Hamer wasn't back in seventy-two hours they would find his battered body on the meadow. Or he would be injured and stranded and unreachable. But he was confident that morning, considering his chances of success to be good. And so, without ceremony, he'd set off.

He had bought the new climbing equipment with some of the money he had been saving for his wedding to Lillian. Her father, Dr Stresemann, had heard about Martin's planned Eiger ascent during an expansive family dinner and had waved his cigar and made comic faces about the money Martin had hoarded.

'I like you, young man,' he had said. 'You've put a smile of joy on my daughter's face. Ach, it's enough, Martin Hamer.' He was a big, florid-faced man with grey hair swept back in extravagant wings above his ears. He could have been a prophet. He could have been an arms tycoon. His practice flourished. Hamer thought his theatrical appearance probably one reason why. The doctor leaned close and whispered, cigar breath and brandy fumes conspiratorial: 'You were disenfranchised by the crime of the peace. I know that. I know my history. You think you have nothing. But you are a good German, Martin. You have a cultured mind and iron in your soul.'

Dr Stresemann drank brandy. 'A father's love

for his daughter should be a selfless thing. This is not easy, as no doubt you will one day discover. It's a more difficult thing still when that daughter is an only child. All I can reasonably ask is that the man she chooses honours her. I believe you will.'

Hamer blushed. He had never heard Lillian's father speak with such frankness. Her father in company preferred the lazy concealment of a bluff and general geniality. Perhaps it was the consumption of drink. It was late, and Lillian's father had drunk a lot of brandy.

'Climb your mountain. Youth occurs once only for a man and calls for a certain extravagance. If ambition demands a price, pay it. A man such as yourself, Martin Hamer, will never be presented with a bill at my table.' Dr Stresemann slapped a heavy hand on his napkin, for emphasis. Cutlery bounced. 'Not at my table,' he said.

* * *

Hamer encountered the corpse on a difficult traverse above the second ice field. He rounded a cornice, supporting his weight on handholds alone, his legs useless, boots hanging in the abyss. If anything, the shock of the body helped. Hamer felt himself electrified by a charge of pure terror. His hands in their shallow fingerholds briefly gained twice their original strength. He traversed. He kicked away a crust of rotten snow and planted his feet on solid rock. He leaned back against the refuge of the ledge he had achieved. He unhooked his water bottle from his belt and thirstily drank. He tried, by kneading his biceps at the same time, to work the numbness out of his fingers and the ache out of his arms. And then he turned to the dead stranger with whom he shared a shallow, temporary space above oblivion.

The dead climber's feet and legs had been rooted in ice. Snow sat heavy in the grooves provided by the contours of his clothing and powdered the whole of him. His frozen face said he had died in the outrage of agony. His eyes, dusted by frost, dulled by death, were wide in their sockets still with pain. A small Italian flag had been sewn on to his upper sleeve. The stitching was clumsy. It had been late, hasty work, probably an impromptu thing done at the inn before departure on the climber's last day alive. There was something awful, Hamer thought, about the size, the plucky optimism of that little Italian flag. Sharing space with the man seemed a breach of his privacy. He'd achieved the ledge, this dead adventurer, after a fall on his rope that had dislocated both his arms. He stood slack-shouldered, the limbs elongated, like those of an ape. He had known there was no way down with this grotesque and disabling handicap. He had stood here, looking at the valley, no doubt thinking of home. And he had frozen to death in this awful place.

Going through his clothing to discover the man's identity would be a further violation. Hamer, deflated by the discovery, wondered what to do with him. Really, there was no choice. He screwed the cap back on to his water bottle and pulled his ice axe from his belt. Here was a grisly test for the new tool, one he would never have wished to perform. It took half an hour to free the man. When he'd done so, Hamer toppled his corpse gently into the void.

* * *

She was pegging washing, one-handed, the bitten arm in a sling made of lint, white in the pallid sunshine against the drab of her clothing. There was recognition in her face as he drew level with her. There was no greeting or acknowledgement, no expression to speak of. He could not have said why it was he stopped. He could not have explained why it was he spoke to her.

'The camp is a temporary measure,' he said. 'Villages and towns are being built. You'll be resettled. You'll have a home of your own.'

She pegged washing awkwardly, wet washing waiting for its turn over her shoulder. She said nothing.

'Dr Buckner tells me you are a Romany. An itinerant. Is one home not as good as another? Nomadic people don't have emotional attachments to the land, do they?'

'As you Germans so famously do.'

She sounded educated. Hamer was surprised into silence.

'I'm sorry,' she said. 'Am I permitted to reply?'

'Of course,' he said. Out of the corner of his eye he could see a thin man at the top of the near watchtower standing very still and observing them. Landau, the sharpshooter, he assumed.

'What is a Romany to you?'

Hamer thought about this. 'A gypsy. A dabbler in the telling of people's fortunes. Histrionic fiddle-playing at the cheaper sorts of restaurant. Horse breeding. Cattle theft. And if you believe the more sinister stories, child stealing.'

'I'm not a Romany. I'm a Pole, born in Katowice. I'm a Pole and a Slav. I'm not here as a punishment for child stealing, sir. I've never committed a theft. I've never committed a crime. I'm here because I'm a patriot.'

Buckner had been wrong, then, about her ethnic origin. But he had been right about her looks. Her features individually possessed too much strength for her to be described as beautiful, but she had a bold, startling attractiveness. Even shorn, ill-fed and attired in clothes well on their shabby and despondent way to becoming rags, her appearance would be pleasing to a man. The thought shamed Hamer, filled him with a surge of embarrassed guilt.

'Do they make you wear that medal?'

Hamer coloured. 'Why do you think that?'

'It's ostentatious. You don't seem an ostentatious man.'

'I'm obliged to wear it, yes.'

'You're the man who saved my life,' she said. 'For that, you have my sincere appreciation.'

What is it that's so winning about her, Hamer wondered. It's her vitality, he thought, as she fixed him with the Slavic slant and focus of her sharp green eyes. The woman has such abundant life.

Buckner's dogs snarled and yelped in the near distance, the indisciplined indulgence of their feeding time breeding in them a natural contempt for those providing them with too much food. Saws barked hopelessly against wet wood in the camp's carpentry shop. Buckner's gramophone carried loud against the chaos. He was listening to the Italian tenor Caruso sob his way in his swollen dotage through an Italian aria.

'You're in the wrong place, sir, I think,' the woman said. There was something else she intended to say, but her nerve deserted her then, Hamer thought, the wit and insolence beyond what she had learned to display in the sometimes lethal game of camp survival. Like vertigo, he thought. Like the moment on a lonely crag when you choose to relinquish the anchoring rope. Except that climbing was voluntary. Climbing was an indulgence and a conceit. This woman had been forced here at gunpoint to open her legs to the pleasures of grunting strangers. Men like Rolfe. Jesus, Hamer thought, men like Rolfe, wishing he had not countered instinct with discipline. He should have killed the man. He had killed a number of men. He was not careless about it. But it was not a difficult thing to accomplish for him. Wind soughed chilly in the sunshine through the camp, and Hamer felt his wound ache like a reproach.

'What's you name?'

'Julia Smollen. I'm twenty-six years old. In a former life I worked as a librarian.'

Hamer heard Landau, or someone, clattering down the watchtower ladder.

'I have to go,' he told the woman.

'To do what?'

There was no honest reply to this enquiry. In the camp, Hamer had no true duties to perform.

'Gypsies don't steal children, sir,' he heard her say from behind him as he walked away. 'They don't steal children. That's just a myth.'

* * *

The storm came in from the north. Hamer felt the atmospheric change afflict his ears, deafening him with the swiftness of the plunge in barometric pressure. He swallowed until his ears cleared and he heard the keening wail of strengthening wind on scats and ledges of rotten snow. He looked to the north, where the darkening sky was frenzied now with approaching cloud. Had he been still stranded on the second ice field, he knew that seeing this weather he would have been watching his death approach. But he was at the foot now of a ramp. He had to ascend, and quickly, to find some sort of shelter in which to hammer the pitons that he hoped would anchor his bivouac. Storms on the Eiger were terrifying in their violence. But they blew themselves out in hours rather than days. If he could survive the night, Hamer believed he could survive. He had to climb, swiftly and well. If he rushed now he would make a mistake and die. If he was too slow, he would be caught in the exposure of the storm and die. He did not want to die. He thought of his father, coaxing him through his first really difficult rockface ascent in the English Lake District. He thought of his father's calm and deliberate encouragement. 'Think of Mallory,' his father had said, a student, an admirer of the English Alpinist. And Hamer had thought of Mallory, and climbed to the summit and his proud father's embrace. He had been eight years old. He gained the summit of that English crag in the spring of 1914. It had been six weeks before the outbreak of war. He had climbed with the deadly certainty of a feral cat achieving a birds' nest. 'Like Mallory,' his father had said, proud. George Mallory was dead now, as his father was dead. Mallory killed on Everest, his father destroyed by the war and the vindictive peace. He thought of Lillian, alone if he did not succeed. The wind shook him, racked him against the tiny handholds and footholds of a ramp of prominent rock devoid of shelter on the Eiger. And Martin Hamer gathered himself and climbed for his life.

⋆ ⋆ ⋆

'Do you know how many Poles we are killing in the General Government, Martin?'

'I've no idea.'

'I have,' Buckner said. 'The commandant was a friend of Reinhard Heydrich. He takes an interest, as Heydrich did, in such statistics.'

'How many?'

'About three thousand a day. Half of them

Jews. A disappointing ratio, I think, fifty per cent.'

'Who are the others?'

The doctor shrugged. 'There's some resistance. In fairness, there's a substantial amount of resistance. But the rest are mostly gypsies, homosexuals, the enfeebled.'

There was a silence between the two men.

'I'm amazed, frankly, that your woman is still among the living.'

Now Hamer was sure about where Landau had taken his incontinent bladder after descending the watchtower ladder.

'Then why don't you have her shot?'

'I'd rather you had her shot. Shoot her, in fact. I'd rather you shoot her, Hamer, as right and proper compensation for my dog.'

'I think you mean retribution.'

'Flaunt your education, Hamer. As you flaunt your medal. God in heaven. Is it any wonder you lack friends?'

'I apologize. I don't want to shoot the woman. Christ Almighty, Herr Doctor. I'll buy you another dog.'

'The deity whose name we both take in vain does not exist any more, you know, Martin. Oh, no,' Buckner said, crooned. 'He has been superseded by a higher power.'

Hamer said nothing. He could never tell whether Buckner was being ironic or not. He suspected the man was drunk but knew he would remember everything.

Buckner puffed on his cigar. The light was so diminished now in Buckner's quarters, at the late hour in which they spoke, that Martin Hamer could hardly focus on his adversary. They spoke over the carnage of the chess table and the remnants of their dinner, delivered to them by an inmate who had cooked in a previous life for the delectation of the Warsaw Chamber of Commerce.

'Is it that you wish to fuck her?'

'Yes,' Hamer said, 'I wish to fuck her.'

'You should have told me, Martin,' the doctor said. 'Carnal appetite and heroism are not incompatible, you know.'

* * *

The night Hamer spent on the Eiger was not the longest of his life. That had been spent as he stood as a child sentinel, by candlelight, in the library of his family home, guarding his father's corpse. He had laid out the body on the large table in their library, his father attired by Martin in the uniform in which he had come home from the war. Tailored for him in his considerable prime, it hadn't fitted and had hung on his body like adult clothing forced for a tasteless joke on a child. Nobody but Martin had seen this, though. He had draped the German flag over the dressed cadaver, partly to honour him but mostly to conceal the self-inflicted wound that had killed him from those members of their depleted domestic staff who still felt the wish to pay tribute to their employer. The cook came. And the gardener and their maid. Martin had found envelopes intended for each in his father's desk.

The old man, scrupulous in death, had willed them gold coin rather than Reichsmarks, a full wheelbarrow of which would now buy only a loaf of bread. It was a long night. A desperate time. Martin thought about it now on the Eiger, suspended from pitons, freezing in his fragile refuge of canvas and goose-down above the impossible void. He thought about it because to do so gave him fortitude. He had delivered himself to the mountain. He had endured without choice the night standing vigil over his father's unhappy remains.

His bivouac, his makeshift hammock, shook and shuddered in the tear of the wind. He had not anticipated how cold it would be. He should have, but he had not. The food he had taken from his rucksack and thawed to make edible now in the warmth of his crotch was dried meat and dried fruit. It would deliver no warmth. He had been surprised by the cold. At this altitude, against obdurate rock, he should not have been. He had climbed in the spring, risking the lethal rockfalls prised from the face by the expanding heat of the afternoon sun, because he had needed, within the limits of his skills, to have clean rock to climb. But he should have anticipated the cold. Would it kill him now?

At least he didn't have Karl for company. Karl climbed a good grade, probably a grade above whatever competence in the mountains Martin could honestly claim to possess. Karl had been enthusiastic; Heidi had pressed his case. But Hamer would have begrudged Karl's company climbing a staircase. He would have wanted to climb in his new uniform; would have wanted pictures and stories about his attempt in the party's yellow press. He would have wanted to plant a swastika, should he achieve his goal, on the Eiger's summit. Martin shivered. The wind shook him, his hammock possessing all the weight and permanence of a fallen leaf. His body batted against shiftless granite. He needed to stay awake through the night, he decided. Should he sleep, the cold would certainly kill him.

All the following day and the following night, Hamer waited, helpless as a swaddled infant, wrapped in his bivouac for the storm to finally abate. His food gone, he was obliged to scrape thirstily for what rotten snow clung to the fissures of the cracks within his reach. Cold racked and tormented him. An hour before dawn on the second night, as he fought fumbling exhaustion, Hamer turned and saw his father, seated on a ledge he hadn't noticed was there before, his father's feet swinging in the void in their Cumbrian boots, under his woollen stockings and his climbing britches.

'Your funeral was a sad affair,' Hamer said. 'Poorly attended considering the man you were.'

'A difficult time,' his father said.

'The regimental association sent a wreath and a bugler. There weren't many of your old comrades.'

'Most were dead,' his father said. He pondered for a moment. 'Blumenthal?'

'A letter of condolence. He didn't make an excuse, but I don't think he could have afforded the train fare.'

'Like I said, a difficult time.'

A silence followed. There was much Martin wanted to say, to ask. His father had lit his pipe, the aroma of pipe tobacco impossibly rich in the thinness of the altitude.

'You have to get off this mountain, Martin,' his father said.

'There's a storm, Papa.'

'The storm blew itself out an hour ago.'

Hamer was aware suddenly of the stillness. The scour of the wind had gone. The stillness that replaced it was profound and terrifying.

'You have to get off this mountain, son,' his father said in the familiar tone of kindly insistence Martin Hamer had missed so much since his death. 'It will be difficult, more difficult than any climbing you have ever done. You are weakened and you are tired. But you can do it. You have it in you if you give it your best. Begin now, Martin. Start right away. There really isn't much time.'

Hamer hauled himself out of the bag and began his descent. He left his hammock where it was. He knew he had no living right to another night on the mountain. He would not require his rucksack. He didn't look back to the ledge on which his father had sat. He knew if he looked back there would be no ledge. And his father would be gone.

She was at the inn. Strain gave her face a worn, ragged look. She ran to him and held him, nearly knocked him down, weakened as he was, with the strength of her embrace.

‘Oh, God, Martin, I was waiting for your body,’ she said.

He grinned. ‘I’ve brought it with me.’

He saw the desperation in her, felt it in the thump of her hammering heart. Her eyes appraised him, filled with dismay. He was gaunt, wind-flayed, had shed twenty pounds. It had been a close-run thing. ‘I’ve finished with the Eiger,’ he said, promised.

‘You’re sure?’ She had known how much it had meant to him. ‘You’re sure you won’t want to have another try at it?’

‘I’m sure of this, Lily,’ he said. ‘I won’t want it to have another try at me.’

‘Karl is up there with two local guides,’ she told him as he spooned broth into himself and tried not to shiver, with a blanket over his shoulders like a shawl.

Hamer choked. ‘How far?’

There was a commotion outside. He heard Karl’s stridency in clipped sentences. ‘We gained the first ice field. The storm has made the avalanche risk appalling. No sign of him. We had to come down. If he isn’t dead, he’s dying now up there. I liked him, stubborn arsehole that he was.’

The owner of the inn was trying to interrupt Karl, without success.

‘Shut up, woman. Don’t you see? They were to be married. This is a tragedy. I doubt the poor girl’s heart will ever mend.’

Karl entered the inn. The swastika stitched to the chest of his climbing smock was smaller than Martin would have anticipated. It was about the size of the flag sewn on to the dead Italian's arm.

Amazement transformed Karl's features. And then a grin of pure joy. Hamer could see that the happiness and relief were genuine. He stood, and Karl subjected him to a hug and several kisses on the cheeks accompanied by murmured words he didn't really catch. Karl's gathering arms were exuberant and his body warm as he pulled Martin Hamer into his embrace.

He's not so bad, Martin thought; a bombastic, unsubtle man, but a man with heart and courage. Martin himself had descended through the Eiger's first ice field in the most dangerous conditions he had ever seen on a mountain after the havoc of the storm. Falling boulders had crashed and hurtled from the heights all around him there, pulverizing snow, triggering explosions of fragmented rock. Each boulder represented an instant, random death, and they had been falling, on that steep and desolate slope in the aftermath of the storm, like rain. And Karl had gone there looking for him.

Maybe there's hope for us yet, Hamer thought as the guides and Lillian with them clapped as though at the sight of seeing lost brothers reunited.

Later the same evening, as Lillian slept after two sleepless nights of anxiety, Hamer and Karl shared a drink.

'How close did you get?'

'Close,' Hamer said. He had told Karl about the Italian. He was not comfortable now, in the bar. He felt too vividly aware of things. There was a smell of garlic strong on the gingham cloth over the table they shared from the debris of someone's earlier meal. The aroma of hops gathered in an autumnal stink over their steins of beer. Shouts and the laughter of others in the bar bruised Hamer's senses in a series of tics and winces of which Karl seemed unaware. The tobacco smoke was thick enough to touch, like whorls and veils of rank, woven cloth. This is how a newly delivered infant must feel, Martin thought, slapped and bloodied, hauled dangling upside down into an alien world.

Karl drank from his stein of beer, licked beer froth with a smack from his upper lip. 'Were you not tempted, when the storm abated, to continue to climb?'

Hamer just looked at him. 'I was finished, Karl.'

Karl drank his beer. 'I envy you,' he said.

'It wasn't just a failure, Karl; it was a fucking disgrace. I had no right to be on that mountain. The attempt was madness. I've learned a very severe lesson. It's one I won't forget.'

'Exactly,' Karl said. 'The truest victories are always forged in the fulcrum of defeat.'

Hamer had to laugh. 'Christ, Karl. 'That which does not kill me?''

Karl nodded.

'You've been reading Nietzsche?'

Karl nodded again, swallowing beer.

Of course you have, Hamer thought. Of course you have.

* * *

Hamer's quarters in the camp were spartan. He would do nothing to change that. He wanted none of the gathered luxuries that made the cosy home from home that Buckner had created for himself. He had known men in the field who could fashion a comfortable abode from little more than scraps of canvas, wagon struts and ration cases. He'd never been one of them. But it wasn't lack of the necessary skills, or a characteristic indifference to his surroundings, that prevented Hamer from settling in. This posting was temporary. He would not distinguish it with the depressing illusion of permanence. He was in some ways a superstitious man. He would not tempt fate into keeping him here a moment longer than he was obliged to stay.

Now, he sat on his cot with his head in his hands in the light of a candle stub. There was a brandy flask beside the candle on the little locker next to the cot. The flask was engraved, filigreed with tiny marks carved into yielding pewter. Together, the marks formed a proud pattern. His family's crest. His father's flask. The flask was filled with good cognac and had been carried through the whole of the Russian campaign without the stopper being once unscrewed. He had carried the flask in the tunic pocket over his heart. It had quickly become the most important of his superstitions. But Hamer had need of the flask now not for any talismanic quality but for the liquor it contained. After what the doctor had told him about his work in his clinic before the war, Hamer had need of the strong anaesthetic of drink.

He unstoppered his flask and drank. The candle flame flared more brightly, fed on the fumes from the flask. Hamer put the stopper back on and the candle spat and its light diminished. He was aware of whimpering from the kennels, or perhaps from the dormitory block in which they kept the women. In the wind on the Polish plain, at night, it was sometimes difficult to source the origin of sounds. A gust strengthened, and the warped wood of his hut creaked in the darkness. Poland was all darkness. It was easy in such a place to imagine darkness encroaching at a stealthy creep across the whole of the world.

'Lillian,' Hamer said softly, pitying himself, at the same time contemptuous of himself for doing so. He always felt alone. It was almost five years since he had shared himself fully with a living human being. He was used to being alone. He considered himself more than competent at coping with his diminished circumstances, his strictured existence. But here, in this camp, he felt the unshifting weight of his isolation like a burden on his soul. He was lonely. After what the doctor had told him, he needed the consolation of company, someone to talk to and, better, to hold. But that was a consolation Martin Hamer knew he didn't deserve. Instead he drank brandy and listened to the mewling of listless animals and the occasional wailing of the wind. 'Lillian,' he said softly to the darkness. 'Lillian. Lily, my love.'

* * *

The machine pistol had become the standard weapon of the German infantry soldier. It was formidable enough in terms of its rate of fire and was sufficiently accurate for the street fighting the German army had been obliged to do so much of during the long siege of Stalingrad. But it was less effective over range, where accuracy and the piercing weight of a projectile mattered more. Some of Hamer's men grumbled about the weight of a rifle. And there was no arguing that the machine pistols were a lot lighter. They were easier in the handling, too, and quicker to load. But their bullets were far less likely than those of a heavy-calibre rifle to find their way through the narrow slot of a Soviet gunsight in a tank or self-propelled gun. And the bigger rifle bullets, with their higher velocity, would ricochet around inside a tank, causing carnage among its crew.

All of Hamer's unit were excellent shots. The ones who hadn't been were dead. It was a process of natural selection Hamer thought more conclusive than any example Darwin had managed to come up with in his scholarly trawl through the animal kingdom.

The same was true, of course, for the opposition. These giant opposing forces had collided and struggled until only the best and the strongest elements remained. The commander had talked about extinction. Perhaps it would come to that. Hamer felt in his mind and heart the dull certainty that the Russians would fight to the last bullet, the last tank, the last man. He walked, dry-mouthed with nervousness, among his soldiers. They sat in clusters smoking, sharpening their fighting knives, loading and reloading the twin five-bullet magazines of their rifles, adjusting gunsights and clipping ammunition pouches and grenades to each man's setup of choice. You put these things not where you were ordered to, but where you would most naturally find them under the bewildering assault of shellfire, as adrenaline convulsed your body and made your hands alien things, clumsy with tremor and sweat.

Hamer had a word or gesture for each of his men as he walked among them. It was not demonstrative; no more really than a wink here, a squeeze of the shoulder there. It was enough. They were Hamer's men and he led them. And they would have followed him anywhere.

The wind had died in the night. In the far distance, to the east, pillars of smoke rose vertically into the sky. On each day of their retreat, the Germans had harried and ambushed the advancing Russian columns. The pattern had not differed the previous night, or that morning. The Russians would get no warning of the counter-attack. When it came, it would come with all the suddenness and ferocity that the Germans could muster. They were still a formidable force. Over a hundred thousand men, thousands of guns and hundreds of tanks would be deployed along the narrow front on which von Manstein had insisted, staking everything. They would drive a wedge through the Red Army, rout them and push the beaten rabble all the way back to Moscow.

The men involved in the battle would have no sense of its scale. Only the noise, the shocking, unsubsiding howl of shellfire, would give any indication of the enormity of the event. You could break a battle down, reduce it to the part you played in it. The human mind insisted on this, perhaps as the best means of saving one's life or one's sanity, Hamer believed. There would be a battle for each unit, each tank crew, each man. For the infantry it would end up hand to hand, as it always did against this enemy, unable to retreat, their own machine guns manned by commissars behind them, ready to kill them if they took a backward step. It would be desperate and bloody. It would end only in victory. Hamer smiled, thinking of Darwin again, thinking how far men had progressed since they had coarse hair growing out of them and dragged their knuckles on the ground.

He found his sergeant sitting pulling a swatch of muslin through his rifle barrel with a filament of thread. Otto Fromm grinned and gestured at the coffeepot on the field stove between his feet. Hamer took his mug from his pack and poured himself coffee. He thought about the cognac in the flask in his tunic pocket, knowing it was a gesture Fromm would appreciate, but decided against it. He would need luck today. The flask over his heart he knew was luckier untouched.

'How are we, Fromm?'

'We're fine, sir,' Fromm said. There was nothing fake about the grin. Fromm enjoyed combat. There were four flashes stitched to his upper right sleeve. Each represented a tank the sergeant had single-handedly disabled or destroyed. He looked at Hamer through grey eyes, implausibly pale and tranquil, Hamer always thought, those eyes, after everything the sergeant had accomplished and seen.

Hamer squatted and sipped his coffee. It was strong and hot and genuine. Christ knew where the sergeant had got it from. 'I feel good about today,' he said, surprising himself, because he meant it.

'We've run far enough, sir,' Fromm said. 'We're soldiers. We came here to fight, not to hike.'

Hamer looked over his steaming mug at the hard-packed snow. 'Wrong weather for hiking,' he said. 'Anything I need to know about?'

'Nothing you don't know already, sir. Bullets are scarce. There's a few of the lads have bad feet. But it's nothing a fight won't sort out. There'll be plenty of boots to choose from and all the bullets we need once we've got those red fuckers running.'

Hamer nodded. He tossed coffee dregs on to the snow. 'Thank you, sergeant. An excellent brew,' he said.

* * *

Martin Hamer was married to Lillian Stresemann in the summer of 1932 and they spent their honeymoon on the Côte d'Azur. They rented a cottage and swam every day. Their skin turned brown and Lillian's hair became white blonde with salt from the sea as it bleach-dried under the sun. They hired bicycles and explored the coastline. Martin climbed a sea cliff in nothing but his bathing trunks and, when he reached its summit, swallow-dived back down to where Lillian trod water at the dark edge of a deep patch of sea. For six weeks they didn't listen to a wireless broadcast or look at a newspaper. They wanted this brief period of their lives to stay unsullied by the bad things brooding, on the brink of happening, in the bigger world. Lillian schooled Martin until he could pick a tune on the guitar. The tune was 'Greensleeves'. Martin coached her at tennis on a clay court attached to a deserted villa, sneaking through a hole each morning in the chainlink fence surrounding the court until she played well enough to take sets off him.

'You're not trying,' she said eventually.

'Of course I'm bloody trying,' he said, shouting back across the net between them.

'I thought you were supposed to be good at this.'

'I am good at this. Is it my fault if you're better?'

They were happy. They were together, and when they lay together at night Martin would pull his limbs into the folds of her sleeping body, arms clasped gently around her waist, willing fate to let him be with her always. He listened to the sound of her asleep. He felt the rise and fall of her breaths, close against his chest. He lay with her in the darkness as night waves broke on the shore and the old stone of the cottage cooled. And he knew that he was the luckiest man living.

There were a number of Americans on the Côte d'Azur that summer. They were happy and friendly, these Americans, chatty and welcoming and utterly incurious about what was happening in Germany. The concept of Europe seemed confusing to them. Many of them seemed to think it was a federation of states, similar to their own country.

'They've forgotten the war,' Martin said to Lillian, after drinks in a bar one night with a gathering of their new American friends. 'Odd, since they took part in it. Odd, since theirs was the decisive part in the peace.'

'They seem very nice,' Lillian said.

'They are nice.'

She touched his nose with her finger, like pushing a doorbell. She was slightly drunk. They both were. 'Since when did you become an expert on Americans?'

'I can tell these Americans are nice, that's all. I've met Americans who weren't.'

They fished with their new friends from a chartered boat. They caught nothing and drank bottles of beer chilled by the Americans in a chest of ice in the galley. The Americans were called Bill and Lucy, and they were from California. Bill was involved in motion pictures. He was a lawyer engaged in contracting people for films. He had been married to Lucy for four years.

'What do you do, Lucy?' Lillian asked.

'Lucy shops,' Bill said.

Lucy kicked her husband. He winked at her through the green glass and condensation of his beer bottle. 'I make Bill happy,' Lucy said.

Martin studied Bill. Bill looked to be in his mid-thirties, the right age. 'Did you fight in the war, Bill?'

Bill shook his head. 'Trained at Fort Bragg. Lot of Yale boys joined up. But the armistice was declared before we got overseas. A lucky escape.'

'Were many of your classmates killed?'

'None I knew personally. But plenty I knew died of the flu on the boats on the way back.'

'Why do you say a lucky escape?'

'Fishing isn't my game, kid, as I'm sure a shrewd boy like you has already surmised.'

Hamer looked at the slack lines draped from their rods. 'I don't seem to be much good at it either.'

'But I do enjoy hunting.'

'Don't you ever,' Lucy said.

'Hunt mostly with a Canadian guy. Davy Robertson. Now Davy did see action. He was at the third Battle of Ypres. Davy Robertson fought at Passchendaele.'

'And he told you about this?'

'Never. But I've shared a tent on plenty hunting trips with Davy. And he talks in his sleep.'

Lillian looked thoughtful. She took the cap off a bottle of beer. 'How do you know the specifics?'

'Technically I'm Davy's boss. I dug his résumé out of company files and it's all there.'

'Sneaky,' Lillian said.

'Guy works for you starts screaming in his sleep, you need to know the reason why.'

'Of course he's sneaky,' Lucy said. 'He's a lawyer.'

'Turns out old Davy was decorated and everything,' Bill said. 'No wonder he doesn't miss a lot of ducks.'

Passchendaele. The word seemed alien, its connotations surreal on the gleaming deck of their white boat, with cold beers in their hands, conversing with nice Americans in English. The sea stretched and glittered turquoise under the sun. The coast of southern France was a sedate, blue-grey smudge in the distance.

'Think there'll ever be another war, Bill?'

Bill laughed. 'A world war? Never. They do say war is a great way to beat a depression. And God knows, Martin, we've got one of those in the States right now. But I can't see us going to fight on foreign turf again. Not in my lifetime.'

'You're not going, anyway,' Lucy said. 'You're going nowhere, honey, without me.'

Martin studied Bill. The man had a spreading paunch and heavy biceps. His exposed forearms were ham sized with bunched veins close to the surface of the skin. It was easy to imagine a younger version of Bill on the football field on a raw afternoon, pitting his strength against the players of Harvard or Notre-Dame. He was a big, strong man acceding to slow decline, a natural athlete ageing with an athlete's genetic reluctance. Lucy, full-lipped, succulent under her careful bob of glossy hair, lit a cigarette. There was an ashtray in front of her shaped like a tropical shell. It was full of cigarette ends. Each stub was stamped at its end with the crimson imprint of her lipstick.

'Have either of you read Hemingway?' Lucy asked.

'Read him?' Bill said. 'I've had dinner with the guy.'

He had met Fitzgerald, too, it transpired, who had lost what careless investments he had possessed in the Crash. Fitzgerald was contracted to spin his elegant dreams for the motion-picture business now. But that wasn't going well. There was a drink problem. A wife problem. And the man couldn't write dialogue that worked in pictures. Bill told his Hollywood war stories to a transfixed Lillian. Martin dozed on the deck of the boat and dreamed uneasily. The Americans had presided over the peace. The French had exacted its terms. Passchendaele was 600 miles away. His father had fought in the horrible mire of that battlefield against the Canadians, the New Zealanders, the British. There was much unfinished business in the world, Martin thought. He sipped beer under the sun and vaguely, at one point, reached for Lillian's hand.

* * *

He had been about to leave Buckner's quarters, late, half-drunk, when the doctor had asked him about what he did before the outbreak of the war. The needle of the gramophone was blunting rhythmically on the inner edge of one of the doctor's recordings. It was an insistent, uncomfortable sound. Martin went across and lifted the arm. The doctor was seated, putting his chesspieces back in their proper positions on the board. It was very late. The camp was as close to silent as it ever got. Buckner was a man with little apparent need for a good night's sleep.

I was a professional soldier, Hamer told him. I was an observer in Spain. I was for a time in Africa. I went into Sudetenland and Moravia. Drilled troops in Austria. Supervised mountain training in the Alps and cold-weather training in the Antarctic.

'Your home?'

'Cologne, with my wife. After her death I sought any posting that took me as far away from Cologne as possible.'

'A beautiful city.'

'For me, unbearably so.'

Hamer had been about to take his leave, had his fingers around the handle of Buckner's warped door, when more out of politeness than curiosity he said to the doctor, 'What about you?'

And the doctor told him about the clinic. His clinic in the forest outside Düsseldorf filled with the children of the idiotic, the alcoholic and the criminally insane. Children taken from the charge of antisocial families when the women of those families were taken to be sterilized and the men confined to labour camps. The children of gypsies were taken there and the children of Jews and whores and those who continued despite the statutes to practise the black art of Freemasonry.

'Do you know about germ plasm, Martin?'

Hamer shook his head. He didn't think he wanted to know about germ plasm.

'Think of it as the corrupt element that causes degeneracy in the collective gene. After the Führer's ascent to power, Germany became a gardening state. We needed to husband our genetic strength, our purity. We needed to grow strong and root out the causes of weakness.'

'What happened to the children in the clinic?'

'Nothing at first,' Buckner said. 'They were merely a drain on resources, another useless, costly channelling of the hard-earned Reichsmarks of a hard-working people.'

Hamer said nothing. His hand had grown slippery with sweat around the handle of the doctor's door.

'The experimental programme was my own initiative,' Buckner said, nudging a black pawn into place with his forefinger. 'The pharmacological cost was negligible. The staff were dedicated. The results of our clinical research were of incalculable benefit. If it hadn't been for the interruption of the war, there would have been accolades and probably awards.'

'What happened to the children?'

'They died. In various ways and at varying speeds. But the children all died. That's what happens to a subject when you introduce and foster in it a fatal disease.'

'For what reason?'

'Vaccines, Martin. We were researching and developing vaccines. For the wellbeing of the people. For the general good of the Volk.'

Hamer said nothing. For no reason he could have explained, he remembered a moment on a military exchange mission to Italy prior to the war. With the rest of the German officers, he had taken part in a parade. They had sat in two open-topped Mercedes cars, polished and resplendent in the Italian sun. The parade was a mixture of civic pomp and soldierly showing off, with much gilt and many swords and cavalry with hats as richly edged as curtain pelmets. A marching band had played, and a ragged troupe of street children had followed in the dust kicked up behind them, laughing and aping the martial musicians, happy in their urchin rags and mischief. The laughter in Hamer's car at their antics had been unanimous and genuine. Degeneracy. A gardening state.

'Where did you put the bodies?'

Buckner laughed. 'What do you think, Martin? That we buried them? Sowed a German forest, sacred land, with virulence and disease? The corpses were incinerated, of course.'

Hamer said nothing.

'Let me tell you something about children, Martin, since you won't be having any of your own. Their trust is instinctive.' The black pawn lay on the open palm of the doctor's extended hand now. 'You don't have to earn it. They just offer it to you, along with their love.' He closed his fingers around the chesspiece.

Hamer still said nothing.

'You are a sentimental man, aren't you, Martin,' the doctor decided rather than asked. 'I knew this before now. I saw it earlier, in the way you played. You lack the stomach for the endgame. It is a flaw in a man so formidable. It is a dangerous flaw, in times such as these.'

'Good night, Herr Doctor.'

'So far, all you have accomplished in this camp is to slaughter a much-prized pedigree animal and deprive a much-valued NCO of two of his teeth and his reputation as a brawler. Your valour in battle is not questioned. At least, not by me. But I know Commandant Crupp wishes to speak to you. And I have to warn you that Crupp is the least sentimental of people.'

Hamer left, leaving Buckner to the pride of his memories and the proliferation of his judgements concerning the nature of other men.

* * *

Lillian's father was a busy man. That much was obvious to Hamer as he sat in the vestibule outside his father-in-law's consulting rooms waiting for the time of his appointment to arrive. Lillian hadn't come. Dr Stresemann had asked for Martin to come alone. Now he sat waiting, turning his cap between his fingers, his shoulders squared by the stiff cut of his tunic and by the nervousness afflicting him. He looked around. It was summer, but cool in the vestibule among the fleshy plants in their ornate copper pots, in the limited light allowed by the brocade drapes over each floor-to-ceiling window. The drapes made an indistinct muffle of the traffic on the wide avenue outside. Hamer looked at the other patients. There was a woman in a cashmere topcoat and cloche hat with a child dressed in the summer uniform of the Hitler Youth. There was a businessman — Hamer assumed he was a businessman — in a beautifully tailored suit. His hands rested on a malacca cane and looked manicured. There was a party pin on his lapel. Across from Martin, ignoring him, a man wearing the uniform of a full admiral sat with a much younger woman and pretended to read a newspaper. Martin saw from the officer's ribbons that his branch of the service was submarines.

Trying to distract himself, he looked at the paintings on the walls. There was an equine study by Stubbs. Two views of Venice painted by Canaletto. And a portrait of the Führer, astride a horse, wearing a field marshal's uniform and flourishing his baton in a manner familiar from a painting of Napoleon that Martin remembered seeing with Lillian in a visit to the Louvre.

The door to the double staircase that descended to the street opened, and a large man with a broad build and boxed-in features entered the vestibule on light feet and lowered himself into a chair. The submariner admiral nodded to the man, who waved a return greeting. Martin recognized him from newsreels. He was an American. He was the former heavyweight boxing champion of the world. Then Martin was called for his consultation with Dr Stresemann.

He knew straight away. Stresemann stood with his back to his desk, facing a window. His hands were linked behind his back and his fingers fidgeted. The doctor's composure and tact were legendary, his skills in diplomacy the envy of his profession. But this was hardly a professional matter. This was a family affair. He turned abruptly, his eyes moist, blinking.

'I'm so very sorry, my boy. So sorry, Martin. For both of you.'

It was strange. Hamer felt almost a sense of relief. At least it was him and not Lillian. At least his wife would not have to suffer the stigma attached in Germany now to a barren woman.

'No hope?'

The doctor spread his hands. 'You can never say never where such matters are concerned,' he said, and Martin sensed the diplomat in him. But then the doctor's face fell again into sadness. 'Viscosity is normal. Quantity is average. But your sperm is delivered to the world dead, Martin. Barring some miraculous breakthrough in medical science, you will never father a child.'

'She should divorce me,' Hamer said.

The doctor shook his head. 'It was you she chose. It was you she married. It is you who makes her happy.'

'You will never hold a grandchild.'

The doctor rocked on his feet and his breath emerged ragged. He was having great difficulty in retaining his composure. 'I won't, Martin, it is true. But it is also true that when Lillian brought you to our door, she brought me home a son.'

The avenue outside the doctor's surgery was filled with sunlight. The air was still and heavy. It smelled of flowers and tobacco smoke and hot engine oil. Hamer put on his cap and adjusted its tilt in the reflection from a shop window. His appearance had never given him any pleasure.

But there was no question that with his physique, in his dress uniform, he looked virile enough.

He looked up and down the avenue. Lillian had taken two days off work. Martin had requested and been granted two days' leave. They were spending the long weekend with Dr Stresemann in his summer house on the Wannsee. Lily was there now, swimming in the lake, a train ride and a walk through wooded lanes away. He decided he would have a drink before catching his tram to the station. Or maybe he would walk to the station. But first he would have a drink.

Hamer sat down at a table outside a corner café and ordered a beer from a pretty waitress with a League of German Maidens badge sewn on to her pinafore. Presently his drink arrived. He drank slowly. The enormity of what weighed on his mind, its implications, were somewhere beyond capable thought. He sipped his beer with a surprisingly steady hand and watched the world. When his first beer was drunk, and his second solicitously delivered, he stripped the glass of the beads of condensation formed on its tall exterior by the contrast between heat and cold. He did it with his thumb. He would never teach the physical laws of the world to his son.

The admiral from the doctor's surgery passed by Hamer's table, he and his young female companion summer pedestrians engaged in heated argument. Whiting had been newly edged on the admiral's cap. His uniform made a splendid sight as his language brawled and the young woman with him began publicly to sob.

He would never teach his son to climb.

Hamer was on his third beer, no longer concerned about condensation, when the boxing champion from Dr Stresemann's consulting rooms passed by. He was in the rear seat of an open-topped Hispanola with a chauffeur at the wheel, gloved, despite the radiant heat. There's a clue in that extravagance, Hamer thought, ordering another drink from the pretty waitress, as to how these prize fighters always end up penniless.

Next in the procession, he half-expected to see the Führer trot by on that white charger, baton in hand, bogus uniform resplendent as the saviour of their nation cantered towards some epoch-making event. Could the Führer even ride? Hamer didn't think so. He himself rode well enough. But Lillian rode better. It was a skill they would never teach their son. He belched. He closed his eyes. He was becoming drunk and sour under the heat and defeat of the day. He needed to go home. Sweat trickled between his shoulder blades and oozed in the afternoon heat through his eyebrows, making him blink. His body did work, he thought then, in at least some essential respects. He closed his eyes, sweat stung, and focused on darkness. He needed to go home.

* * *

There was a commotion on the corner opposite the café. It cleared, and Hamer saw a small figure standing in an unseasonal overcoat. The men who had surrounded him, Brown Shirts, the cause of the commotion, spat in their own aftermath and jeered. Hamer rose, put money on the table, notes anchored under the heavy lip of a glass ashtray, and crossed to where the figure stood.

He stood with a cardboard sign across his chest on a piece of string depending from his neck. There were gobs of phlegm on his coat lapels. His nose was bleeding. Otherwise he looked respectable, Hamer thought. His trousers were pressed, although there was a tear at one knee, which looked fresh. And a pavement scrape had stripped the shiny leather from one of the toecaps of his scrupulously polished shoes. Medals hung in a neat row from the left breast of his overcoat. Hamer recognized the ribbon of an Iron Cross. It was torn, the decoration itself gone. The man was trembling. His nose dripped blood on to his coat. The sign around his neck said: WAR VETERAN. JEW. LOVER OF MY FATHERLAND. WHY DO YOU TREAT ME AS A CRIMINAL?

'Go home, sir,' Martin Hamer said.

The man shook his head. 'I have no home to go to.'

'Go home.' Hamer said this gently. 'Please.'

'I had a tobacconist's concession at the Zoo Station. They took a Zionist premium from me. Then they took the concession. I have nothing, sir. Nowhere to go.'

'Where did you earn your Iron Cross?'

'Those men just now took it from me. They

said for me to wear it was a violation.'

'Where did you earn it?'

'The last offensive of the war, sir.'

Hamer groaned. 'What's your name?'

'Jew.'

'What's your name?'

'Jew.'

Hamer put a hand on the man's shoulder, felt the shudder of fear through fabric too thick for the time of year. 'Please, soldier. What's your name?'

'Weismann, sir. Jacob Weismann.'

'Go home, Jacob Weismann.'

'You are drunk, sir, with the respect your rank accords,' Weismann said.

And that was how Martin Hamer first encountered a Jew.

* * *

Their fighter-bombers began the battle, flying from airstrips to the west on the other side of the river. Their commander had promised hundreds of planes. He had delivered on this pledge. The squadrons of Stukas dived vertically out of the clouds, stippling the snow with machine-gun fire, sowing the ground with bombs in endless, screaming, staccato attacks. Then came the blizzard of shells fired by their heavy artillery. As the columns of Russian tanks became diesel-fed pyres, the sky turned black and the snow was burnished to the east with what looked to Hamer, through his field binoculars, like a series of orange suns setting cruelly across the land.

His men rode the tanks into combat, dropping off in clusters and fanning out across the edge of the battlefield in the moments before the panzers engaged.

Smoke boiled and pitched over the steppe. Using his field compass to orientate himself, Hamer led his men in a strung-out line. They would attempt to broadside a Russian column, attack its tanks and lorries where their targets couldn't find space to roam and manoeuvre. They would still come under shellfire and machine-gun fire from the rotating turrets of the T-34s, but this most lethal of Soviet heavy weapons was far less dangerous to an attacking infantryman when they were wedged motionless, their caterpillar tracks unable to churn and crush at will.

They heard their column before they saw it. They heard the screams of burning tank crews and the stippled ricochet of machine-gun fire from the dive-bombers still howling out of the sky. Machine-gun bullets bounced off plates of heavy armour and rattled through tank tracks, and Hamer heard the wet punch of them hitting men still stranded on wooden seats under the canvas coverings of troop lorries.

A zipper pattern sewed itself into a snowy rise to Hamer's right, and he realized they had come under automatic weapons fire, the trappers trapped, ambushed. He saw a flush of red illuminate a copse of spindly trees in the gloom to his left, and a tank shell exploded thirty feet from him as he dropped to the ground and looked for any scrap of cover on the frozen earth. Instinct overwhelmed him then, and he scrambled up the rise that had taken the row of bullets and heard another machine-gun burst and felt the deathly breath of a bullet on one cheek as he dived into a shallow depression on the other side.

Sergeant Fromm shared the depression, conscious, bleeding in arterial spasms from the ragged wound where his leg now ended, just below the left knee. He was pale, his grey eyes vacuous with shock. Listening for the change in engine noise that would signal a gear shift and the tank's approach, Hamer unbuckled the sergeant's belt and secured it tightly around his leg above the knee joint. He fumbled for morphine, cursing his rebellious hands. Once he'd got the morphine into his sergeant, he risked a glimpse over the edge of their cover. A burst of fire came from the copse of trees and thudded into the berm of frozen earth in front of him. He scrambled back down, grabbed Fromm by the tunic, lifted him into a sitting position and slapped him hard across the face. The sergeant's eyes cleared.

'How bad is it?'

'You've lost your lower left leg. You'll live if you do as I say.'

Fromm closed his eyes momentarily, opened them again and nodded.

'I need a field of fire, sergeant. Anything you can do. There's a T-34 in a copse of trees a hundred and fifty feet beyond this bluff. From where you are now, it's precisely at four o'clock.'

Fromm's trained eyes went to the spot. 'If its commander knew how lightly armed we are he'd have churned our entire patrol into meat. That's assuming anyone else has found cover.'

'I don't hear any of our lads attacking the tank,' Fromm said.

It was hard to know how much of this stoicism was courage and how much of it morphine. Hamer didn't think it mattered. The penny was going to drop with the commander of the Russian tank. They had to go for him before he came for them. They had to do it now.

'I'll leave you all the ammunition I've got except for what's in my magazines,' Hamer said, unclipping his pouches. He pulled his water bottle free and took a couple of swallows. 'I'll leave you this. I'll leave you two grenades. Lob the first as soon as I make my break. Here, I'll help you into position. And I'll come back for you, Sergeant Fromm. Alive or dead, I'm bringing you back.'

'Get going, sir,' Fromm said. He gripped the handle of his stick grenade and winked.

It's courage, Hamer decided. Morphine has fuck all to do with it. He gathered himself and leaped for the lip of the bluff.

The bullet that hit Martin Hamer almost jerked him out of his boots. It took him in the chest, on the left side, above his heart and the token protection of his father's hip flask. Its impact felt like a full blow from the blunt head of a heavy hammer. It saved his life, because it pulled him out of the path of the other bullets sprayed by the tank's machine gun and dumped him in a drainage ditch where he hoped the Russian tank crew thought him dead. He could see along the ditch. It lay under the smoke of battle and he shared it with the dead. He could see bodies in the spectral, almost luminous light of the snow, German dead, members of his own patrol. He put his fingers in his wound, which was clean and apparently too deep to bleed. If the impact had been a hammer blow, the pain was like someone gouging him repeatedly with an ice axe. He'd given his morphine to Fromm; could not have used it anyway, needed to be alert, had to move if he didn't want to die like the men collapsed like rag dolls in uniforms sharing the ditch with him. He heard the T-34 grind into gear. The sound came from a point further on up the ditch and to the left. If he could prevent himself from fainting with pain, he could approach the tank in cover, perhaps surprise them. He took off his helmet and scooped snow into it and softened the frozen crystals with his fingers and then packed his wound with snow. He had lost his rifle. He put his helmet back on and took his pistol out. He began to run.

He could hear a steady series of rifle reports and the plink of heavy-calibre bullets against the armour of the tank, interspersed with the roar of return fire. It was his opinion that the Soviets were an enemy profligate with their ammunition. He supposed that a slave population ensured such a high rate of productivity that they would not fear shortages. The Russians under Stalin would rather make bullets than bake bread. He thanked God for Fromm and the dogged belligerence of his sergeant's courage. The tank was moving. He could hear it close now, feel the fifty-ton mass of it shuddering on the frozen earth. It was moving slowly because of the lack of visibility caused by the smoke and because the mopping up of infantry was a deliberate and methodical task.

Hamer emerged from his ditch to the left and to the rear of the tank. As he clambered on to the back of it, he heard something shift and snap inside him and his wound began to bleed, pink through its packed dressing of snow. He hauled himself up to where the tank commander, head and shoulders out of the open turret hatch, tapped signals with his feet on to the shoulders of the man controlling its steering mechanism. Praying that Fromm was no longer shooting, he put two bullets into the back of the tank commander's neck and hauled the body free of the hatch as waves of pain made the panicked cries of the tank crew faint and distant. He dropped two grenades into the turret, fired in a few pistol rounds, slammed shut and locked the hatch and crouched down beside it with his hands over his ears. There were screams and then a dull crump and a thrum of vibrating metal through his feet. Then there was silence. There can never be silence in a battle. But for Hamer that day, when he took his hands from his ears, it seemed for a blissful moment that there was. He climbed down carefully from the metal tomb he had made for the Russian tank crew. He was very thirsty. He took the water bottle from the belt of the tank commander's corpse and put the bottle to his lips. He spat and grimaced. It was filled with vodka. He tossed the bottle on to the snow. Martin Hamer went to gather his surviving men and to keep the promise he had made his sergeant. He would retrieve his rifle too. He was sure he could find the spot where the weapon had been torn so rudely from his grip. The smoke was choking, and explosions boomed above him in the black sky. The battle had only begun. He had earned, without knowledge of it then, an early place in its mythology.

* * *

She sat on the bed and rolled a cigarette with the tobacco she had requested he buy her. He lit it for her. She inhaled deeply and held the smoke in her lungs. Then she let it out in a long downward plume through her nostrils, her full mouth and eyes closed as her body and brain thrilled to the spread of nicotine.

'The flowers are a nice touch,' she said.

He had picked them in the woods a mile away from the camp. He didn't know if the remark was meant sarcastically. The wild spring blooms made his quarters look even bleaker than before.

'And it was kind of you to buy the books.'

'They're not proscribed.'

'I know that, sir. I was a librarian. I was there for the burning.'

'Of course you were.'

He wanted more than anything to touch her,

to have her hold him, to feel the touch of skin and hair in an embrace.

'Do you want me to take my clothes off?'

'What would you like to do, Julia?'

She smoked. Her eyes shone, green in candlelight through smoke. 'My choices are somewhat limited in the circumstances, sir.'

Her shoulders were slender under prison drab. Her skin was pale, and she was thin with undernourishment. She sat on his bed and rolled another cigarette. Her legs were crossed at the knee. He could see the shape of a calf. She stared at him.

'You don't fear me, do you, Julia?' It was a question posed as a statement. He must have learned the habit from Buckner, he realized with a stab of self-disgust.

She licked the gummed paper of her cigarette.

'Is it hate you feel?'

'I don't hate you, sir. Sometimes I hate myself. But that's normal, don't you think?'

Hamer could not believe how much he wanted her. The collision of feelings in him practically made him gasp. Her proximity, a few feet away, within touching distance on his bed, seemed terrible and wonderful at the same time. The circumstances were bizarre and grotesque, but a part of her at least seemed willing to be here. He was aware, in the raw thrill of her presence, of how isolated and solitary a man he had become, of the years and years of willed isolation, of starving himself of feeling, of his abject surrender to grief. He wanted to touch and stroke and kiss this woman. He wanted to lick and enter her. 'Nothing is normal,' he heard himself say.

'What I'd really like to do, sir,' Julia Smollen said to him, 'is to have a bath — in hot water, with real soap.'

'Of course,' he said.

'And then we can do whatever you wish.'

* * *

They travelled on a fishing holiday to Scotland with Karl and Heidi. Heidi was five months pregnant with their twins. Lillian joked that Karl would have to find some khaki wool so that the new arrivals could be knitted uniforms. Karl laughed at the joke. He can afford to be generous with his laughter, Hamer thought. His marriage isn't barren. He thought it brave of Lillian to make the joke. He knew that her humour concealed pain. She had a selflessness. He loved her all the more for her possession of this quality.

They were still at the breakfast table in the small hotel on its hill above the loch. They had breakfasted on kedgeree at Karl's happy insistence. The dish owed its origin to British India, Karl informed them; it was a product of empire. Hamer thought the stuff disgusting, thought that if this was the benefice of empires, then those empires weren't worth the struggle of subjugation. The women had gone for a walk through the pure Scottish air, the breath of heather and pine around the peaty stillness of the loch. It had become a ritual over the seven days they had been there. It had become the way in which Heidi countered her daily bout of morning sickness. Maybe she threw up in the loch. Whether she did or she didn't, Lillian was far too discreet to say.

Karl's jaunty mood had disappeared. His face was concealed by an English newspaper. A Scottish newspaper, Hamer corrected himself. Karl was concealed behind the pages of the *Edinburgh Gazette*.

'Bad news?'

'Unfortunately, yes.' Karl's voice was tight in his throat. 'My God, Martin. And they came so close, those boys.' He handed Hamer the newspaper. There was a photograph of a young climber, dead, bent from the waist, his outstretched hands two frostbitten claws, his body suspended in the void from his abseil rope.

'I don't have your facility with written English,' Martin said, handing back the newspaper. He said it gently. Karl was visibly distressed.

And so Karl read out to him the account of the attempt on the Eiger's Norwald made by Hinterstoisser, Ranier, Angerer and Kurz. The Scottish newspaper carried a comprehensive account.

'You knew them all.'

'I've climbed with all of them,' Karl said.

'I'm so sorry, Karl.'

'That brilliant traverse made by Hinterstoisser? They're going to name it after him. As they properly should.'

'It condemned them.'

'They were unlucky,' Karl said. 'Unlucky with the storm.'

'Would you climb it, Karl?'

'Not now.' He smiled but didn't look at Martin Hamer. 'My children need their father. Heinrich Harrer plans an attempt. Heckmair will probably accompany him. Harrer asked me if I was interested in having a crack at it with them. I said no. But it needs to be a German who conquers the Eigerwand. It should be one of us.'

'Heinrich Harrer is an Austrian,' Hamer said.

'An outmoded view, Martin,' Karl said, leaning across the breakfast table, the kipper from his kedgeree vile and fishy on his breath. 'We're all good Germans now.'

I'm always cajoled into fishing on holidays, Hamer thought much later, in the boat, with Karl. And never catching anything. It is a failure predetermined by fate. It is like some doomed quest. I'm fated to fish in every fishing water in the world and never catch a bloody thing. You'd think I could lure and land a fish. I mean, it isn't as if I'm questing for the Holy Grail. He laughed at the absurd fancy of his thoughts. They had dropped the women at tea time at the little wooden jetty that served the hotel. He thought the fanciful nature of his brooding now might have been brought on by the sunset, an extravagant flush of orange cloud ribbed above the purple Scottish mountains. It was a vista fit for epic dreams.

'What's funny?' Karl said, his head a halo of summer midges, his attention on the baiting of a hook, between attempts to bat the midges away.

They heard their piper test his reed and begin a lament.

'Not a bite all day and now that bloody noise,' Karl said.

Both men turned and looked at the piper, slow-marching up and down the hotel jetty as he played, the sound of the pipes amplified across the waste of unruffled water separating him from them.

It was their eighth evening. For the eighth time Karl said, 'I'm mystified by a people who consider that banshee wail to be a sound acceptable to human ears.'

Tonight, Hamer decided to say nothing. He was enjoying the sunset too much for debate. He'd endured much chapter and verse about the inferiority of the Celts to those of Aryan descent. He liked the sound of the bagpipes. At least, he liked the laments. He had heard from his father the stories of the Scots, the Seaforth Highlanders, the Black Watch, their murderous advances over battlefields in their fighting kilts, their bayonets fixed; to the fierce skirl of the pipes. But he liked the laments. They echoed to him the solitary beauty of the Scottish landscape. They hinted at the tragic history of a country left largely emptied by that tragedy.

'And I can't understand them wearing skirts,' Karl said. 'I mean, can you imagine any more ridiculous garment than a plaid skirt on a man?'

Hamer thought about the question. 'From a Scottish perspective?'

'If you wish,' Karl said, batting midges.

'Lederhosen,' Hamer said. 'I think they'd find

lederhosen pretty funny, the Scots. I have to confess I always have myself.'

Karl didn't respond to the humour. His own mood had been combative, when it hadn't been gloomy, all day. He was brooding on the fate of the climbers who had perished on the Eiger's north face, Hamer knew. Sedimeyer and Mehringer the previous year, now these four brave, ambitious boys. The newspaper picture of Toni Kurz was haunting, the story it depicted heartbreaking. After the falls to their deaths of his climbing companions, he had somehow endeavoured to scramble and clamber solo for hundreds of feet down a makeshift descent that most would have considered impossible. But he was a greatly gifted Alpinist, Toni Kurz, who wanted very much to see his thirtieth birthday. He had managed to get within twenty feet or so of the viewing windows hewn out of the living rock for passengers on the railway that ran through the mountain. But the viewing windows had been cut high in the sheer face of the Eigerwand and there was no way for his would-be rescuers to reach him. As night fell and the rescue party were worn down by the cold and the anguished pleas of the freezing, stranded boy, they were forced to retreat for the night. They came back the following morning. He hung there, suspended, his gloves lost, hands contorted into shapes resembling lobster claws by frostbite. Kurz made one final, exhausting attempt to free himself and reach the men grasping for him from their vertical rectangles of light and hope in the mountain face. But it couldn't be done.

'I'm finished,' Kurz said. His body bowed then, defeated on its rope, and he died.

It was later discovered that a knot on the rope had caught between rocks and snagged it. Had his rope not caught, he would have reached his rescuers and survived.

'Let's row in,' Karl said, the sun setting, dusk diminishing the view around their boat. 'I've had it with today, Martin. I very much want it to be tomorrow.'

It was close to midnight when Martin found Heidi, alone, reading in the conservatory of the hotel, her swollen feet on a cushion on a chair in front of her. She smiled and gestured for him to sit, slamming shut the book she had been reading. Her eyes were bright in moonlight and her skin had a pale, lunar lustre, smooth and perfect. She brushed hair off her face, but heavy, abundant, it just slipped back again, glossy in the night, spilling on to her shoulders. Her feet might be swelling a bit, he thought, but pregnancy suits our Heidi very prettily indeed.

She reached out and squeezed his hand. 'How's Lillian?'

'She's fine,' Hamer said. Heidi was far from insensitive to their situation. She had introduced them, after all, was his wife's best friend. Late in the evenings, there was an honour bar in the lounge. Hamer had signed a bottle of whisky out of it and brought a glass with the bottle to the conservatory. The smell out here, if he closed his eyes, reminded him of his father's conservatory, the same smell of stored sunlight and pungent soil and cooling greenery. It was a smell too redolent of his youth for him comfortably to endure. He poured whisky into his glass and sniffed the whisky's banishing smell of northern rain and peat. It was why he had bought the bottle from the bar.

'How are you, Heidi?'

'Happier than I'd be on a Strength Through Joy trip,' she said.

'Is that what Karl wanted?'

She hesitated, careful with her language. 'It works both ways, Martin. I'm pregnant with twins, which is a cause for general celebration. The paediatrician is free. The midwife will be free. The post-natal care will be solicitous and free, and so will nursery provision. But there is always pressure to do what is thought most proper, particularly now that Karl works for the party full-time.'

'Do you think it's changing him?'

Heidi laughed. 'Be honest, Martin. You found him pretty insufferable before.'

'He has his qualities.' Hamer sipped whisky. 'Do you, though?'

Heidi was silent. 'When we decided we would come to Scotland,' she said, 'I told Karl that I would like to go to Glasgow while we're here and see the school of art there that Mackintosh designed. It's a bus ride from the village on the other side of the loch. It's a not unreasonably long bus ride, and it passes through some of the most glorious country in the world, by all accounts. But Karl scoffed at the idea. He said that Mackintosh was soft and of a decadent school.' She hesitated. Hamer sipped his whisky. 'The answer to your question is I think it's changing all of us, Martin. It's doing so subtly, in ways we don't even see.'

After kissing Heidi good night, Hamer put back the whisky bottle on the bar, built in one corner of the lounge to resemble the wood and brass prow of a boat. The hotel lounge was full of clutter. Bric-à-brac, he believed the British called this happy chaos of mementos. There were pipe racks on the mantelpiece and stuffed fish and fowl in glass cases on the walls. There were flat display cases filled with insects and butterflies and fishing flies. A set of antlers as thick as his fist at their base spread regally above the doorframe. There was a large Chinese vase filled with walking sticks fashioned from ash and spruce and yew. Some of these had the names of their owners stamped in silver and mounted close to the head of their shafts, the plates secured with tiny, jewellery makers' screws. Then there were the bottles on the honour bar itself. Hamer had drunk a whisky called Oban. He'd thought it very fine, its smoky flavour possessing more taste and character than any schnapps he'd ever drunk. There were others, whiskies from distilleries with names he could never have pronounced, in his not-much-better-than-schoolboy English. These were the souvenirs of happy times, here in this place, he thought, gathered as the knowing, collective shoring of experience. These artefacts were the happy proof of a way a people lived, of the small intricacies and pleasures of their civilization. In the far corner ticked a longcase clock, its long pendulum and weights visible through a glass panel in its wooden body. Hamer went over and studied it, expecting to see Geneva, or perhaps London, inscribed on its face. Instead, scrolled proudly, in italic script, were the words 'Made in Edinburgh'.

There was a guest book, inviting comments on the hotel. 'Rains interminably,' one guest with a French name had written in October 1922. 'Serves you right, Georges Laval, for coming in October,' Hamer said aloud. He wasn't overfond of the French. 'Caught four trout in an afternoon!' an ecstatic Mrs Siobhán Connolly recorded in June 1929. That's four more than I've caught in my life, Martin thought. Perhaps that was just the luck of the Irish. He went through the earlier part of the book, half-anticipating his mother's small, neat script, detailing a visit paid by his parents. But in his mother's abbreviated life, they had not, it seemed, ever been here. If they had, they had not recorded the fact.

And then Martin noticed the toys. There were balls and a skipping rope and a clockwork warship built for the bathtub. There was a toy fire engine fashioned from tin and a carved balsawood aeroplane. There were wooden building blocks with letters and numbers painted on their faces and a doll's house and a tiny lace-lined crib. Lastly there was a miniature set of bagpipes, scrupulously crafted to suit the dimensions of an infant child.

Hamer crept as softly as he could back to their room. He hadn't needed to worry, though, about waking Lillian. She lay on her stomach in darkness, crying very quietly into her pillow. Clouds from the mountains concealed the moon now, and the room was inhabited by a darkness close to absolute. He took off his clothes and draped them by touch alone over the brass rail at the foot of their bed. He hesitated for a moment before climbing in beside his wife. He did not ask her what it was she was upset about. He did not need to ask Lily why she was crying.

⋆ ⋆ ⋆

Hamer collapsed, finally, through blood loss as he and a corporal tried to carry Sergeant Fromm back through the line of advance to one of their mobile dressing stations. The short, sapping journey was a struggle against the tide of every sort of military vehicle. There were tanks and churning half-tracks and trucks and motorcycles with sidecars, metal spikes protruding from their tyres to grip the snow. Marching soldiers occupied the salted, gritted, make-shift roads in double ranks of three, singing. Their voices were strong and their windburned faces resolute. It was like the blitzkrieg days at the start of the campaign, when they had first invaded this incalculable country, such was the pace and relentlessness of the Reich army's forward momentum. Hamer and the corporal were forced to walk back through the heavy snow at the sides of the route occupied by their advancing forces. Fromm kept struggling in and out of consciousness. The sergeant was a heavy, unquiet burden, as belligerent carried, dying, as he had been in the fight.

Hamer came to on a truckle bed in a field hospital, reeling from the smelling salts they had used to revive him. The commander stood over him, a smile tight on his face. Hamer tried to salute, but he was too weak to raise his arm fully. The commander took his half-lifted hand and placed it gently across Martin's chest. He squatted, boots groaning stiff in protest. He was still holding Martin's hand. The calfskin of his gloved fingers felt as soft as butter. A salvo of rockets launched from behind where Martin lay made the canvas ripple and shudder, and snow was slapped from the roof above their heads.

'Kharkov,' the commander said. 'We'll advance to Kharkov and beyond, thanks to the efforts of men like you, Martin Hamer.'

'Fromm? My sergeant?'

The commander shook his head. 'Our field surgeons are the best. He was hit twice providing your covering fire, apparently, as you approached that tank. The life bled out of him. You did as much as any man could have.'

Hamer saw blackness encroach on the edge of his vision. Another rocket salvo shocked him into alertness. 'My wound?'

'You were shot through. There's a hole in you. It's clean, but the infection risk is high.' The commander stood. 'You're going home. You've earned a rest, Martin. A rest, and with it your due reward.'

He saluted. He walked to the canvas and Perspex door of the field hospital and called over a man in a white coat and surgical cap. The man had on rubber gloves, and gore reached halfway up his biceps. The rubber gloves reminded Martin of lobster claws. For some reason he thought then of the Eigerwand. Karl had been right: Harrer had been the man to climb it. He had done so successfully in 1938, with Heckmair and Vorg and Kasparek. What a propaganda coup it had been for the Führer! Karl had been right about that as well. Wiggerl Vorg was dead now, of course, just as poor Karl was dead. Vorg had been one of the more prominent early casualties of the war on the Eastern Front. A minefield? A sniper bullet? Hamer could not recall the detail of Vorg's death. Its manner had been mundane, and there had been so many deaths. Now Otto Fromm was dead, whom Hamer had thought indestructible. There was another salvo of rockets. Christ, we're giving it to Kharkov, he thought. The commander pointed a calfskin finger in his direction and the medic with the lobster claws beside him nodded gravely. Martin saw a drift of black again at the edges of his vision. And his wounded body surrendered to it.

* * *

She lay above him in candlelight on his cot, her weight supported taut on her slender arms. She was naked, and he could see the dark pool of her nipples conclude the small white curve of each breast. She sighed. He was fully inside her. She contracted, and he gasped. She moved, cupping his balls between her thin, closed thighs.

'What shall I call you?'

'My name is Martin.'

Her lips brushed his. 'Do you want to kiss me?'

He tried not to come, not to bucket inside her like some convulsing, adolescent boy.

'I do.'

She brushed his lips again, tobacco and urgency on her breath. Her thighs contracted tight, and her tongue probed wet and warm between his lips.

* * *

He met Crupp at Crupp's insistence for dinner in Poznań. He walked from the railway station and had no difficulty in finding the restaurant. All the street signs were written in German. There were many uniformed Germans on the streets of the city. Most of these were SS. There were far more black than field grey uniforms. Twice on the way to the restaurant he saw civilians, their eyes averted, step off the pavement in deference to a uniformed German coming the other way. Obvious signs of conquest were absent. None of the buildings was ruined by shellfire or pockmarked by street fighting. He saw no battered-in doors or broken windows. No corpses hung from streetlights or the makeshift gallows he'd seen erected on street corners in Russian towns. Poznań had not been conquered;

it had been subsumed. It was a once-Polish city in the General Government. It was part of Greater Germany now.

The restaurant was busy. Most of the men were uniformed. The women with them looked prosperous and Germanic. The bleach bottle had been busy in the hair salons of Poznań, Hamer saw. There was not a woman who was not immaculately blonde. One wall was decorated with an extravagant fresco of the Führer. He was dressed this time as a medieval knight, taking a surrender from some weapon-denuded, humbled warrior chief. Hamer studied the face of the Führer in the fresco. He looked stern, in the mood to exact a punishing peace from his beaten adversary.

Crupp was not a man who suited a uniform. This was true, Hamer thought, of many of even the highest in the party hierarchy. Himmler had the furtive look of the secret policeman that instinct had made him whatever he wore. Goebbels, to Hamer's mind, had the carriage and manner of a provincial clerk. Göring, it was rumoured, had before the declaration of war had his uniforms tailored in London's Savile Row. The cloth cutter's skill, if it were true, had done little to disguise the field marshal's obesity. Crupp's uniform was immaculate. But there was nothing remotely martial about his bearing. He looked like a fellow on the make. He reminded Martin Hamer of spats and cheap cigars and jazz recordings kept in greaseproof-paper sleeves.

Crupp rose and smiled to greet him. His handshake was surprisingly firm, and the smile seemed genuine. 'The Reich hero of Kharkov,' he said. 'Finally we meet.'

Hamer coloured.

'I saw the medal ceremony on a newsreel,' Crupp said. 'I thought, Now there's a man who looks the part. But in the flesh, my God!' He slapped Hamer on the back. 'Let's have a drink. Champagne, I think, to sharpen our appetites. I can promise you a feast tonight. This is the best restaurant in the city, and you are my honoured guest.'

The menu was written in German. Hamer studied it, thinking that this was the strangest start to a dressing-down he could ever remember. If Crupp really was angry or indignant at his conduct in the camp, he had an unconventional way of showing it. Hamer could recall some epic bollockings from his army past. It was a part of the military culture. He'd been hung out to dry on more than a few occasions. This did not so far resemble any of them.

'May I call you Martin?'

'Doctor Buckner — '

Crupp raised a hand. He had hazel eyes and sallow skin, and his hair was combed scrupulously over his pate from a low parting. 'Please. Talk of Buckner is seldom pleasant and never less than complicated. Let's have our champagne before we confront any difficulties concerning the good doctor.'

So Buckner had been lying. Whatever Hamer was here for, it was nothing to do with his demeanour or actions in the camp.

They ate their dinner to the accompaniment of a string quartet playing Brahms and Schubert. They performed beautifully, but Hamer was slightly disconcerted by the volume during some passages, by the shuddering vibrato of some of the deeper bass notes. Shellfire, he knew, had done this to his nerves. He would in time recover from it.

'Students from the music academy here,' Crupp said, gesturing at the quartet. 'At least, they were. We've closed it, of course. We can't very well subsidize the musical education of Poles. That would be ridiculous. War has a wonderful way of clarifying economic priorities, don't you think?'

Hamer looked towards the musicians. 'Do you pay them?'

'They get to eat in the kitchen when they've finished their performance. It's an arrangement I'm sure delights them.'

* * *

It had been after midnight when he had taken her back to the women's block. She had left her smell on his pillow and sheets. He had bitten her, drawn blood on her breast trying not to cry out the first time he came.

'You've never paid for sex, have you, Martin?'

'How do you know?'

'Prostitutes don't kiss.'

'You're not a prostitute.'

She had laughed, then, in the darkness. 'I'm here, aren't I?'

He could not get the scent and touch of her out of his mind.

* * *

Crupp was saying something about Joseph Goebbels. 'I'm by no means the man's biggest admirer,' he said. 'He has his faults, like we all do. He's chronically vain, for one. He's a relentless philanderer. But the interest he takes in conditions in the field is genuine. It's why he seeks out men like yourself to meet and to listen to.'

Hamer quietly put down his knife and fork. 'Joseph Goebbels wants to meet me?'

'That's what I've been saying, Hamer. You're to be flown to the Wolf's Lair. It's all been arranged. And then you'll visit some of our wounded in various hospitals at home. And you're to speak at a few key youth rallies. You're quite famous in the Fatherland, you know.'

'When?'

'A month from now: a six-week tour of duty. Then back here to our camp. What's the matter?'

'I have no experience of public speaking.'

Crupp speared a piece of veal on his fork and popped it into his mouth. The morsel of meat looked so tender that it barely seemed to Hamer to need chewing. He felt a nostalgia, which he knew was insane at that moment, for field rations. He had drunk a single glass of champagne.

'I don't wish to be offensive, sir, but I was hoping at some stage to return to combat duties.'

Crupp dabbed at his forehead, which was perspiring, with a napkin. He put the napkin on the table and nodded. 'You're a soldier and the war here is won. You feel obsolete. Quite so.'

Hamer waited, knowing there was more. Crupp was cleverer than he had first supposed.

'Reinhard Heydrich was a friend of mine.'

Hamer nodded. 'Buckner intimated as much.'

'Ariel Buckner is a cunt,' Crupp said. 'An aberration.' He ate more veal.

'Heydrich?'

'You'd agree he was an important man?'

Hamer could barely remember a time when Reinhard Heydrich had not been an important man. He had been second in command to Himmler in running the SS. At the time of his assassination he had been governing Czechoslovakia.

'Reinhard flew combat missions over Russia,' Crupp said. 'Did you know that?'

'I remember rumours of the sort,' Hamer said.

'Goebbels could not make it up, Martin. I recognize the warrior mentality. I know you thirst for combat. I know that men like you will be the winning of this war. You're here only to recuperate. Then, I promise you, promotion and a return to the field will be yours.'

And Hamer believed him. He felt he had misjudged the Herr Commandant Crupp. The man was no soldier, obviously, but he was a plain-speaking fixer who had offered Hamer something other than the aphoristic crap he got from Buckner in the camp. His eyes strayed to the fresco depicting the armour-clad Führer. The man prostrated before him had a walrus moustache and carried a horned helmet. The Führer appeared to be accepting the surrender of a Viking.

A party approached their table and asked if they could have their picture taken with Hamer. The man was an SS Obersturmführer, the two females with him a plump woman with a nervous giggle and a lantern-jawed harridan burdened by much ersatz jewellery. He introduced them as his wife and his sister respectively. Crupp had them pull up chairs for the picture, to create the intimate lie of a shared dinner for the photograph. Hamer smiled, nursing the unsubtle bulge of an erection brought on by the insistent recollection of Julia Smollen lying naked in his bed.

More people approached them after that. The commandant was all charm and accommodation. Everyone knew Crupp, Hamer realized. Or more pertinently Crupp knew everyone. Last before they left, Hamer signed his first autograph, for a Hitler Youth leader up way beyond the boy's bedtime. He did it with a flourish and a smile. The boy walked away from the hero of Kharkov happy.

'You called Buckner a cunt, sir.'

Crupp groaned. 'And it's been such a convivial evening. Don't spoil it, Martin. Let's leave the sorry story of Ariel Buckner for another time.' He gestured to a waiter for his coat.

He expects me to pay, Hamer thought, more amused than affronted. 'Wait, sir. We haven't got the bill yet,' he said.

Crupp winked at him. 'There is no bill, Martin. What's the point of ruling the world if it doesn't bring a few perks?'

* * *

Karl had come to love the ritual of Nuremberg. The rallies left him tremulous, wet-eyed, spent. Hamer attended only when his military duty made doing so unavoidable. Karl evidently thrilled to the common strength of the single voice and choreography of a quarter of a million men moved to the will of one cause. Martin Hamer heaved in the heat as the body odour of Masurian peasant boys, drunk on aggression, mingled with the endlessly beery breath and cheap cigar smoke of the urban Brown Shirt mob. He was a professional soldier, and Nuremberg, however polished the ceremony, pandered annually to the instincts of the thug.

He hated what the mob called Hitler weather, the humid, windless heat and metallic light that always seemed to greet the Führer's more extravagant public appearances. It was odd, uncanny, the way that Hitler's presence seemed to still the very breeze, so that swastika-bearing banners the size of stitched-together football pitches hung behind him without a ripple as he roared and murmured and cajoled. The singing and the bugle fanfares had been so loud that Hamer knew he would be hard of hearing for another week after the crushing intensity of the noise in the stadium.

Nevertheless, they were there. And so as the

celebrants from the hinterland filed hungover on to their buses and coaches and trams, they shared a drink at a bar near the railway station, where queues of impatient sons of the soil would now be stinking out the overcrowded platforms. They were lucky enough to find a seat at a table towards the rear of the bar. They were both heavy-legged from the length of ceremonials, which each year seemed to grow longer and more elaborate.

'I thought he was quite magnificent,' Karl said. 'It's the best I've ever heard him speak.'

The Führer had arrived in a silver aeroplane, a glittering craft of polished aluminium. To top that, next year he'll have to descend to the podium from the heavens in a chariot, Hamer thought.

'How are Hansel and Gretel?' They were Martin's and Lillian's pet names for the twins.

A grin lit up Karl's face. 'They're adorable. Now they're walking and saying the odd word, they are much easier on Heidi. Honestly, Martin, they're like two perfect little people. And it's as though they've been around for ever.'

Hamer nodded and smiled back. He shared the general view that nothing was so boring a subject as other people's children. But Hansel and Gretel were everything to their father and mother.

'How's Lillian?'

'That promotion she's been offered has caused a lot of resentment.'

Karl frowned. 'I can't see why. She's as well qualified as anyone at the store.'

'There's some nasty gossip going around. It's a story to the effect that she's sacrificed her duty to motherhood to further her career.'

'It's a malicious lie,' Karl said.

Hamer shrugged. 'Malicious, yes. But damaging, because people are choosing to believe it.'

'You think it threatens the promotion?'

'I think it threatens her job, Karl.'

'Is there anything one can do?'

He means, Is there anything I can do, God bless him, Hamer thought. Karl was sometimes hard work as a friend. But he was nothing if not loyal. 'Mrs Beck, her departmental head, is one of Dr Stresemann's patients. He's going to have a word with her and explain it's me who is the villain of the piece.'

'That's all right, then,' Karl said.

'No, it isn't, Karl. The whole thing is sick. It's sick and it's demeaning. Frankly, I'd like to get out of Berlin. There's a posting in Cologne. If I can persuade Lily, I'll take it.'

Fresh steins of beer were delivered to their table by a waitress wearing the inevitable League of German Maidens pin. It was so ubiquitous now that it no longer put Martin in mind of a stupefying Berlin afternoon and a man with a bloodied nose wearing a cardboard sign in the street.

'You've made a mistake, miss,' Hamer said. 'We haven't finished the drinks in front of us yet.'

'I haven't made a mistake, sir,' she said indignantly. 'These come with the compliments of the table over there.'

She indicated with a nod of her head before turning away with her tray. Hamer looked. A table of Brown Shirt boys gazed back at him. One of them, eyes shy under a flopping blond fringe, smiled nervously.

'They're queers,' Hamer said, incredulous.

'A case of mistaken identity,' Karl said. He smiled, but his lips stuck to his teeth.

'Well, we'd better clarify matters. Or we'll be pestered by flirtatious boys all night. Bloody hell. As if being in Nuremberg isn't penance enough.'

'Let's just drink these to be polite and leave,' Karl said. 'I agree with you they might very well be queer.'

Hamer laughed. 'I don't think there's too much doubt,' he said.

'And they might be very well-connected queers,' Karl said.

Martin Hamer nodded. Even in Nuremberg, it was a point well made.

* * *

Crupp insisted on a cabaret club. Two Germans with facial scars flanked the entrance. Hamer was pretty sure that they were off-duty SS earning a bit on the side. They stiffened when they recognized the commandant. He barely nodded at them. They didn't look at Hamer, whatever the temptation. Curiosity was not so strong a reflex as fear, after all. Hamer had begun to sense some of the power that came off Crupp, with his polished ways, his easy charm and fraudulent manner with a comb. He would be an easy man to underestimate. But Hamer had begun to sense that you would get the opportunity to do it only once.

The cabaret was terrible. Patriotic folk songs were blubbed out by fat men in lederhosen. A violinist hacked his way through highlights from the Paganini canon. A woman dressed and made up to look a little like Marlene Dietrich proved conclusively that she could not sing with any of the style or skittish emotion of the woman she impersonated. There was a magician, who was skilful enough, though magic bored Hamer generally. And there was a series of tableaux depicting Germany's most recent military victories. It climaxed with the counter-attack on the river Dnepr. A spotlight was then shone on Martin Hamer, who was obliged to stand, blinking, blinded by the glare, as an ovation gathered around him.

'It's your idea, isn't it, Herr Commandant, this audience with Goebbels, this tour?' He was doing it again: couching questions as delivered verdicts, in the manner of Dr Buckner. It was an obnoxious habit. In present company, it was also dangerous.

But Crupp didn't seem to mind. 'Not entirely. Goebbels did express a wish to meet you. I suggested that an itinerary could be built around the meeting. We should maximize our advantages. We should make the prosecution of the war as efficient and effective as we can.'

You're looking for another sponsor, Hamer thought. You need another champion in the hierarchy, now that Reinhard Heydrich is dead.

‘What I did in the counter-attack wasn’t that extraordinary.’

The commandant raised his eyes to heaven. ‘I think it was Napoleon, when asked what makes a good soldier, who said ‘Give me a man without imagination.’ But I believe most men, shot, would have stayed in that ditch.’ He lit a cigarette. Hamer noticed that he didn’t inhale. ‘It wasn’t so much what you did, Martin, as the circumstances in which you did it. You got up and saved your unit from annihilation. The Führer himself has commented on it.’

Thus you, Hamer thought. Thus Goebbels. Thus the whole, clambering bandwagon. He felt intense home-sickness then, in a wave, for the harsh simplicities of Russia and the winter and the front.

He stayed that night, at Crupp’s insistence, in a Poznań hotel. It was not as though there were urgent duties in the camp awaiting him. There was a picture in the hotel lobby of the Führer. It was huge, of course, and took pride of place. In this representation, Hitler had travelled effortlessly through time to the present day. And his mood had changed. He was no longer stern, but melancholy. Clearly the weight of destiny was proving a heavy burden on him. But there was stoicism in the way he gripped his gloves in one fist. A landscape of Wagnerian crags and rivulets worthy of nymphs extended behind the epic pose he struck. Studying the picture, Hamer saw that the brushwork was terrible. But how did any artist fill so much vacant space? Other, lesser Germans were represented. There was a portrait of Bismarck and one of Frederick the Great. There were depictions, too, of Napoleon and Nelson, men from hostile countries whom the Führer was known slyly to admire.

Hamer rang the bell on the reception desk and a smiling German girl turned around the hotel register for him to sign. The volume was handsome enough, hand-tooled in leather and printed in Heidelberg. It occured to Hamer that he might be in Berlin, or Leipzig, or Dresden. There was nothing to suggest that this had ever been a foreign country.

In his room, there was a telephone. He looked for and found a directory. It was slim, the directory, printed in German, with a swastika in a circle lightly described in silver relief on its cover. There were no Polish names when he looked through the book. The name 'Smollen' was as absent as any other that might enable him to telephone an ethnic Slav. It was as though Poland had never existed, Hamer thought. Karl had often, in the old days, talked about the fulfilling of German destiny. Martin Hamer had been far more interested in the righting of injustices committed in international collusion against the German people. But what was happening here, what had happened here, he thought, was neither of those things. Poland had been made to disappear. The history of a nation had been eradicated and its people disenfranchised, barred from its future, made invisible. It was the General Government now, an open kingdom for men like Wilhelm Crupp to colonize and profit from.

She had described herself as a Pole and a Slav. She had described herself as a patriot, and in the night settled over the ghost of her country she had kissed him on the mouth. Hamer felt the force then of Julia's hatred, knew the gagging, loathsome compromise of her will for survival, her encompassing fear. And he felt ashamed of himself. And he, a soldier, honourable, he believed, felt further ashamed for wanting her still.

* * *

They went to a clinic in Lucerne run by an old colleague of Lillian's father. The cost of the treatment was high, the treatment itself tedious. But Dr Stresemann negotiated them a special price, and Martin endured his uncomfortable series of daily injections taken from the glands of animals. There was deep-tissue massage and special baths in darkness during which the water tingled around him with electric current. A thick paste was daily applied. He was given volumes of erotic fiction to read, stuff written in such an arcane style that it was difficult to keep track of what was supposed to be going on. He didn't know why he'd been given it at all. Desire had never been a problem.

'I think they're a bit confused here,' he said to Lillian.

'Confused?'

'They can't differentiate between cause and effect.'

She smiled at the joke. But in truth it was a

melancholy time for them in Switzerland, demeaning and futile.

The country was beautiful. They took a boat on the lake. They went out and ate dinner with a view of the mountains. But after a week of this, Martin couldn't remember the last time he had heard Lillian's laugh. The loveliness of their surroundings seemed like a reprimand.

'Let's go to the mountains and ski,' he said to her, reaching across the table for her hand, at dinner on the eighth evening of the fortnight that had been booked for them.

She took his hand, returned his grip. 'What about the treatment?'

'Quackery, with every respect to your father. Honestly, Lily, if I have one more shot of sheep's urine, I'm going to start to bleat when I see grass.'

That made her laugh, finally. 'It's June, darling. Where are we going to find snow in June?'

But they did find snow. They managed to hire skis. They took a cable car to the top of a glacier. They stayed in a rescue hut built for stranded climbers from logs and skied each day from early morning until the afternoon, when they picnicked and grew drowsy and slept on a canvas groundsheet under the summer sun.

In the evenings they kindled wood fires, and the air in the cabin grew dense and cosy with pine sap from the burning wood. They drank wine and ate cheese and cured meat they'd bought in the village at the foot of the mountain and brought up with them in the cable car.

'My father would be furious,' Lillian said. Her hair had streaked in the sun. In the firelight, now, her hair fell in cream and amber coils across her bare shoulders. She sat naked in front of the fire, tawny-skinned, gorgeous. Martin could smell her skin in the warmth of the firelight.

He sipped wine and looked at her. He never tired of looking at her.

She laughed. 'I'd say, with that expression, you were undressing me with your eyes. But you can't be, can you? I'm naked already.'

'I love you,' he said.

She looked at him. Her eyes were pale, but they were not transparent. Sometimes her thoughts were hard for him to read. 'You're enough for me, Martin.'

'Shush, Lily — '

'It's the truth. You make me happy. You're all I will ever need.'

They were resting after struggling through soft snow on a steep descent in the partial thaw of the afternoon, when they saw the climber. He was climbing solo and was such a tiny dot on the light and shadow of the face he climbed that you lost him if you took your eyes away for a moment.

'He's not putting any gear in,' Hamer said to himself, incredulous.

'Gear?'

'He's not putting pitons in the face, securing rope. He's free-climbing solo.'

'My God.'

'He must be very good,' Hamer said.

They watched the climber. He *was* very good. His progress was deliberate and relentless up the blank grey vastness of the face. They watched him, and he was very good almost to the summit of the climb, very good right up to the moment that he fell. He didn't seem to Hamer to make a mistake, though from this distance it was impossible without binoculars to be sure. One moment the climber was poised to take a step, the next he was dropping through space. He was very high on the face, and he fell for a long time. Beside him, he heard his wife gasp and whisper something in shock. There was no other sound. A scream would have carried, Martin thought, would have amplified off the solid rock and echoed around the valley. But the climber did not cry out. He just fell, continuing to fall until the impact at the bottom of the mountain and the end of his adventurous life.

* * *

'There's no easy answer,' Julia Smollen said. She held herself, huddled on the bed between her gathering arms, her knees clenched against her chest. But it was warm enough, with the paraffin stove, in Hamer's quarters. It was not cold that provoked her posture.

'You allowed me to kiss you.'

'You're an attractive man.'

'We've destroyed your country. Taken everything away from you.'

She laughed. 'All accomplished a long time before you came. There's a pun there, by the way, Martin.'

He said nothing.

'Have you tobacco? May I build a cigarette?'

He took the tobacco, papers and matches from the drawer on his bedside table. He handed them to her. She could have easier reached for them herself.

'Do you know it's a capital crime for a Pole now to own matches?'

'Why?'

'Sabotage.'

'You must despise me. Yet you let me kiss you.'

'It's like this,' she said, taking a long drag on her built cigarette. 'I was taken by Rolfe, by Landau, by a dozen others, Martin Hamer. It's all stopped now. You've no idea how much they fear you.' She screwed up her eyes, burnished emeralds, as she inhaled. She blew out smoke. 'They do, you know. They think you're an accomplished killer of men.'

Hamer said nothing.

'Are you?'

Hamer said nothing.

'He'll come for you, by the way, will Rolfe. He's a most vindictive man, and cunning.'

'Then he'll die. Why did you kiss me?'

'I've been ostracized by the respectable patriots in the women's dormitory since Buckner had me held down over a table so that he could watch me being fucked a day after my arrival here. I've been a collaborator, in their eyes, since then.'

Hamer groaned.

'He didn't take me himself, by the way. I don't think he's capable of it. In direct contrast to you.'

Hamer tried again. 'Why did you kiss me?'

'You kissed me, Martin. I allowed you to.'

'Power, then?'

'You have all the power. That's why I'm wearing this dress.'

He had bought it at a shop in Poznań, guessing the size. He had brought it back into the camp wrapped in brown paper tied with string. It was too big for her, but she looked beautiful in it to him, nevertheless.

'What is it if it isn't power?'

She didn't answer for a moment. 'Pity,' she said. She spat tobacco shreds on to his warped wooden floor. 'You saved my life. I feel sorry for you. I don't believe I've ever encountered a man in my life more alone.'

* * *

Leaving their flat in Berlin was hard for Martin and Lillian. They had bought their home with many expectations. Most of those expectations remained still unfulfilled as they piled and labelled their possessions for the removal men. Lillian had hoped to lure Martin away from the army and into a civilian career. But civilian careers had diminished in the society in which they lived. Martin had hoped to achieve a rank that gave Lillian the choice of whether to work or not to. But as Germany had been transformed, as the paramilitaries had blossomed and flourished under Hitler's rule, Martin's rank and pedigree had become debased and his worth as a soldier had apparently declined. He could fight invisible in the wastes of the Antarctic. He could blow up railway lines with bombs conjured from ingredients available in the average domestic kitchen. He could parachute from an aeroplane. He could fly the bloody aeroplane for other men to parachute from. He could field-strip any infantry weapon used by the army, blindfold. And yet he earned less than Karl, who organized Strength Through Joy excursions and supervised summer camps on the Rhine for the Hitler Youth.

He was depressed, disheartened, as he carefully placed crockery in tissue paper and the pictures from the walls of their flat in boxes cushioned scrupulously with straw. When he inventoried their possessions, it seemed they had achieved little against the bright expectation that lit their earlier lives. She had wanted to be Brett Ashley on the day they had met. Where would Lady Brett be now? In a sanatorium, Hamer thought, nursing a liver ruined by gin. At least it hadn't come to that.

Lillian walked into the room with a mug of coffee in either hand. She saw his mood immediately, looking into his face, and tilted her head to one side with an expression of sympathy. 'Don't be sad, darling.'

They had pulled down and packed the curtains, and in the bright light through the window her hair, eyes and skin shone. How can any man who shares his life with such a woman feel despondent, Hamer asked himself. But he did.

'It could be worse,' Lillian said, deadpan. She blew on the surface of her coffee to cool it and sipped. 'You could be Arthur Boscombe.'

It was gallows humour, something they said to each other when the occasion arose, a grim joke between them. Boscombe was the man they had seen fall from the sheer face of a Swiss mountain. He was an Englishman and a noted climber. His business had failed and he was facing a trial for fraud and a prison sentence. His death had turned out to be a suicide.

'Poor Arthur Boscombe,' Hamer said. He looked around. Their things were packed in boxes. Boxes were filled with their clothes, their photographs, their bedding and books, their cups and plates. It didn't seem to take many boxes to contain a life.

'It's always like this,' Lillian said. 'We moved a lot when I was a child, before my father had saved the money for his own practice. It is a wrench, Martin. It makes you feel shiftless and insecure.'

'And worthless,' Hamer said. 'As though we've achieved nothing.'

Lillian's eyes hardened very slightly. 'It could be worse.' This wasn't the Arthur Boscombe joke. They both knew what she meant. They could have been forced to sell their possessions for knockdown prices. They could be fleeing a home whose walls had been daubed with the slogans of race hatred, obliged to take a one-way trip to an uncertain future on a tramp steamer bound for South America. It had happened to the family of a girl Lillian had worked with at the store. The girl had been popular there and good at her job. But she worked there no longer. Her family had fled the country after their eldest son had been beaten up by a Brown Shirt gang in the street.

We'll just go on like this until we're old, Hamer thought, hating himself for thinking it. We'll just go on like this, the things we once found attractive and beguiling about one another dulling and diminishing until we're like two elderly strangers unable to remember quite what brought us together. But that won't happen for a few years yet, he conceded, looking at the honey splash of sunlight in Lillian's corn-silk hair. He reached out and stroked her hair, and she took his hand and kissed his fingers and smiled.

'What would make things better, Martin?' She had secured a job at a new store in Cologne with no trouble at all.

He thought about the question. 'A war,' he said simply. 'I'm supposed to be a soldier. My arms are stiff with the bearing of banners and my ears sore with rhetoric. A war would sort things out. I'd feel useful. I'd be appreciated and I'd be properly paid.'

'You could still leave the army. It's not too late.'

'And do what? The corners of our cities have their fill of shoeshine boys and match sellers.'

She smiled, but there was strain in the smile. Lillian was a woman who liked to make things better, and this was a situation unsuited to her gift for accomplishing that.

There was a knock at their door. Hamer opened it. It was Dr Stresemann. He kissed his daughter and slapped Martin heartily on the back. He reached inside the coat of his suit and pulled out an envelope. 'A little something to oil the wheels, since you're on the move,' he said.

Hamer knew that the cheque would be generous. They always were. Usually the doctor's cheques signified a holiday. But the destinations were starting to run out. There were fewer and fewer places in the world where Germans were welcome any more. He smiled, shunting himself out of his despondency. It wouldn't do. Lillian's father was a thoughtful and generous man. He deserved the grace and hospitality he always showed to them. Martin would fetch glasses and schnapps. He could remember where he had packed them. He would fetch glasses and schnapps and they would drink a toast to the doctor's generosity and to the adventure of their new life in Cologne.

As he located the glasses and the schnapps bottle, Hamer thought about Arthur Boscombe. His body had never been recovered. He wondered sometimes if Arthur Boscombe had simply gone on falling, for ever.

* * *

The tailor made chalk marks on Martin Hamer's back. The new greatcoat felt heavy on him. 'I don't think it needs any alteration,' he said to

Crupp, who sat and watched.

'The Führer is very fastidious about the dress of his officers,' Crupp said.

'It's Goebbels I'm meeting, isn't it?'

Crupp shrugged. 'It's the Wolf's Lair. The Führer's movements are not planned in advance. He could be in residence. He might visit for a day. There's no point in having him unnecessarily antagonized by the sight of an officer wearing an ill-fitting uniform.'

Hamer unbuttoned the coat.

'How is your wound?'

'Healing.'

'Good. That's good. The Führer is a very approachable man.'

'Yes?'

'But if you do encounter him, you do not attempt to engage him unbidden. Make no eye contact unless he directly addresses you. Be clear on those points.'

'I am, Herr Commandant Crupp. Will you tell me now about Buckner?'

Crupp turned to the tailor. 'Leave us.' The man nodded and retreated with his tape measure and chalk and Hamer's new greatcoat, marked up for alteration.

'You're like a dog with a bone, aren't you, Martin?' Crupp said. 'I like you. I believe our association can be of benefit to us both. But you are sometimes like a dog with a bone that won't let go. I suppose it's an advantage, tenacity, in the field.'

'Buckner?'

'I'm getting to Buckner. Sit down.'

They were in the barracks in Poznań. They were in Crupp's office in the barracks, where he had a large desk with a telephone and a scrambling device. There was also a picture of the Führer on the desk, and it was signed. A cast of Reinhard Heydrich's death mask, in bronze, had been hung on the wall. It was clear that Crupp's business extended, roamed, as he did, beyond the confines of the camp.

'Before the war he ran a clinic.'

'He told me that.'

'Don't interrupt.'

It was a story of clinical procedures ignored. Of ambition gone mad. It was a story of murder.

Buckner had developed a vaccine he claimed was effective against tuberculosis. He wanted recognition of his achievement, and he wanted his proper reward. Neither would be forthcoming without the implementation of a vaccination programme. So Buckner began to petition the city's health and education authorities to begin just such a programme. Implementation was entirely the prerogative of the authorities. But neither was prepared to implement without a comprehensive run of clinical trials.

This was too slow for Buckner. He believed in the science, the epidemiology of what he had created. He began a campaign through the newspapers, saying that by dragging their feet the authorities were in effect killing innocent children. It was a dangerous tactic, said Crupp. But it was one that caught the public mood at a time when there was intense pressure on every German family to breed and rear healthy children for the fulfilment of the nation's destiny.

I know all about that pressure, Hamer thought, listening to Crupp. It had begun to rain against Crupp's windows. Rain fell in large drops that streaked and splashed against the glass.

A child died of tuberculosis, as was eventually inevitable, in a public hospital on the outskirts of Düsseldorf. Buckner's campaign grew hysterical. The authorities partially relented. They would try the vaccine. They would try it on the children of an orphanage. If there were no ill effects after three months, far longer than the incubation period for the illness they were trying to prevent and eradicate, they would vaccinate wholesale.

Only there were side effects, Crupp told Hamer, as the sky outside darkened. Rain on the windows dripped and splashed. The vaccine triggered a mutant virus that liquefied the lungs. The vaccinated children were all dead within twenty-four hours.

'It had the same effect on them as trench gas,' Crupp said. 'Those children died in agony. The only small consolation was that there wasn't a parent there to have to see it happen.'

'I'm amazed Ariel Buckner wasn't barred from practice. I'm surprised he wasn't put on public trial and sent to prison.'

Crupp's eyes were on the bronze death mask of Heydrich, his former sponsor. He turned them towards Martin Hamer and spoke quietly, the trademark jocularity completely absent from his tone. 'There would never have been a trial, my friend. Our attitude towards science in the Reich would have prevented that. Science is our saviour and our friend. We have the best scientists in the world, toiling to enable our golden future. And Buckner had contacts. He wrote prescriptions for two or three influential people with a fondness for treatments that couldn't simply be obtained for cash over the counter of a street-corner pharmacy.'

'They were prepared to put themselves out for a man guilty of what he did?'

Crupp smiled. 'If they had a choice. I doubt Buckner would stop at the threat of blackmail if it meant saving his skin.'

Hamer rubbed his face between his hands, as if washing without water. 'No wonder you called him a cunt.'

'I inherited Ariel Buckner,' Crupp said. 'He checks the women of our small Joy Division for venereal disease. He treats the camp guards for the bruises they acquire when their singsongs get too drunken and robust. He probably pulled himself together for a bit of a show when you arrived. But most of the time I suspect he has his head over the ether bottle.'

'I thought, when I met him, he was clever.'

'He is, Martin, which makes him worse.'

The rain was torrential now. Electric lights had been switched on in various rooms and buildings of the barracks, and they shone yellow and bleary in smudges through the wet panes of Crupp's office windows. Rain drummed on the glass. Hamer wished with all his heart that he had never asked about Buckner, had never met the man, had never come to the sad and desolate country he now knew Poland to be.

'I'll organize a car to take you to the station,' Crupp said. 'We can't have you turning up at the Wolf's Lair with a cold.'

* * *

Hansel and Gretel played on the mat, seemingly oblivious as their mother sat shaking on the sofa in Karl's and Heidi's chintzy sitting room. Martin passed her the tea he had made. She needed two hands to steady the cup. She tried to smile, but the reflex was no more than an ugly jab in her pale, pretty face. At her feet, wholly consumed by their invented world and one another, the twins sat back to back, building a wall with wooden bricks around themselves. Martin sat down next to Heidi and took the untouched tea from her and put the cup on a table at the side of the sofa. He hugged her then, hard, fully, and she sobbed into his chest as the twins clucked and cooed and spoke the wordless language of their tiny domain.

Somewhere outside he could hear an oompah band playing. Heidi and Karl lived near a tea garden and when the wind was right the sound carried. Screams of children, disembodied, playing in the tea garden floated through the opened window, through the lace curtains, into the heat and light and clutter of the room.

'It was good of you to come.'

'Shush, Heidi. What else would I do?' he said. He held her. He could smell the lanolin in her hair and the scent of soap on her skin and the smell of terror, under it, in a sour secretion from her glands. She was struggling to regulate her breathing, trembling in the uncontrollable way a small mammal will when held in the palm of a human hand.

'What's to become of us, Martin? What's to become of my children and me? What in God's name will we do?'

It was the same question he had asked himself endlessly on the laboured journey from Cologne. He wished Lillian were there. Lillian would better know what to say and do. But she was still in a hospital bed, recovering from an operation to have her wisdom teeth removed. Martin's wife lay with her face swollen, cotton swabs stanching the bleeding in her ripped mouth in a darkened room, and he had not thought it fit even to tell her of the catastrophe. He had told her he was going to Berlin on military business. It was the first lie he had told Lily in their marriage. It did not sit well with him. But given the circumstances, it sat better with him than the truth.

There were flowers in the room. They were in a heavy vase, the flowers decorated with a painting of a girl in a swing in the fussy style of Fragonard. They looked a day or two old. Karl was a man who often bought his wife flowers. He would, of course, have bought these. He would never buy flowers for Heidi again. These would wilt and die, the water holding them turn brackish, and they would never be replaced. It was hard to take in, the enormity of it. The suddenness seemed appalling. In unison, the twins began to cry.

'I haven't made them their lunch,' Heidi said.

'They're hungry, poor darlings.' She started to sob again. The house sounded suddenly as though it had been invaded by grief. Which it has, Hamer thought; which it has.

'I'll make their lunch,' he told Heidi. She didn't respond. She just sobbed into her hands and shook, a string of saliva extending from between her fingers towards the floor, a woman abandoned to grief. Hamer got up and walked into the kitchen. He began to open drawers to discover where things were kept as the children he thought of as Hansel and Gretel bawled louder to be fed.

⋆ ⋆ ⋆

One of the books he had bought at Julia's request was a volume of *Grimms' Fairy Tales*. He had thought it an odd, whimsical choice. She did not seem a whimsical woman. She did not seem the sort of woman to be transported in her imagination by tales of enchantment and elves.

'Have you read these stories?' she said to him.

'When I was at school, perhaps. I don't remember them.'

She looked at him. 'These are the grown-up versions. They don't have happy endings, these fairy stories, Martin.'

He thought of Hansel and Gretel then, poor Heidi's twins.

'Are you sure you haven't read them?'

'Quite sure. Why?'

'The expression on your face just now. Recollection and, with it, sorrow.'

'I'm going away for a few weeks,' Hamer told her.

'I know.'

'How?'

'The whole camp knows,' she said.

'Will you be all right?'

She laughed. 'I doubt I'll come to further harm than I have already.'

'The war won't go on for ever,' he said. 'One day you'll have a home. Settlements, villages are to be built.'

'Believe that if it makes you feel better,' she said.

* * *

The attempt on his life was made as he gained his own quarters after escorting Julia Smollen back to where she slept. He had struggled to walk her there on trustworthy ground through the force of the unrelenting rain. Purchase on the soaked, giving earth was a sort of lottery. His balance was the poised gift of a man who had climbed naturally since boyhood. But as he slid and scrambled he wondered why duckboards had not been improvised in the camp. It was Crupp's blithe unconcern. It was Buckner, oblivious. It was his own fault, swanning off to Poznań to have a new uniform tailored for his audience with Joseph Goebbels.

He was almost absorbed in his own progress, but not quite. Hamer had the alertness of a combat soldier and this never truly left him. So when he saw the chop of a hand in the flare of light from Landau's tower, to his right, it was probably a signal they thought deadly, and discreet. He would show them different, Hamer decided. He would show these conniving bastards what it meant to wear the uniform.

The swing of the blow came from behind him as he opened his door. It came from his left. He ducked under it. The weapon was a pick handle. It collided with the door of his quarters hard enough to make wet wood squeal and buckle and splinter in the doorframe. Hamer was up then, his elbow jackknifing into his assailant's face. The man held on to the pick handle, tried to swing it again. But it was no weapon for close combat. Hamer stepped inside its clumsy arc, turned his attacker and smashed the man's head against his door with the flat of his hand. They sank to the floor of Hamer's porch, wet, slithery after the deluge of rain that had fallen during the day.

'Hello, Rolfe.' Hamer hauled the sergeant to his feet in a choke hold. He eased just fractionally the pressure of his grip.

'How did you know?'

'Your stink gave you away. You have bad breath. I could smell you. When a man is forced to fight, Rolfe, as you have never fought in your entire, squalid fucking life, he comes very much to rely on his senses.'

Rolfe tried to struggle free, tried to wriggle his torso and kick shinbone with the heel of a metal-shod boot, but between Hamer's hands his head and arms might as well have been clamped between brackets of iron.

'I knew a man who shared your rank, you miserable piece of shit.' Hamer hauled Rolfe back, on to his toes. 'Otto Fromm was his name. I'd love you two to have met.' He couldn't help thinking of poor Karl, then. He didn't know why. Perhaps it was the earlier talk of the Brothers Grimm, who had included the harsh parable of Hansel and Gretel in their collection of fairy stories. 'Too late now,' Hamer said sadly in the rain. 'Too late.'

'You can't kill me,' Rolfe said. He didn't sound confident. He sounded like a man incontinent with fear.

'Yes,' Hamer said, 'I can.' He wrenched Rolfe in his grip, breaking the man's neck with a sound as sudden and fatal as the snapping of an abseil rope.

He walked straight to the quarters of Ariel Buckner. He knocked on the door and then entered, urgency superseding protocol. The smell of ether almost made Hamer reel. The doctor sat slack-eyed, slumped, with Wagner playing on his gramophone.

'I've killed Hans Rolfe,' Hamer said.

Buckner's head stayed buried on his chest. His eyes, alert now, swivelled. 'A clash of personalities?'

'He attacked me with a pick handle.'

'Ah.' The doctor blinked, revived. Closed his eyes. 'It doesn't matter. Crupp has taken to you. That's what matters.'

'You should lay off the ether,' Hamer said.

'How was this death accomplished?'

'I broke his neck.'

'He broke his neck, poor man, in a fall,' Buckner said. 'A big man who'd drunk too much and stumbled.' The swell of strings and horns from the gramophone was an absurdly dramatic soundtrack to the bland delivery of Buckner's lie.

'I'm going to talk to the commandant about having Landau transferred to the Eastern Front, where his gifts can be more practically applied. I'm telling you this, Herr Doctor, as a courtesy.'

'You know, things worked well here prior to your arrival, Hamer.'

'Did they?'

'Like clockwork,' the doctor said. 'Like clockwork.' He shook his head. He sounded honestly nostalgic for a less eventful time.

* * *

They had Karl in a holding cell in a station house in a drab suburban section of the city Hamer had never had cause to visit before. It was stiflingly hot in Berlin that day, the sky like zinc, the pavements glazed and the street trees defeated under their burdens of still foliage. It was a day when traffic trundled and even noise seemed blunted by the heat. Sweat crawled under Hamer's uniform, and his collar felt far too tight. His pistol weighed stiff and heavy in its holster on his right hip, and his feet were sore in their boots.

He was to meet Hessler, the Gestapo man who had been summoned to the telephone when he had called the station, given the number by

Heidi. Hessler was too important a man to be based at the station house. He had been sent there from headquarters to deal with the matter of Karl. He didn't tell Hamer that, hadn't needed to; Hamer had known it from his manner on the telephone. Hamer was made to wait thirty-five minutes in an anteroom for his audience with Hessler. The room had no windows. It was lit by an electric lamp set into the ceiling. It was a small room filled with the blank heat of the day and the bitter odours of stale tobacco and terror.

He was shown in to see Hessler, who rose to greet him, shaking his hand. Hamer's file lay on Hessler's desk. It was, presumably, what had been occupying the Gestapo man for the thirty-five minutes Hamer had waited to see him. Hessler offered him water from a carafe, and Hamer accepted a glass. In such circumstances, in such company, men were always dry-mouthed. Hessler gestured for Hamer to sit, then sat himself.

'You've spent a lot of time abroad.'

'Most of it in a uniform.'

'How was Spain?'

'Savage,' Hamer said. 'Blood feuds fought with modern weaponry.'

Hessler nodded. 'Is yours a sham marriage?'

Hamer shook his head. 'Quite the opposite. We have no children only because I'm infertile.'

'That's a shame,' Hessler said.

It's also in my file, Hamer thought.

'This business comes as a surprise to you?'

'A complete shock,' Hamer said.

Hessler looked thoughtful. He was about thirty years of age with an open, intelligent face and blond hair that he wore rather long on the top and carefully constrained with a neat side parting. Martin Hamer had no doubt that he was sitting in front of the most dangerous man he had ever met.

'What will happen to him?'

Hessler looked briefly annoyed at having his thoughts interrupted, his mental calculations with their checks and balances, their infinitely subtle calibrations. Then he smiled, amiably enough. 'He'll be sent to Buchenwald, and they'll work him to death in the clay mine at Berlstedt. Or he'll go to Mauthausen and they'll work him to death in the stone quarries there. He'll be dead in six months if he doesn't possess a strong constitution.'

'He does.'

'A year, then.'

So Karl was to spend the last year of his life splitting stones for some public monument built by Albert Speer in tribute to the Führer's surpassing vanity. He would never see his wife again. He would not see his children grow another day.

'There's no possibility of a reprieve?' Hamer said.

Hessler pinched wax from his ear between finger and thumb. 'We're both men of the world. A lot goes on it's pragmatic to turn a blind eye to. Homosexuality didn't end as a perversion in Germany the night Ernst Röhm was sent to meet his maker. But the boy your friend was caught with was only nineteen years of age. And his father, who is outraged at the seduction of his son, has given much of the profits from his factories over the years to the party. There can be no reprieve. On the contrary, he'll be made an example of.'

Hamer thought of the boy simpering in their direction from his table in the bar in Nuremberg. He hadn't looked like someone who needed much seducing.

Hessler looked at his wristwatch. 'They're sending a van for him in half an hour. You can see him now if you like.'

A jailer let them into Karl's cell. Karl sat on an upright chair, the cell's only furnishing other than a wall-mounted cot, but he stood when Hessler and Hamer entered. The jailer locked the door behind them. Karl had been beaten. One of his eyes was surrounded by a purple and yellow swelling, and when he tried to smile at Martin he was missing a tooth. Martin put his arms around his friend and hugged him. Karl's hands were not bound, but he did not return the embrace. His body was rigid, and he was trembling in an effort to control himself.

'I'm so sorry, Martin,' he said. 'I've let everyone down.'

Hamer took a step back and looked at his friend. Karl was crying, trying not to. To Hamer's left, Hessler stood leaning against the locked cell door with his arms across his chest. The jailer was next to Hessler, standing to attention with his keyring hanging from his right hand. Karl was staring at Hamer's pistol with a hungry expression of impossible hope. In one easy, practised movement, Hamer pulled the gun free of its holster and chambered a round. To his left, he heard the jailer gasp. Hessler remained motionless. Hamer closed the fingers of his left hand around the barrel and extended the weapon, grip first, towards Karl. Karl took the gun, held it to his right temple and, with his eyes on Martin, squeezed the trigger. The shot sounded very loud in the confined space of the cell. A fine mist of blood, bone fragments and brain matter sprayed a pink, circular stain on the wall to Karl's left as his body slipped to the floor.

The silence in the cell was profound in the aftermath of the pistol report.

'Retrieve your side arm, Hamer,' Hessler said.

Martin prised his dead friend's fingers from the stock and trigger guard of his gun. He ejected the spent shell and put the pistol back in its holster. 'I expect there'll be a charge?'

'No,' Hessler said. 'I was rather hoping for something of the sort. It's why you weren't relieved of the weapon, as is customary, at the front desk.'

Hamer nodded, his expression sad, his eyes on the corpse.

'Whatever else, your friend died well enough,' Hessler said. He turned to the jailer. 'Clean up the mess.'

Hessler escorted him to the front office of the station house. He was talkative now, one of those men made garrulous, perhaps excited, Hamer thought, given pleasure by the sight of a violent death. If so, the Gestapo man had surely discovered his perfect vocation.

'There's an American theorist of the mind,' Hessler said, 'a psychologist from Chicago who believes that no person can know another person well. Not really well, I mean. He thinks intimacy is an emotional conceit. He believes that, at heart, people are and always remain strangers to one another. It's a seductive theory, no?'

'No,' Hamer said. 'It's a vision of hell.'

Hessler chuckled. 'You soldiers. You're such a sentimental lot.'

Martin Hamer signed himself out of the station house and walked through streets glassy with heat on his way to tell Heidi that her husband, the father of her children, was dead.

* * *

He dined with Crupp on the eve of his departure for the Wolf's Lair. The Herr Commandant was on ebullient form. He told Martin about the unbelievable appetite the Propaganda Minister had for sexual affairs. It wasn't even as if Magda Goebbels could be described as undemanding in the marital bed. The five children born to the couple were ample proof of that. But she wasn't enough for her husband. He had enjoyed a series of mistresses. Some of them had been famous as actresses and singers. One of them had been a glamorous journalist. Even a dressing down from the Führer had failed, really, to stop for very long this catalogue of lubricious adventures.

Hamer was bored by this gossip, and it must have shown. Crupp shoved into his mouth what looked like meat so rare it had barely stopped moving and said, 'I understand you're conducting a tryst of your own.'

'Hardly a tryst.'

'I'm told she's very pretty. For a Pole.'

Hamer sipped his wine.

'Don't be coy about it, Martin. It's a question of practicality. A man has needs. I've known men fuck Jewish women. You might not believe it, but I have. The English have a phrase: any old port in a storm.' He forked in some more of his food. 'It's a good expression, no?'

Hamer nodded. 'It has some merit. Some wit.'

'I like the English, that's my secret,' Crupp said. 'I think it a good thing we've eradicated Poland, a pity we're fighting the English. The Führer likes the English too. That's his secret.' He swallowed food, sipped wine. 'Where do you stand on the subject?'

'I used to travel to England with my father as a child. It's a beautiful country. I'd never been to Poland before the war.'

Crupp laughed. 'And now you have a Polish mistress.'

I killed the wrong man, Hamer thought. I should have broken Buckner's neck. 'Tell me more about Joseph Goebbels,' he said. 'Tell me what you think makes the man tick.'

But the camp commandant wanted to hear about the war in the east. They were all fascinated by the war in the east, Hamer had concluded, these men with not the slightest intention ever of going there. Part of it was the stories about the Russians, some of them true.

Stories of their fierceness and fanaticism, their cannibalism, their contempt for their own lives.

Martin Hamer knew plenty of stories. He had witnessed many things and been the instigator of a few. But he felt that he lacked the language to describe the war in the east. He felt it would take a Dante, a Goethe or a Milton to bring the terrible reality of the Russian campaign to life in words. Even then, in his heart, he thought the story would probably emerge counterfeit or overblown, as rhetoric. The language had not been coined to describe what had happened, what was happening, in Russia. Or maybe, more simply, it was not a fit subject for language to describe. What men did there was urged on by instincts that predated language. What men accomplished there was something words could never justify, or do justice to. So he told a few of the sort of war stories experience had taught him men like Wilhelm Crupp liked to hear. He told him stuff about the superiority of German weapons and tactics, the superiority of German training, the indomitable spirit of the German fighting man. He sang for his supper. He must have done it well enough. The subject of Julia Smollen was not raised by the commandant again.

* * *

Lillian and Martin spent their last ever holiday as guests of Bill and Lucy on the West Coast of America. It was an extravagant trip. But the cheque given them by Lillian's father on their unhappy final day in their Berlin flat was a very generous one. He's spending the money on us he would have lavished on his grandchildren, Martin thought, realized, when Lillian tore open the envelope, paled at what she saw and showed him the amount Dr Stresemann had determined to give them.

It was six months after the death of Karl. Martin had steeled himself in the loathsome heat on that Berlin day to break the news to Heidi. But when he had turned into Karl's and Heidi's street there was a police car parked outside their house. He could hear from where he stood her screams of bereavement through the open windows.

Somewhat to his surprise, Martin was granted a week's compassionate leave. He always felt afterwards that Hessler had a hand in this, perhaps grateful for the neat way in which Hamer had helped abbreviate a potentially messy business. He stayed in the house with Heidi. He slept in the sitting room and looked after the twins. Again to his surprise, he proved to be very good at this. And his two godchildren adored him. Lillian joined him after two days, her mouth still swollen and seeping blood. She did what she could to console her friend. One night after Heidi went to bed, they decided to offer her the money Lillian's father had given them when they left Berlin. But Heidi neither wanted nor needed it. German law had guaranteed her husband's death. But German law made very generous provision for the mothers of fatherless children. There were Karl's savings and even Karl's pension. 'I don't need your money,' Heidi told them. She tried to smile. 'I needed him. But he's gone.'

So they kept their money and then spent it six months later when they went to America and stayed with Bill and Lucy, the friends they had made what seemed like a lifetime ago during their honeymoon on the Côte d'Azur.

'Good God, Bill, look at you!' Martin said, when he met them at the airport. Bill smiled. He looked older around the eyes, where a cluster of crow's-feet spoke of a life lived in the sun. But his belly was flat and hard, and in his short-sleeved shirt his biceps were heavy with muscle, arms stripped entirely of the excess flesh he had carried in France.

'You have cheekbones, Bill,' Lillian said. 'They're very becoming.'

Bill laughed. 'Not half as becoming as yours, honey,' he said. He kissed her on the cheek. There was a breeze from the big propellers of an aeroplane taxiing close by. It blew off Bill's fedora and the three of them chased and caught the hat, laughing.

'Christ, it's good to see you,' Martin said.

'Come on, you guys,' Bill said. 'The missus is practically apoplectic with excitement at the thought of our European guests.'

They got into Bill's Packard.

'You seem to be ageing in reverse, Bill,' Martin said. 'What's the story?'

He was sitting in the back of the car with Lillian. She dug him with her elbow in the ribs for his deliberate use of the Americanism. They had sworn a pact on the aeroplane not to do it. He saw that her shoulders were shaking already with suppressed laughter.

'Ouch,' he said. 'So what's the scoop, Bill?'

Lillian hit him again. Any more of this and he'd break a rib. And his wife would asphyxiate.

'Lucy will explain,' Bill said. 'My darling wife will make everything abundantly clear.'

Lucy met them on the large porch of their property. She was wearing sunglasses, and her bob, intact, was now a sudden shade of auburn. She looked tanned and happy and heavily pregnant with Bill's child.

'It was an accident,' Bill said as they drank a celebratory toast in iced beer for history's sake by the pool.

'A miscalculation,' Lucy said. She lit a cigarette.

'But a happy one,' Lillian said brightly.

Bill looked at Hamer. 'When we got the news I had myself checked out. Overweight. Blood pressure through the roof. Kid deserves a dad can play ball with him in the park, I thought.'

'Or her,' Lucy said.

'Or her,' Bill said.

'This tastes disgusting,' Lucy said. She tamped out her cigarette. 'Funny thing about pregnancy, Lily. Nothing tastes the same. I've been mad for polk salad. Maybe I just have hillbilly genes.'

'You ever heard of Gene Tunney?' Bill was still addressing Martin Hamer.

Hamer smiled. He knew about Gene Tunney. Tunney was the American marine who had come back from the war and taken the world title from the elemental boxing force called Jack Dempsey. Dempsey had spent his youth walking into saloons in shantytowns filled with gold and oil prospectors and offering to fight for money the toughest man in the bar. He was a Pole, Dempsey. He'd take an Irish name as a fighter to guarantee gate money and popular support. Tunney, the boxing scholar, the pugilist able to quote Shakespeare, had beaten him twice. It was Gene Tunney he remembered seeing now in the vestibule of Stresemann's consulting rooms. He had been wrong, on the street in Berlin, outside that café. Tunney was not the sort of champion who would ever lose his money.

'Martin?'

'Sorry, Bill. Away with the fairies.' Lillian kicked his ankle and coughed. That one had been completely unintentional. Anyway, wasn't it an English saying? 'Of course I've heard of Tunney.'

'Guy who trained Tunney trains me,' Bill said. 'I won't be an embarrassment in a public park to my boy.'

'Or girl.'

'Or girl,' Bill said.

'How did you meet Tunney?' Hamer was impressed.

'Hemingway's place in Bermuda. Tunney thinks you can absorb culture by osmosis. The return part of the deal was some very gentle ringwork Tunney did with Hem.'

'Wow,' Martin said. Lillian kicked him. It was getting to be like Pavlov's dogs, Martin thought.

'Needed to be gentle too,' Bill said softly,

perhaps to himself. 'You wouldn't believe how hard these heavyweights can hit.'

Lillian said, 'Would you ever introduce us to Hemingway?'

Bill sipped his beer. 'Honest answer? No. Hemingway likes a fight. He'd fight with Martin about Spain, eventually.'

'I went there as an observer,' Martin said.

'Sure,' Bill said. 'So did he. But there's observing and there's observations, kid.'

It was the only time on the trip they came anywhere close to discussing politics with their host.

They had a good time with Bill and Lucy in America. They enjoyed the West Coast weather, their proximity to the sea. They hiked in Marin County. They swam and played tennis and ate food cooked on a griddle by Bill's and Lucy's pool. Martin sparred a lot with Bill. Naturally they nicknamed him Maxie, after Schmeling, in the gym Bill used, though Martin didn't in the slightest resemble the German champion.

Towards the end of their stay, Lucy tired, and out of consideration and tact they hired a car and said they wanted to drive to Colorado to see the mountains. 'He needs to be alone with his wife,' Lillian said to Martin. 'She's frightened, poor thing. She's frightened at the thought of giving birth.'

'How do you know?'

'Because she told me,' Lillian said.

Martin drove. The road was huge and empty. 'They have a good life out here.'

'She didn't need to tell me,' Lillian said. 'I

could see she was afraid.'

The peaks came into view on the horizon, high, like a spiked and frosted mirage. 'I don't even want to hear the word Boscombe uttered,' Lillian said. 'You're not even permitted to say Arthur.'

They climbed to picnic at a place that reminded Hamer of a book of photographs he'd seen of Lillian's. The landscape wore a proud, gaunt enormity. Remote on a far crag, an eagle's nest described a thorny crown. There was no wind, only a subdued stillness. The silence about them seemed to him a provocation.

'Ansel Adams,' Lillian said. She chewed egg and cress sandwiches cut and wrapped for them by Bill.

'You always know my thoughts.'

The sandwiches were thickly spread with mayonnaise. They had everything in this country.

She looked at him. Her long legs were folded at the knee and her weight rested on her hips.

'I know what you're thinking right now,' he said.

She stopped chewing.

'That Gatsby stuff,' he said. 'That fatal innocence.'

Lillian swallowed.

'You accused me of it once.'

She looked at him. 'Why did Arthur Boscombe kill himself, do you think, Martin?'

'I thought — '

His wife tore grass in her clenched fist from a fissure in the rock on which they sat. The grass was sinewy stuff and stubborn, the wrench of its tearing audible. 'Why?'

They weren't supposed to mention Arthur Boscombe. 'He lived a lie, I suppose,' Hamer said. 'He lived a lie that became so big for him that he could no longer endure the living of it.'

Lillian nodded and breathed with a depth that raised and visibly sank the volume of her chest. Grass strands fell from her fist, and Martin saw green streaks staining her fingers. She shed from them, delicately, newly dead filaments of grass. 'Do you think that we live lies?'

'I don't like or admire the man, Lillian. But I want my country back. I want my nation restored.'

Lillian laughed. The sound of her laughter was a small reproof in the vastness of the space they shared. He did not know for what. He'd seen the Ansel Adams pictures she admired and thought them so scoured of life they might have been moonscapes. His wife's head rocked back and bowed forward and tears ran down her face. 'I'm not talking about the running of our country and your army, Martin. I'm talking about us.'

'Us and what?'

Lillian shuddered and sobbed into her fingers. Martin could smell the salt in the tears on her cheeks. The air in Colorado was that fresh, gave the senses that immediacy.

'I'm not Jay Gatsby,' he said.

She sniffed. There was snot on the back of her hand. He had never seen his wife before display so little self-possession.

'I'm not Arthur Boscombe.'

Laughter briefly broke the sobbing.

Hamer gathered himself. 'Are you unfaithful, Lillian? Is there someone else?'

She raised her eyes. The mountain light was pitiless, and her eyes were bloodshot, torn and flecked.

Was it remorse?

Lillian sniffed. She shook her head. 'No one,' she said. 'There's no one but you, Martin.' She laughed again the Arthur Boscombe laugh. 'There never has been.'

He sighed, despite himself. 'Then there is no betrayal.'

Lillian smiled at him. There were grass stains on her hands, and she rubbed at them absently.

'Thank God,' he said. He kissed her mouth, then, her eyes, as if to try to heal and soothe.

* * *

Bill dropped them at the airport, embraced them both. Martin stepped back. 'That's the first clinch you haven't come out of hitting me.'

Bill laughed at the joke, but there were tears in his eyes. He was a big, generous American man and he didn't know when he was likely to see his good friends again.

'Goodbye, Lillian,' he said. He was saying his final farewell to her. He would see Martin only on one further occasion. He would stand in three months' time in the rain at Lillian's graveside, one strong arm around his shoulder as Martin wept at the cleaving sorrow of his loss.

* * *

The spring had barely fingered East Prussia with sunlight or warmth. Frost was still on the grass. Hamer felt the crunch of it under his feet as he climbed out of the aircraft and stretched his legs. Men in Waffen SS uniforms, carrying machine pistols, met them in a column of cars at the landing strip. The cars jounced along a cart track stubborn with frost. The Wolf's Lair was a fortress of gaunt concrete slabs, greying with rain stains in a clearing amid dense Prussian forest.

The birds at least recognized that it was spring. They whistled and sang in the forest canopy. The only other noise was the occasional barking of a leashed Alsatian dog as their black-clad handlers urged them through the trees. Nobody spoke in Hamer's car. His aircraft had flown through the night, and he was stiff and sleepy. The flight had been far too noisy, far too cold to permit the luxury of a nap. He was hungry and needed sustenance and a shave.

An orderly fetched coffee and bread rolls and then offered to shave Hamer with a straight razor. The rolls were fresh and they were served with freshly churned butter. Hamer commented on this as the orderly lathered him and then stropped the edge of his blade. We're self-sufficient here, the man told him. We're equipped for a siege.

His audience with Goebbels lasted for just short of two hours. The man asked intelligent questions and listened intently to the answers Hamer provided. He was dark-shaven and had the mannerism of fingering his chin in thought. He was a dark-eyed man, sallow-skinned, better looking in the flesh than in the photographs of him. He had the suggestion about him of great energy. But he was short in stature and seemed to be totally without a sense of humour. Hamer thought the Reich minister's lady-killing career probably relied heavily on his influence and rank. Crupp had told him that the two women he had really wanted had both of them turned him down. He was well informed, and nursed no illusions, though, about conditions on the Eastern Front. You had to give the man that.

After his interview, to break the tension, Hamer went for a walk in the woods. He looked back to where the Wolf's Lair brooded darkly on the land. And he saw the Führer, briefly, a pale figure walking towards the concealment of a corner in a long leather coat with his hands clasped behind his back and vacancy in his eyes, his mind evidently elsewhere. Hamer was sure he wore the coat he had worn on his leisurely stroll through the conquered city of Paris three years earlier. Hamer had seen the photograph — every German had — the Führer serene at the centre of his senior officers, the girders and gantries of the Eiffel Tower rising in blurred focus behind them. Hamer had caught only a glimpse, just now. But in three years it seemed to him that the man in the leather coat had aged a lifetime.

An officer who shared his rank approached him through the trees. The man wore a knife or bayonet scar livid on one cheek and had four tank flashes sewn to his sleeve. There was a Knight's Cross hung around his neck.

'I could murder a drink,' the officer said to Hamer, smiling.

'You're still to see him?'

'I'm next,' the officer said. 'And to be frank with you, I'm crapping myself.'

Hamer took his father's flask from his tunic pocket and handed it to the man, who took three hefty swallows and handed back the flask.

'You're a gift from God, my friend,' he said.

'Martin Hamer,' Hamer said, extending his hand.

'Ludwig Kurtz,' the other man said, shaking it.

'They've planned an entertainment for this afternoon,' Kurtz said. 'Have you heard?'

'No.'

'Do you hunt, Hamer?'

'I used to shoot a little with my father. Snipe. Not for years.' At least it isn't fishing, he was thinking.

'Wild boar,' Kurtz said. 'It will make a change from shooting at Russians.'

'Wild boar are prettier, less fierce.'

'Slower moving too,' Kurtz said.

Hamer frowned. 'I didn't know wild boar were indigenous to East Prussia.'

'They weren't,' Kurtz said. 'They were specially bred and then put here to suit Field Marshal Göring's fondness for killing them. Nature isn't that which you inherit, Hamer. Nature is that which you create.'

It wasn't possible to tell whether Kurtz meant his remark ironically. Hamer suspected that he did. He looked back towards the Wolf's Lair, where the orderly who had shaved him had told him the water pipes froze solid in the winter and where in the summer the mosquito plagues would eat a man alive.

'We'll be all right on the boar hunt, you and I,' Kurtz said to him. 'One's appetite for melodrama is an individual thing. But both of us can shoot.' He smiled. The drink had relaxed him. He had a broken nose, and his face formed bleak, hard planes around this damaged feature. Hamer would not have wanted him for an enemy. 'We can both shoot, Martin Hamer. If we couldn't, by now we'd both be dead.' Kurtz winked, relaxed with the brandy inside him, and departed for his audience with the Reich minister.

Crupp had told Hamer about the most recent setbacks in the east, in Italy, during their dinner on the eve of his departure. But watching Kurtz walk over the frost-crisped ground to the Wolf's Lair, Hamer wondered how, with men like Kurtz in the fight, the army he fought for could ever seriously contemplate the losing of the war.

* * *

Martin Hamer was able to identify his wife's body. He was able to do so from the labels in her torn and bloodied clothes, from the texture, when he stroked it, of her hair and, most conclusively, from a ribbon he had tied in her hair with his own fingers. He had never learned to tie a proper bow. Since childhood, he had tied his shoelaces with an improvised double loop of his own devising. He had tied the bow in

Lillian's hair in the same individual fashion. But he saw nothing of his wife, really, in what remained of her on the steel table in the mortuary.

The car had not caught fire, which was a blessing for him he was told by a hospital medic later reprimanded for the tactlessness of the remark. But the vehicle had fallen and rolled for several hundred feet in its plunge from the narrow ribbon of road from which it had skidded. Lillian had been bounced around the car's interior, repeatedly colliding with its steering wheel.

'Lily wouldn't wish to be seen in this condition,' he told the surgeon and police officer in attendance. 'Cover her now, please. Please keep the body of my wife covered.'

Her bag had been retrieved from the wreck once their car had been hauled out of the ravine. They gave it to him, and he took it to a small room in the mortuary bare but for a table and chair and a sepia portrait of the Führer on the wall. He opened the bag and spread the contents on the table. First he picked up her purse. The bag he had bought for her in Paris, the purse in a small village in Italy near Lake Maggiore in the hills above Milan. With the coins and banknotes in the purse, tucked and folded into a pocket probably intended for bus tickets, was a single-column story cut from an English newspaper. It was an account of the public inquiry in a court into the death of Arthur Boscombe. The paper was yellow and the cutting fragile in its folds, compressed by confinement in

Lillian's purse. Boscombe had left two children, Robert, six, and three-year-old Veronica. The names had been underlined in pen and some comment scribbled beside them. Martin recognized his wife's handwriting, but the ink had run in the porous newsprint and whatever she had written was illegible now.

There was a dog-eared photograph in the bag, a portrait of the writer Scott Fitzgerald, with his thin Irish mouth and dated, matinée idol centre parting. The words TO LILLIAN, WITH TRUE AFFECTION FOR A DISCERNING READER! had been written on the back of it in the novelist's large, hasty scrawl. Bill had given it to her during dinner at Bill's and Lucy's house in America. He had slipped it across the table in an envelope.

Her sunglasses were in the bag, the sunglasses she wore when they endured the heat and reflected light of the Wannsee at her father's place, or walked through snow in the high valleys of the Alps in the spring. They were tortoiseshell and darkly complemented the light and shade of her hair. Martin tipped out of the bag his wife's comb and lipstick and library membership card. He spread these things out on the table in front of him, and when he breathed in they were possessions thick with the perfume and sense of her, each gathered, random item like a small but vital piece of evidence suggesting that she had not gone at all. At any moment he would hear familiar footsteps approaching along the corridor outside. She would put her lovely head around the door, and her eyes would widen in mock outrage at the pillaging of her handbag. But of course that would not happen. She had gone. She had slipped for ever from the earth and from him.

'I can't do this, Lily,' Martin said, his head in his hands. He sobbed and shook. 'I can't do this, Lily. I can't.' He rocked and wept and the Führer looked down on him from the wall with an expression that was stern but did not seem altogether unkind.

⋆ ⋆ ⋆

It was dusk by the time the boar hunt finally got started. There were eight of them, eight heroes of the war, Hamer presumed, from the number of badges and flashes and campaign wings and medals and general decorations on display as the men joked and chatted, unbuttoning their tunics, taking off britches and boots. They changed in a lodge built from wood and thick with the scent of pine sap from an open fire warming the place in the gathering chill of the Prussian night. Sconces lit the lodge, patches of scorched, hardened wood behind each roiling flame. There were drinking horns in elaborate stands on a long wooden table. Bleached animal skulls stared balefully down from high displays.

'Where are we?' Kurtz said to Hamer, who was getting changed next to him. 'Fucking Valhalla?'

They were given hunting clothes to wear woven from coarse, heavy green cloth. The jacket offered to Hamer was stiff at the edge of one cuff with dried gore. They were given gaitered boots and Tyrolean hats to put on their heads. Hamer looked at the hat, with its jaunty brim and silk band and small plume of osprey feathers. He was fussy about what he wore on his head, had been since encountering a man with teeth stained by chewing tobacco who concealed his scrofulous scalp under the sinister cover of a straw boater. He hailed from northern Germany, from the border with France. He thought the sartorial style of the south of his country sometimes laughable.

Ludwig Kurtz confirmed this when he put his own hat on. 'What are you giggling about, Hamer?'

'They're not going to let you into Valhalla wearing that.'

Kurtz took off the hat.

They were schooled quickly in the use of their weapons. These were single-action hunting rifles with a bolt mechanism and an accurate range of three hundred metres. Each man was given a cartridge belt filled with the long, slender bullets manufactured for the rifles. They were housed in polished brass, these projectiles, and looked to have been hand-turned. Hamer hefted his weapon. Kurtz, who was working the action of his, raised an eyebrow. 'Ammunition of this calibre and velocity wouldn't bring down a jack rabbit.'

Hamer was inclined to agree with him. The gun was beautifully made, the walnut stock oiled and smooth. But it felt alarmingly insubstantial between his hands, used as he was to a rifle designed for tank killing.

* * *

Beaters with pitch-dipped torches led their way through the dark tangle of forest. They held a torch high in one hand and a staff in the other to try to panic and goad the beasts they were stalking out of their cover. It was a moonless night, the stars remote through thin cloud cover.

'I'll stick with you, if you don't mind,' Kurtz said to Hamer.

'Likewise,' Hamer said. He licked his lips.

They had been told that the animals they were hunting grew to a mature weight of half a ton. They were covered in coarse hair that hung over hides so thick that nothing indigenous to the forest could penetrate it. No thicket was too dense or thorny for these beasts to hide in. And they were cunning at concealment. Their method of attack was to charge suddenly and rut and tear with the curved teeth of underhanging jaws three or four times more powerful than those of a Doberman. They aimed for the groin, for the inner thigh, seemingly with a sense of where the femoral artery lay waiting to be torn and to bleed a man to death. But they could kill equally with the weight and momentum of these sudden charges from the hides they occupied. Over a short distance they were lethally quick. When they got to their target, they ripped and trampled, enraged.

The boars were also carnivores, the men were told. They favoured human flesh as carrion. But they would eat out the stomach of a living man, once they got him down.

Nothing happened for an hour. Then there was a hoarse, juddering squeal and the tear of bone as a beater went to ground a hundred yards in front of where Hamer and Kurtz stood together, sneaking a sip each of Hamer's brandy. The two men dropped to the ground, kneeling side by side, shouldered their rifles, aimed and began to shoot. They each got off two rounds as the shape grew rapidly towards them. They heard their bullets hit their target and ricochet off the bone of the animal's skull. They could smell it as it came on, feel the ground shudder under its furious feet. Without a word, each man reloaded.

'Hold,' Kurtz said. They stood their ground. The boar was closing, ten feet away from them, fury burnishing in its black eyes, its head heaving, blood-flecked foam gathering in an angry stink around its teeth.

'Now,' Kurtz said.

Hamer rolled to his left and Kurtz to his right as the boar careened into the space where its targets had been. Struggling to still its own momentum, it juddered to a stop and started to turn. It had travelled twenty feet beyond them. Both men fired as the animal wheeled for a fresh attack, hitting it in the flank, high in the chest where they judged its heart would be. The boar groaned and its front legs folded under the huge weight of its head and chest. Blood was looping out of the two neat holes punched in its side, purpling the ground, rich smelling in puddles on the ferns and pine needles and grass. The animal panted and stank. Kurtz worked the bolt of his rifle, ejected a spent shell, inserted a fresh round and fired into the brain of the animal through an eye. It died, and Hamer and Kurtz saw the hair on its hide come alive with fleas leaving the beast as its great carcass started to cool and the beaters approached pulling knives and saws from scabbards and packs.

Hamer walked over to retrieve his flask, which he had dropped on the ground.

'Let's get a beer,' Kurtz said, as the beaters prepared their flaying tools. 'I've seen my share of butchery.'

'Funny way to hunt,' one of the heroes said, approaching. Hamer thought the voice belonged to an airman.

'That must be how they do it in Russia,' someone else said, as their fellow hunters gathered to look at the kill.

'Fuck off,' Hamer said to him. 'Have you any idea how ridiculous you all look in those hats?'

There was no more banter from the group as he and Kurtz retreated to get their beer.

* * *

The funeral was an occasion he endured largely mute, incapable. In the bewilderment of his pain, his instinct was to reach for Lillian so that she could comfort him. Wasn't it Lillian who always offered him comfort? Her absence was so sudden, the loss of her so overwhelming, he could find no perspective to help him to deal with what had happened. He was a strong and disciplined man, but the source of his strength, its inspiration, had been taken from him. For a while, he was sure later, he was mad with grief. Heidi and Bill united to orchestrate the ritual of Lillian's interment.

She was buried in Berlin, in the family plot bought by her father. She was lowered into the ground in a coffin of yellow wood in the rain. The wreath carrying the parting message Hamer had written his wife lay on top of the coffin. The coffin had handles of polished brass. The mourners dropped clods of earth on to the coffin, and the rain pattered on to the heaving shoulders of men and women at the graveside, crying, grieving. Lillian had been a lovely woman and she had been a woman much loved. Hamer could believe none of it.

He didn't believe it until a month after the burial, when he had sold their house in Cologne and sought and been granted a new assignment near Dresden. He had emptied the house of their furniture, burned Lillian's clothes, given her collection of books away as keepsakes to various of their friends.

He went finally into the attic of the house, where he never went, just in case some item had been overlooked. He remembered a sewing machine. He had not been able to locate the sewing machine and thought that it might have been stored by Lillian in the attic.

It hadn't been. There was a painted wooden rocking horse in the attic and a crib on runners and a doll's house. The doll's house had been scrupulously furnished. There was a tin battleship built for the bathtub. Martin remembered the battleship. He had seen it before. It had come from the lounge of the hotel in Scotland where they had stayed on holiday with Karl and Heidi. Now it sat in an attic in Cologne in secrecy, under dust, brought here under God knew what false hope of ever finding a use in the hands of the boy they could never have had. Martin picked up the tin battleship. He ran a finger along the bump of fake rivets lining its hull. And he knew then, finally, that his wife was dead, dead with her dead hopes and cherished illusions about what they could in life have accomplished together.

'Goodbye, my darling,' he said. He would take the boat to an orphanage. He would gather the toys and take them where the unloved and deprived could gain some comfort from them. 'Farewell, Lily,' Martin Hamer said.

* * *

At the funeral, in the rain, Martin Hamer could not look directly into the face of Dr Stresemann. He did not want to see what it was the loss of his only child had done to the doctor. Stresemann had always talked of how, in Martin, Lillian had delivered him a son. Martin's view on this was clear. It was an extravagant claim used to make him feel more comfortable about his failure to produce a grandchild. He liked the doctor, who was a generous and ebullient man. He was grateful that Stresemann was so accepting of him and of his relationship with Lillian. But he had never felt particularly close to his father-in-law.

He still felt the absence of his own father, a man whose grace and intelligence had gifted Martin's life until he had been broken by the peace that followed the war and chosen to end his own life in a stand of silver birches on the land they were about to have taken away from them.

He did not possess a living relative. He would have liked someone like Bill for an elder brother sometimes. There was Heidi, of course, but his feelings for Heidi were complicated by how attractive he had always felt her to be. He had never been remotely tempted to betray his wife. But he knew he did not look upon Heidi in quite the way a man would be comfortable thinking about his sister.

Stresemann approached him then. He stood in front of Martin Hamer at the graveside and the grief was ghastly in him. Nothing worked properly in the doctor's face. His facial muscles seemed pinched, and his skin appeared granular and grey. He twitched. His eyes were bloodshot. He seemed to half-stumble into an embrace with Martin and then gathered himself and changed his mind. He could not remember how to behave. All the suave presence of mind, the professionalism on which his success and reputation were built, was subsiding like the clods of earth under his feet that fell and tumbled down on to his daughter's coffin.

Hamer patted Dr Stresemann's shoulder and turned away. He wanted his friend, Bill. He needed the comfort of Bill's strength and understanding.

'Martin?'

He turned back.

'Try to find it in your heart — ' the doctor interrupted himself. 'Try to find it in your heart,' he said, and he attempted a sympathetic smile.

'I saw Gene Tunney in your waiting room one afternoon,' Hamer said, not knowing he was going to say it until the words were out of his mouth. 'Why was he there?'

'Tunney,' Stresemann said to himself. 'Tunney.' Rain pattered on the shoulders of his coat, and the expression on his face showed what could have been a kind of gratitude for this small diversion. 'Rheumatic pain,' Stresemann said. 'I treated Tunney for rheumatic pain in the knuckles of his hands. You see, Martin, the human hand was not designed to function as a weapon. Mr Tunney had damaged his hands using them as clubs to hit other men.'

'Thank you, doctor,' Hamer said. He turned and went to look for Bill, who was his friend.

* * *

There was some effort to skewer the boar on a spit and roast the beast over logs and charcoal. But the carcass was too fresh and needed to be hung. The meat had no maturity. Blood dripped and spat into the logs and then congealed on the muscles of the flayed animal until it smoked and charred and smelled of burn. Eventually cold cuts of lamb and beef were begged with bread and pickle from the kitchen of the Wolf's Lair, and the heroes hauled the boar away on its spit, dumped it in a depression in the forest and sat around the fire eating their impromptu picnic, drinking and talking.

Late, very late, in front of the grey-orange ashes of the fire diminishing now in the hearth of the lodge built for boar hunting in the forest near the Wolf's Lair, Hamer and Kurtz sat drunk, drinking beer from a barrel with a tap on the table, out of drinking horns fashioned for the purpose and mounted in scrolled silver. Each of the other Reich heroes had one by one staggered off to bed in the adjacent bunkhouse. Kurtz had more recently been in the fighting on the Eastern Front than Hamer. The counter-attack had stalled after the fall to the German forces of Kharkov. There was talk of a looming tank battle, massive, decisive, the biggest of the war.

'Do you still believe in what we're doing?' Hamer would not have asked the question sober.

Kurtz steadied his gaze, focused his eyes in concentration. 'The methodology, you mean, or the motive?'

'Aren't they two sides of the same coin?'

Kurtz smiled. 'We owed Poland a fight, and France, after what they did to Germany following the peace. I never liked the prosecution of the war in Russia, though. Couldn't see what was wrong with treating prisoners well, if they'd fought to the limit and surrendered honourably.'

Hamer nodded. He more than agreed.

'After Stalingrad, everything changed,' Kurtz said. 'I'm good at war, Hamer. I can fight. But I have two boys growing up with their mother at home in Saxony. They're great lads. They're my beautiful boys. I'd like something better than war for my boys. I'd like them to know their father.'

Hamer sighed. 'You talk as though it will go on for ever.'

Kurtz was looking around the lodge interior in the feeble light of the fire and the sconces guttering on the walls. The walls were decorated with broadswords, battle-axes, spiked maces on black metal chains. A portrait of the Führer, full length, glowered against a blood-flecked sky. An SS banner, the fabric rent and ragged with bullet holes, brooded in one corner.

'I think it's all we've come to know,' he whispered.

Hamer looked at the engraving scrolled in silver on his drinking horn. A Teuton knight laid about him with a broadsword, inflicting carnage on an enemy horde with a firmly Asiatic look.

'You've no one, have you, Martin?' Ludwig Kurtz concluded. Ariel Buckner had come to the same judgement what seemed like a lifetime ago, but was in fact only a few weeks. Was it something he gave off, like a smell? He thought of Julia Smollen, then, the woman in the camp. She would be sleeping now, under a thin blanket on a thin mattress filled with straw. Perhaps before sleep she had read a story from Grimm, or a chapter from Conrad. All the Polish books had been burned. Asking for a book by Joseph Conrad had been her small act of defiance, he knew. Hamer had read Conrad, had enjoyed stories written by the English author from Poland.

'When we met, I wondered what class of enemy you would make,' Kurtz said.

Hamer smiled. 'I did the same.'

'We'd be evenly matched, I think. We both got off two rounds against the boar. Two wasn't bad in the circumstances. All four bullets found their target. We both held our ground and, when we turned him, either of our third shots would have proved fatal.'

'Your conclusion?'

'I wouldn't like to fight you. We'd be evenly matched, but you place no value on your life. It gives you something.'

'It gives me nothing,' Hamer said, the sentiment heartfelt. He was drunk, though not too drunk to know it.

'I'd hate to fight you, Martin,' Kurtz said again. He slapped Hamer on the back. 'I like you far too much.'

* * *

Lillian had been in the ground six months when Martin agreed to have dinner in Berlin with Heidi. He was in the city to attend a series of seminars on the new tactics concerning rapid deployment and movement of tanks and tank infantry. There was great excitement about these tactics and a rush to make everyone from senior to junior commanders conversant with them. He had just come from a two-week stint in the Austrian Alps and was tanned from the sun in the mountains.

He telephoned Heidi as soon as he got to Berlin. He was godfather to the twins and took his responsibility very seriously. Karl had been dead for more than two years, and the twins had grown and developed and changed beyond recognition. They now piped a language he could understand in their angelic little voices. They had no recollection of their father. They loved their uncle Martin. But he had not seen them since Lillian's funeral because he hadn't felt able to do so. He was keen when he got to Berlin to make up for lost time.

* * *

He took the twins to the tea garden and bought them ice creams and spread them a picnic tea on the grass and played with them until dusk. They fell asleep in his arms as he carried them back to the house. It surprised him that Heidi had not thought fit to move after that awful, broiling Berlin day when Karl had taken his life. But then the twins would have had their friends at kindergarten. And he supposed it would not have been easy for a single mother to make new friends in a different locality.

* * *

She had changed by the time he knocked on her door knocker carrying the sleeping Hansel and Gretel. The babysitter answered the door. He washed his face in the sink in the kitchen and brushed his hair into place with his fingers. She walked into the sitting room as he sat waiting for her, reading a magazine. Heidi had on a satin wrap dress that exposed an inch of creamy cleavage. Her hair was pulled up into a sable coil behind her head. She wore an amethyst necklace and perfume. He stood.

'You look stunning,' he said, which was only the truth. She smiled and held out the keys to her car.

They dined in a restaurant on the river. Electric lights had been strung on poles above the tables, and the light reflected in shifting patterns on its surface when the breeze blew and the waters of the river rippled. The lights had paper shades so they moved even when the wind blew gently. Their reflections on the river were very pretty. Heidi was beautiful. It was a lovely evening. She reached across their table and put her hand on his.

'You still miss her terribly, don't you?'

Martin didn't say anything. Heidi withdrew her hand. 'I'm sorry. That was crass.'

Martin reached for her fingers, linked them with his. 'What's that saying the English have? Life goes on.' He raised his eyes.

A man had approached their table, two men, both in the uniform of the Gestapo. Hamer recognized Hessler, whose hair was shorter now than the last time they had met, cut into the style American college boys called a crew cut. The man with him was younger, slightly thicker set than Hessler. He seemed either embarrassed or coy, trying to conceal his face under the peak of his uniform cap. He suppressed a belch and said sorry under his breath. The Gestapo men had both clearly been drinking.

Hessler clicked his fingers. 'Hamer,' he said.

There was a short silence. 'Aren't you going to introduce me to your beautiful dining companion?'

Hamer pushed back his chair with his legs and stood. 'Heidi,' he said, 'may I present to you Hauptsturmführer Hessler of the Gestapo.'

Heidi nodded briefly and smiled.

'Hauptsturmführer Hessler, this is Frau Heidi Jodl, an old and treasured friend.'

Hessler beamed. Evidently he enjoyed the formalities of social occasion. He did not bother to introduce his own companion, a Gestapo Untersturmführer who stayed slightly behind the senior officer to his right.

'Your choice in friends is better than it was,' Hessler said to Hamer. He and his friend walked away. At least he hadn't insisted on kissing Heidi's hand.

'What did he mean by that last remark?'

'I don't know.'

'Why did you introduce me by my maiden name?'

'Because he's Gestapo and might have remembered Karl's.'

'Why was he here, Martin?'

'To eat, I suppose. This is a fashionable restaurant. I imagine all the coming men have it on their list of necessary places to see and be seen.'

Heidi looked doubtful. Hamer linked his fingers with hers again and squeezed her wrist gently with his thumb. The touch of her wrist was smooth and warm. He felt the beat of her pulse under the skin.

'He's a Gestapo man I met years ago,' Hamer said. 'His presence here is nothing more than coincidence.'

Heidi said, 'I'm a civilian and I live in Berlin. Where the Gestapo are concerned, I don't believe in coincidences.'

* * *

The last port of call on Hamer's trip through Germany after his audience at the Wolf's Lair was at a college at Bremerhaven. He wondered now how he had ever been nervous about the prospect of public speaking. If he found his young audiences unnerving, it was because of their appearance and the preconceptions they all seemed to share, rather than any inadequacies concerning his style of delivery. True, he was not a histrionic speaker. But then he hadn't needed to be. He had done things and seen things most men, even most Germans, would only ever dream or, more accurately, have nightmares about.

And it was not as though the questions forced him to think. They were the same, informed by the same propaganda and myths and smattering of hard information wherever in the Fatherland he travelled. No, the Russians did not eat their own young. Yes, they frequently pretended to surrender only to spring an ambush when the Germans rose from cover to take them into captivity. Yes, the Russian women fought. They were not used as strike troops but they drove transport and were often used as fighter pilots and snipers. No, your pee did not freeze into a golden column when you relieved yourself in the Russian winter. But a wise soldier would relieve himself in a latrine, if he could find one, rather than in the teeth of an Arctic gale on the frozen steppe. And it was a very ill-advised soldier who took a crap on the steppe.

They never laughed at his jokes. Maybe it was because his attempts at humour were feeble. But he looked at his audience, at the army and naval college cadets and Hitler Youth, and he never saw humour on their rapt, earnest faces. There was a uniformity about their expressions as well as about their dress. In one way it was impressive; in the way perhaps in which Karl had responded in the rallies before the war, in Nuremberg. But in another way it was sinister. They look like they've all come out of the same bath, Hamer thought to himself at Bremerhaven. The same bath or the same pod.

After the sustained ovation that followed the last speech of his tour, he had four hours to occupy in Bremerhaven before his train. He was offered tea and cake in the college staff room. He drank the tea and left the cake. Hamer was not a man with a very sweet tooth. He picked up a newspaper and flicked through its pages. Almost every story it contained could have been described as a call to arms or a plea for further sacrifice. Hamer looked at the cake on his plate. The faces of the boys in his audience had been gaunt, bright-eyed not just with enthusiasm but with the effects of rationing, which shrank and tightened facial skin and made the features bigger in a hungry child's face. He looked with guilt at the cake on his plate. Somebody would eat the damned thing. He covered it with his napkin so that it would not harden and stale. Then he saw the news story, the authentic piece of news in the paper that defined Bremerhaven in his memory for the rest of Martin Hamer's life.

He walked down to the beach. The port of Bremerhaven had dirtied the sea with slicks and spillages from ships. The water was thick, really, with filth from bilge tanks and the flotsam of wrecks and the spoil released safely, in harbour, after weeks under the water, from the navy's homecoming U-boats. But the wind that scoured off the North Sea was clean. Hamer blinked against the grit of shifting sand. He listened to the wind as it buffeted the beach. He smelled the salt on the wind and closed his eyes and listened to the gulls scream and the sea toil on the shoreline. He squatted and sat on a tussock of grass.

The newspaper picture of Ludwig Kurtz had not been of great quality, but it had not needed to be. You did not forget such a face. His air transport had been shot down somewhere between Kharkov and Kursk. The death of the crew and the army passengers aboard had been instant, said the report. But then it would, wouldn't it, Hamer thought. Kurtz would not see his wife or Saxony again. He had seen the last of his beautiful boys and they of their father.

Hamer was aware suddenly that he was not alone. He turned and saw the principal of the

Bremerhaven college standing there in the uniform of an officer of the naval reserve. The man was about sixty, pale and dignified. Martin had not heard his approach because it had been against the direction of the incoming wind. About a further fifty feet behind the principal, two cadets stood to attention. To Hamer's astonishment, he saw that they were armed.

'You followed me?'

'Please, sir,' the principal said. 'It's a precaution only. Please do not take offence. Men come from the Eastern Front to speak to our colleges. It's hard sometimes for them to adjust to the fact of returning. There have been suicides.'

The wind whipped sand on the beach. The principal of the Bremerhaven college took a handkerchief from his pocket and held it out to Hamer.

'What's that for?'

'For your eyes, sir. For your face. You are crying.'

* * *

The twins slept in the same bed. Heidi had bought them bunk beds once they had outgrown their cots but had fought a losing battle trying to keep the infants apart in the night. They lay in fleecy pyjamas, limbs intertwined, breathing softly, dreaming innocent dreams.

'You've worn them out,' Heidi said in the darkness.

Martin ruffled Gretel's hair and the boy stirred in his sleep.

'I'll go and make us some coffee,' Heidi said.

* * *

A tiny, skilful arrangement of hooks and eyes secured the wrapover dress that Heidi wore. Now she used the fingers of one hand to open it and her shoulders to shrug the dress to the floor.

'Heidi — '

She unclipped her brassiere and eased the straps off her shoulders. Her breasts were high and full and cream-coloured in moonlight. Her shoulders moved with the weight of her breathing and moonlight sculpted shadows above her collarbones.

'Heidi — '

'At least hold me, Martin,' she said. Her voice shook. 'At least hold me and kiss me, once.'

He closed the distance between them and held her and kissed her. Her lips were soft and her teeth sharp against his tongue. He could smell a dark tang of arousal under her perfume.

'It wouldn't be any good.'

'You are hard for me, Martin. I can feel you.'

'Every time I look at you I'd be reminded of her.'

'You wouldn't be.'

'I would. I am.'

He held Heidi in his arms, wondering how such a woman had not been enough for Karl.

'Bastard,' Heidi said, as though reading his thoughts. She ground herself closer to him. Her breath was hot, and he felt the raw warmth of her.

'The twins — '

'Don't say it, Heidi. Please don't.'

'I'm sorry. God, I shouldn't even have thought it.'

'It's all right,' he said. It wasn't as though he had not thought it himself.

They pulled apart. He picked her dress up from the floor and handed it to her. She put it on but didn't bother to fasten it. She laughed. 'Who would have thought things would ever come to this?' She went to him and stroked his hair and kissed him on the cheek. 'I'll make you some coffee. Or a brandy if you prefer. I'll pour you a brandy. And then you'd better leave.'

* * *

Crupp and Buckner ate dinner together. Their shared repast was taken late, in a Poznań restaurant closed to other diners. The food was good and the wines they drank with it were well chosen. But there was no ceremony, no string quartet of gifted student Poles to play for them.

'I need him,' Crupp said to his cousin.

'He's a fucking criminal,' Buckner said.

'Goebbels was impressed.'

'Because he's the Aryan fucking pin-up boy.'

'Rolfe apparently thought the same,' Crupp said. He swallowed some wine. 'Where is Rolfe now?'

'Back in hell, where he was spawned.'

'Hamer is the genuine article,' Crupp said.

'He's a hero of the Reich.' Crupp chewed a morsel and then swallowed some wine, in thought. Buckner watched him and said nothing.

'These notions, heroism, sacrifice, nobility — '

'Bullshit,' Buckner said.

'If you interrupt me again, Ariel, I'll kick your arse out of that door and you'll walk back to the camp. You've long missed the last train.'

Buckner took this in.

'I told Hamer you were a cunt,' Crupp said.

Buckner's face fell. 'Why did you tell him that?'

Crupp chewed on something moist. He swallowed. 'You have to be honest with a man sometimes if you want to earn his trust.'

Buckner said nothing.

'So, these notions, heroism and so on. They can become ours by association if we hang on to Hamer and use him shrewdly. It's an open secret that migration to the General Government is not proving to be as popular as was hoped. We get Hamer to campaign for the cause, to say that after the war he wishes to make Poznań his home.'

'I thought he was in a hurry to go back and get killed by the Russians in the snow.'

'He is. But his departure will be delayed. Soldiers are philosophical about delay.' Crupp pondered. 'How's his wound?'

'Little more than a legacy of scar tissue. His health is restored. The man is frighteningly strong. He broke Rolfe apart with his hands.' Buckner shuddered.

'Just so,' Crupp said. He smeared the food

around his mouth with a napkin. ‘A hero of the Reich should not be made of cotton wool.’

* * *

Julia Smollen lay in her bunk with the taste of blood on her tongue. Her mouth kept filling with blood. A kick in the face had forced one incisor into her gum, and the wound was too deep to heal quickly without the stitches with which it would not be treated. She tried to be philosophical about the deep cut in her mouth. She was lucky still to have all her teeth. She had strong teeth, still white and firmly rooted in her gums despite the food and neglect of the camp. She was bruised, but she had been bruised before, in worse circumstances, during the reign in the camp of Hans Rolfe, who was now thankfully dead. Had Rolfe been alive to hear the rumour the women in the camp had heard, and he would of course have heard it, she would be dead now, Julia believed. And her death would have been a drawn-out and squalid event.

They had taken her books. They had taken her precious volumes of Grimm and Conrad and torn the pages out for lavatory paper and to wad into sanitary towels. In part, Julia did not blame them for that. Books here were an indulgence and reading a conceit. There were necessities in the camp that came before reading. But the books had been her escape, in her imagination, from this place and its realities, and they had robbed her of that and it was a blow to her. She had not even had the books for very long. He had bought them to her only a month before his departure from here.

She blamed them most for shaving her head. She had gone with the German officer to save herself from Rolfe, who had been killing her on a sort of instalment plan. The officer, Martin Hamer, had been kind to her. He was a kind, handsome man who had gentle hands. She honestly thought the motive of the women, most of them, was as much envy as patriotism. They hadn't been fucked for years. How many of them could honestly say they had ever been fucked by a man who looked like he did? Patriotism was to her mind the most abused of causes.

These were vindictive, childish thoughts, she knew. Lying swallowing blood in her bunk, it was hard not to feel them, but they were feelings that would pass. What she really hated the women for was for proving that she had not conquered her vanity in the way that she had thought she had. She had been dismayed when they had shaved her head, when she had seen her own sunless scalp, the skin as white as a grub worm, exposed. They had held up in front of her face the small mirror they coveted and she had seen her naked head and her eyes, green and frightened, larger without the frame of hair she had worn around her face, and she had been shocked at her own appearance.

The rumour had come and gone with the speed only rumour possesses. Hamer was dead, had been killed in his crashed air transport. Her protector had perished in a pyre of aeroplane fuel, they told her gleefully, cackling in a shrinking circle around her, making fists of their filthy, calloused hands.

Then, after she had been shorn and beaten and her books torn from their place of safekeeping under her mattress, he had come back to life again. There had been nothing Christlike or miraculous about Hamer's resurrection. It was another hero of the Reich, another visitor to the Wolf's Lair with him, who had died. Julia lay there and she ached and she bled. She wondered if the man whose death had prompted her pain and degradation was worthy of the unintended tribute. She doubted it. She had heard them creeping up to her bunk to try to reconstitute the pages of her books not already smeared with blood and shit. The pages were piled now in a sad heap on the floor below where she lay.

She'd felt nothing but fear and foreboding on hearing of Hamer's death. She had believed the rumour, as all of them had. They believed all the rumours. To do so was a symptom, a reflex, a condition of life in the camp. She had felt no pity or disappointment at the news. She had felt only the selfish instinct of fear. This meant that the camp was succeeding. She had realized early on that one of the principal ways in which it stripped its inmates of themselves was to deaden them to emotion. She could have pitied him, at least, in death. Hadn't pity been what she felt foremost for him in life?

Her head could not really have the whiteness of a grub worm. That was how the shock of it had appeared in a snatched glimpse in the looking glass they'd held before her. But feeling her scalp now, it was rough in places with scratches and cuts and clusters of small scabs. The cutting had been done with animal shears smuggled in from the farms they were sent to sometimes to shear sheep for wool. They were a blunt, rusty implement. And they had been used on her with a vindictive clumsiness. Julia smiled through bloodied teeth to herself. Hamer had not died. But she had lost her protector. He would not want the grotesque version of herself they had turned her into now. She screwed her bruised body into what scant comfort her mattress afforded, lying foetal, her elbows on her belly and her hands in small fists under her chin. In the circumstances, that was ironic. In peace there might have been something tragic about the circumstances. But then they would not have occurred in peacetime. And Julia Smollen had come firmly to believe that irony was the truest expression of this war.

* * *

Hessler asked Hamer's permission before he asked Heidi out on a date. Heidi's parents were dead. She had no brothers. So perhaps there was a courtly logic to the protocol. Hamer didn't think so. He thought it a gesture made by Hessler to amuse himself. He stood there with the telephone receiver in his hand in the officers' mess in the infantry barracks at Dresden, inhaling the familiar mess atmosphere of floor wax and cigarette smoke and listened as the

Gestapo man listed his qualifications as a possible suitor for Heidi.

'She knows none of the detail of the death of her husband,' Hamer heard himself say. Outside in the courtyard, feet drummed on cobbled stones, practising drill.

Hessler's laugh was a relaxed, confidential chuckle. 'She won't learn any of that stuff from me,' he said.

Hamer pictured Heidi, in the night, shrugging a sheath of satin from her dimpled shoulders to the floor. He felt a stab of envy then, keen and deep.

'Don't hurt her, Hessler.'

There was a silence. 'I'm surprised you can even suggest such a thing, Martin,' Hessler said. 'I mean, my God.' He sounded more than affronted. He sounded genuinely hurt. Hamer realized that Hessler had the advantage over him of knowing his Christian name. He certainly didn't know Hessler's.

'It's Jacob,' Hessler said, 'by the way,' as if reading Hamer's mind. He had recovered. His voice had already found its easy tone of intimacy again. 'If things go the way I hope, Martin, it will be Jacob from now on.'

It was a warm afternoon in Dresden. Sunlight shafted through the floor-to-ceiling windows of the officers' mess, dust motes turning them into solid-seeming, slanting pillars. Hamer's sole duty for the afternoon was to attend a seminar on a variant type of rifle ammunition thought to be more accurate at higher altitudes. He felt he had listened to everything he ever needed to learn about killing men in the mountains. He signed the excuse book and fetched his tunic and cap from the mess coatrack and wandered out of the barracks into the streets of the city, dazed.

It was hard in Dresden to escape the sound of music. Dresden was a city giddy with strings and horns. Music seemed to pour forth into the light from every vacant doorway. Hamer wandered without destination through its plangent, sweet-sounding streets, panic replacing the numbness that was the first response brought on by the mock obsequiousness of Hessler's telephone call. He sat heavily on a chair in a small square outside a café. He ordered a coffee and a cognac. People spilled by him, swastikas fluttered above him and birds added their voices to the cacophony of the square. Martin was aware of none of it.

If things go the way I hope, Hessler had said, it will be Jacob from now on.

If things go the way he hopes, Hamer thought, I won't see my godchildren any more.

* * *

The flight that had taken Hamer to the Wolf's Lair had been necessitated by the hectic schedule required of and kept to by a Reich minister. It was no honest reflection of the status enjoyed by a soldier, even of a soldier such as Hamer, who enjoyed the transient status of a popular hero. Thus, provision had been made by some military clerk in Poznań for his return journey to the camp. But it was not an urgent journey demanding scarce resources such as pilots and aeroplanes. It was a dawdle by connecting trains through a kind of wilderness; one of the bleakest, most desolate, least developed parts of rural Germany.

Bremerhaven was a German town neither too remote on the map nor even on the rail network from Poznań. But Hamer couldn't help wonder whether it had not been chosen for his final public appearance mostly because, of his entire itinerary, it was the place in Germany from which a deserting soldier could least easily abscond.

The thought owed a lot to his encounter with Ludwig Kurtz. Hamer had not known Kurtz for very long. But he did not believe he had ever met a braver man or a better soldier. There was nothing counterfeit about Kurtz. Hamer had encountered often enough the medal hunters, the flamboyant seekers of glory that professional soldiers derided as men with chest pains. Ludwig Kurtz had not been one of them. He had been a man of true courage.

Yet Martin Hamer was in no doubt now about just how disillusioned Kurtz had become, by the time the two men met, with the prosecution of the war.

He did not believe any more that Kurtz had sought a swallow of cognac to steel his nerve for an audience with the Reich Minister for Propaganda. He wondered how he could ever have been dumb enough to believe it. Kurtz had worn four tank flashes on his sleeve, for Christ's sake. Such men did not need alcohol to steel themselves for a confrontation with a peddler of correct opinion, regardless of the status the peddler enjoyed. This was a man who had crossed the steppe in his boots with a rifle on his back to fight on foot against oncoming Russian tanks. Hamer believed now that Kurtz had wanted a stiff drink only to mellow his temper and prevent him from speaking his mind. He dared not speak his mind, didn't Ludwig Kurtz. All the man had really feared was the reprisal his furious honesty would surely have delivered his wife and his boys back in Saxony, once it had stripped him of his rank and had him shot, for dissent, or hanged, for treachery.

These were gloomy thoughts. The train rocked and travelled over featureless wastes too boggy, too heavily sown with salt from the sea, to give labouring the land an honest return. Hamer drank from his flask. The principal at the Bremerhaven college had insisted on refilling it from his own drinks cabinet, having heard his rueful anecdote from the podium in the lecture hall about how its talismanic qualities had failed to save him from the bullet on the morning he was shot.

'Why are the boys armed?' he had asked the principal of the college on the beach.

'We followed you here because it is hardly the place or the weather for swimming, sir.'

He handed back the principal his handkerchief. 'And if I'd tried to drown myself, they'd have done what? Shot me out of the water?'

The principal shrugged.

Hamer regretted embarrassing him. He was

clearly a man of integrity. You could see it in his face, in the starch and revitalizing brush which had been applied with such scrupulous care to his fading uniform.

'I apologize for my last remark, which was trite and undeserved.'

'They're excellent swimmers, these two. Carrying weapons is an instruction we're obliged to obey. They'd have stacked their rifles one against the other on the sand and followed you into the water.'

Hamer looked at the waves, heaving, viscous, breaking as if in slow motion on the filthy shoreline. 'Into that?'

'Into that,' the principal said.

He signed autographs for the boys. He tore off a tunic button each for them, one from a pocket and one from an epaulette. The college principal looked appalled at this. But the two boys seemed delighted by their souvenirs.

The train rocked and Hamer dozed.

He revived, and with him his thoughts. Part of the problem with his conclusion about Kurtz was that he himself had willed the war. His will hadn't caused it, but perhaps his had been part of the collective German will that had. Did he believe in the collective will? He didn't know, had never given the matter sufficient thought. You could do that in the army. You could hide behind collective irresponsibility. It was encouraged. Why not? It was an efficient tendency. What he did remember with certainty was saying to Lillian on the deflating day they left their Berlin flat that a war was just what his career required.

'Jesus,' Hamer said to himself now in the train carriage. He rubbed his face and looked around. In a uniform, a profanity from a man was a small sin. But it did not appear to matter anyway on this train. There did not appear to be anyone within earshot to hear him commit the offence.

He was probably drunk. There were sandwiches in his bag. Perhaps he should eat them. But he felt bad enough about having them. They had been presented to him by the principal of the Bremerhaven college at the point of his departure. And Hamer had known that there had been no food provision made for him by the organizers of his itinerary, that this had been the man's lunch, prepared probably that morning by his wife. Martin Hamer had only come to understand the established pretence of this custom after the fourth engagement of his tour. He had opened his dedicated lunch then, and opened as a napkin, and then read, a loving and impromptu note from the wife of the man who had handed him the meal. He'd had no particular bad conscience about that. The note made it clear that the man deprived that day of black bread, cheese and pickled cabbage had been someone with far more than Hamer had to look forward to when he got back to his family home.

* * *

Night had fallen when Hamer next awoke, and the train was pulling into some dim station too obscure for the distinction of a placename lit by electric lamps. A man in the field grey uniform of the Abwehr got on to the train. He sat with his back to Hamer, this soldier, but he was a big man, and Hamer could see his thick neck and thick, neatly shorn hair under his field cap above the seatback. The mass and colouring of the man reminded him of an episode on his last holiday with Lillian in America. Hamer had not eaten his sandwiches. He was still slightly drunk. I should eat, he thought. But he didn't. Instead he closed his eyes and surrendered to the luxury of reminiscence.

He'd been sparring with Bill in Bill's gym. His American friend was exactly the Ivy League athlete Martin had always supposed he would be. There was no vindictiveness or spite in Bill, nothing petty or mean-minded. But he was tough when it came to sport, and when he played he played to win. Martin stood in the corner between rounds with his gumshield gripped in one glove and his gloves over the top rope. He spat blood into the bucket in the corner and smiled.

'You've got nothing to smile about, trooper.'

The words were indignant. They came from the ring apron. Hamer stood with his arms rested on the top rope, waiting for the completion of the minute interval on the gymnasium clock, for the bell signalling the start of the next round.

'Get your arms off that fucking rope,' the voice said. 'Give your lungs a chance to open, for Christ's sake.' Hamer disentangled and dropped his hands. He opened his lungs, his eyes.

'Breathe, kid. Fuel the engine. Feed the fire.'

The bell rang.

'Don't rely on your strength,' Tunney said. It was Gene Tunney. It was an apparition. Bill must have hit him fucking hard, Hamer thought. 'Get up on your toes. You'll ship less punishment mobile. You can punch on your toes, boy strong as you are, kid.' The old champion looked like a god. It was real. It was no apparition. The god winked. 'It's how I beat Dempsey,' Gene Tunney said to Martin Hamer.

Bloodied, beggared before this visitation, Hamer put Bill on the canvas twice in their final round. Bill's coach, also Tunney's coach, was a picture of mystification.

'Character,' Bill told his mentor, sated by defeat, wiping blood from his nose on the bandages over his fists, gargling blood from his mouth at the lip of the water bottle in his corner. He'd had the best of it often enough, over the course of their sparring. This was a setback he'd learn from.

From his stool on the other side of the ring, Hamer looked at Bill, the white lint on the bandaged hands of his friend pinking as Bill used his hands to try to stanch the bleeding caused by damage inflicted by Martin's fists.

'Pretty good, kid,' Tunney said, winking at Hamer, turning for the portal of sunlight at the gymnasium door, magnificently dapper in his brown three-piece pinstripe, in his wingtips and his hat, carrying his cane. 'I know people would have happily paid to see you and the big fellow scrap just now. You can fight, kid. And you're still improving.'

We're wrong about the Americans, too, Hamer thought on the train. The Führer had said somewhere that they were good at manufacturing razor blades and automobiles. And they are very good at those things. But we take them far too lightly.

The soldier who had reminded him of Dempsey came over then; towered over the drunken hero of the Reich and asked him for his autograph. You've probably sons, Hamer thought, like Ludwig Kurtz. You've probably daughters. He signed his name on the scrap of paper the man had brought over, drunk. The man retreated seemingly happy enough. I should eat my Bremerhaven sandwiches, Hamer thought. I need their ballast.

Dempsey and Tunney had become friends after the two bouts that made them both famous and rich. After the second fight, after Tunney's relentless jab had turned his eyebrows into gore, Dempsey had groped blindly for his manager's guiding hand and said: 'Get me over there. Get me to Tunney's corner. I want to congratulate the guy.'

Hamer remembered the famous picture published a decade earlier of Dempsey and Tunney and their mutual friend Ernest Hemingway, dining in Dempsey's steak restaurant in New York. How friendly still, he wondered, would the two great boxers be? Jack Dempsey was the Pole with an Irish name. Gene Tunney was one of Germany's most vocal foreign friends.

Hamer nodded with drunkenness and fatigue and the somnambulant rhythm of his train on its rails. What did he care about all this stuff? He didn't care. He didn't give what Bill would call a flying fuck. He was a hero of the Reich. He carried in his lap a meal that he wouldn't eat. And the recollection of Julia Smollen festered somewhere in him like a welcoming wound.

⋆ ⋆ ⋆

Martin took Hansel and Gretel to the zoo. It was a sunny day in Berlin, and the children loved to go to the zoo and see the elephants and the big cats and the hippos wallowing ugly in their wet and muddy enclosure. Martin tried to see the animals in the zoo through the five-year-old eyes of his twin charges. The world must seem enormous to them, he thought. The zoo must seem the size of a city. The elephants must appear colossal, twice as big and tall at least as they appeared to him. And louder, he thought, as an elephant trumpeted, the beast adopting a warlike tone, confronted by dozens of glazed brown buns extended from tiny hands through the bars of its cage.

Child logic fascinated Hamer. Two weeks previously he had taken them to a wood, telling them it was a place of spells and enchantment. The twins had looked about bold-eyed with expectation. But apart from some trees contorted by nature into ghoulish shapes, sinister holes with spider webs stretched over their apertures in twisted trunks, there was nothing particularly magical for them to wonder over or be fearful at. So he'd called them over to a fallen log sunk half its thickness deep in the needle- and moss-strewn forest floor. There'll be creepy-crawlies underneath it, he promised, and the children crouched with their hands on their knees and their eyes wide in anticipation. He expected worms, slugs and woodlice, a little hamlet bustling with pale and slimy horrors for the twins to be properly disgusted by. He lifted the log. And lying under it, two inches long, was a bright yellow newt with a green crest and black, astonished eyes. Martin gently picked the creature up and put it into the palm of Gretel's extended hand. It was perfect in its detail, from the tiny talons on its four claws to the almost microscopic pebbling on its bright skin.

'What is it?' Gretel asked.

'A baby dragon,' Martin said.

'Can we keep it,' Hansel asked, 'to watch it grow?'

'They only grow in the dark,' Martin said. 'That's why we have to put it back now.'

But he had been far more astonished by the find than the children had. They had never before seen a fallen log prised from the forest floor. It was the sort of thing done by children older than they were. And so the twins simply assumed that every fallen log in the forest concealed a baby dragon, growing in the dark towards its fire-breathing maturity.

In the same way, they thought that every penguin in the world lived in a concrete enclosure with a pool, surrounded by a laughing audience of children, thrown herring from a bucket by a keeper in oilskin waders.

It is how they reach their accommodation with the world, Hamer thought. They can't hope to understand its mad complexities. So they have it conform to rules built around the small store of what they know and have precedent for.

The thought made him smile. The thing was, he knew adults who did this too. But he didn't think it particularly funny that one of them was wooing Hansel's and Gretel's mother.

He bought toffee-apples and lemonade for the twins and coffee for himself, and they sat and ate and drank thoughtfully, the big cats next on their list of attractions to see. He always punctuated their visits to the zoo like this. He felt that the lethal animals captive there, the hunter-killers from Africa, deserved a special moment in the order of the day. He didn't mind the children thinking there was a dragon under every mouldering log. He thought it important, though, that they were properly awed by the languid power of a predatory jungle king.

And he enjoyed this part of the zoo day best himself. Shortly after they met, Lillian had read out loud to him the introduction to Hemingway's famous African story set at Kilimanjaro, the bit about the carcass of the frozen leopard lying unpicked by the vultures high on the slopes of the peak. He had not questioned the legend in his mind. He'd wondered what lonely prey the leopard had stalked there. He wondered what it was had caused the death of the cat. He had found a corpse of his own on a mountain. High on the Eiger, in a storm, he had almost become one. He came with Lillian subsequently to look at the leopards at the zoo. He looked at the pumas, the cougars, the lions and finally the tigers. He was never charmed by these animals, for all their feral beauty. They carried their killing natures in their poise, their patient gaze and the heavy odour they secreted. Hamer was never charmed by these animals. But he did think there was a lot to be learned from their careful study.

'He's doing it again,' Martin heard Hansel say around a mouthful of toffee and apple flesh. 'He's daydreaming again.'

'What do you think he daydreams about?'

'I don't know,' Hansel said. 'Do you?'

'Yes,' Gretel said.

'What, then?'

'Sweets, of course,' Gretel said. 'Uncle Martin daydreams about sweets.'

'Come on, you two,' Uncle Martin said. 'The tigers are expecting us.' He took a sticky hand in each of his. 'And not a word to your mother about those toffee-apples.'

'Mama said it's all right for you to spoil us,' Gretel said.

'She said that?'

Hansel and Gretel were nodding at him, both. When they spoke, they spoke in unison: 'She said it's your job.'

When he looked at his watch as they left the tiger enclosure it was twenty past four. He had promised to have the children back at six. They had enough time to take a rowing boat on the lake, or have a ride in a landau behind a trotting horse in the park. He suggested they choose. A frown troubled each of their faces. He squatted down for a serious chat with them, eye to eye.

'Don't you like those choices?' He said it chucking their chins, his voice gentle. He loved the twins.

'We want to play with you,' Gretel said. And so they played hide-and-seek. They played tag. Hamer wondered if Jacob Hessler ever played tag with Heidi's twins. It was not something he could easily picture in his mind. He could not have known then, of course, that one day he would play a lethal game of hide-and-seek himself with Jacob Hessler.

* * *

'Will you come in for coffee?'

'Best not, I think.'

The twins had kissed him goodbye and run into the house past their mother, headed for their playroom. She wore a blue cardigan over a cream silk blouse and had her hand above her eyes to shield them from the descending sun. Her breasts tugged at the buttons of the blouse. Her hair spilled like sable over the shoulders of the cardigan.

'How long is it now?'

'Another month.'

He was halfway through an eight-week posting in Berlin. In one way he hated being in the city. But he got to see his godchildren here, to take them out. Ever since Lillian's death, he had dreaded the free time most soldiers looked forward to. But that time was better spent in Berlin than Dresden, despite his dislike of the place, its imperial atmosphere, its sense of permanently being a city on parade.

'The time's gone quickly.'

'It has.'

'The twins adore you.'

'Yes, well. That's mutual.'

'He's nothing like as bad as you think.'

Hamer smiled. He kissed her on the cheek. 'You can't make a constant habit of justifying the men in your life to me, Heidi. Be with whoever it is you want to be with.'

She averted her eyes, then, and shook her head.

'I'll phone,' he said.

* * *

'It's like this, cousin,' Crupp said, his arm avuncular around the shoulder of Ariel Buckner as they walked the perimeter of the camp. They walked casually. Their progress might more accurately have been described as a stroll. Landau stalked them, twenty feet to their rear, with a machine pistol balanced between alert, agile hands. 'We're going to have a prize-giving in Poznań.'

'Prizes? In Poznań?' Buckner looked bewildered.

'You smell strongly of peppermints,' Crupp said. 'Have you been at the ether, cousin?'

Buckner reddened. 'I swore off the stuff when the murderer Martin Hamer stormed into my quarters and confessed to the killing of Rolfe. You know I did.'

'Yet you left your meal untouched in Poznań the other night,' Crupp said.

Buckner stopped. 'I'm not sniffing ether. I'm partial to peppermints. In Poznań the other night I quite simply did not like the food.'

Crupp made a noise in his throat or nose. It was a small, inconsequential sound that could have meant anything. He ushered them on. Behind them, Landau followed.

'Joseph is with me on this.'

'Joseph?'

'Goebbels,' Crupp said, who had found his new sponsor. 'Agriculture is at the heart of our culture. Agriculture is the home and hearth of the Volk. So we gather our pioneer farmers for a fair. We allocate prizes for the biggest potato yield per acre and the best-performing semen bull. And we have Martin Hamer, hero of the Reich, sworn to live here after the Reich victory, hand out the prizes from the podium.'

'It's good,' Buckner said, nodding.

'You're trying to find a flaw in all this, aren't you, cousin?' Crupp said.

Buckner nodded. 'Of course.'

'And is there one?'

'Hamer won't be happy when he sees what's been done to the woman he fucks,' Buckner said.

'The point of the prize-giving,' Crupp said, 'is to breed real pride in the pioneering achievement of our settlers. I intend to make it an annual affair. Joseph has pledged me the funds. The prizes will be substantial, as befits the importance of real economic achievement in Greater Germany. None of this is going to be jeopardized by a Pole.' He smiled. 'But your fears are groundless, cousin. Hamer is a man without self-love. Love is a stranger to his bleak little soul. It's not as if he has feelings for this woman. If she's been shorn, made to look ugly, he'll pick another one.'

Buckner nodded and sucked.

'Better, I'll find him a Poznań whore. Then we'll have his gratitude.'

* * *

Hamer thought the encounter with Hessler in Berlin a day before returning to duty in Dresden an innocent matter of chance. He remembered what Heidi had said, after her first introduction to the man, about coincidence and the Gestapo. But Hessler was a policeman, not an actor. And when the two men were confronted by the sight of one another in the changing room at the gymnasium on Friedrichstrasse, Hessler looked genuinely surprised. He was accompanied by the coy officer who had been with him on that evening at the restaurant by the river. Both men had faces reddened here and there by the impact and friction of leather. Hessler had a nick on one ear Hamer assumed had been caused by rubbing from the laces of his opponent's glove. They had been boxing, the two of them. And they looked as though they had been going at it hard.

Hessler spoke garrulously as he towelled off after his shower and then put his uniform back on. He was in very good shape, Hamer saw, sinewy, his athletic body as lean as ripcord. He explained to Hamer that self-defence was a passion with him. He'd practised judo and French foot-fighting. He'd done quite a bit of Chinese boxing. He was, by his own account, formidable on the wrestling mat. He'd even spent a month on the course run by the SS at Lübeck to learn how to fight with a knife and kill with a rope.

He'd got the better of his sparring partner today, Hamer knew. He remembered that violence cheered Hessler up, made him talkative. But he didn't think the man would be half so exuberant had he come off the worse of the two against his bashful opponent. Hamer looked at the junior man. He was strong, too, but he lacked Hessler's honed physical sophistication. Hessler had the clever musculature that came from frequent, skilled training. He looked quick. Hamer thought he could imagine exactly the sort of boxer Hessler would be. His work in the ring would be sharp, varied and vindictive. His Gestapo colleague was strong, with the brutal strength of a farm boy. A Westphalian farm boy, he realized when the younger man opened his mouth to ask Hessler for the key to the valuables locker they were sharing and Hamer heard his accent.

The junior man returned with their wallets, watches and pistols. Hessler used a towel to rub condensation off a mirror and, when it reflected his image clearly, began to wet-comb his hair. His crew cut had grown out, and he was wearing it longer again. Addressing Hessler's reflection, Hamer nodded to the gun now strapped to his hip. It was a standard-issue Luger. If it were fully loaded it carried eight nine-millimetre bullets.

'I'd have thought foot-fighting a redundant skill if you carry one of those.'

Hessler's reflection laughed back at him. 'We're headed for war, Martin,' he said. 'When it comes to methods of killing, I think we'll come to discover that none is redundant.'

Eventually he stopped combing his hair. He tilted his head this way and that. After deliberating, he seemed satisfied. He put the comb into the breast pocket of his shirt. 'Join me for coffee, why don't you? Anselm here has filing duties to attend to. But I have time for coffee if you can spare half an hour. There's a matter I've been meaning to discuss with you.'

Of course there is, Hamer thought. Of course you have. His soul sank, leaden in him.

There was a bar in the atrium at the top of the building in which the Friedrichstrasse gymnasium was housed. They ordered their coffee from a waitress and Hessler sat back in his chair. With his combed-back hair and the steam-room lustre of his skin, he reminded Martin Hamer of a sleek blond seal.

'What did you do here today?'

'Some floor exercises. Some stretching. Some work on the climbing wall.'

'You have a very fine physique, Hamer. Have you ever done any boxing?'

'A little, in America.'

'Were you coached?'

'A little.'

'By whom?'

'By Gene Tunney.'

It was about the twins, of course. Hamer had known it would be about the twins. Hessler told him that he was shortly to propose marriage to Heidi and was confident that Heidi would accept. As her husband, he would of course become legal guardian to her children. He felt the substantial role taken in their lives by Hamer put an obstacle in the path of his growing close to them. The present situation was confusing for the twins and likely to lead to disruptive behaviour. As their stepfather, Hessler would need to discipline them. This would be difficult if he did not go unchallenged as the dominant male in their lives.

'I have some expertise on this subject,' he told Hamer. 'As you may have concluded, I take a professional interest in psychology.'

Hansel and Gretel, Martin thought. My poor little darlings. But they were Heidi's children, not his.

'I'll see far less of them when I go back to Dresden,' he told Hessler.

'Good.'

'But I'm their godfather. I'll write letters and send cards. I'll never give up on them.'

'Just so long as I have your assurance that you'll determine to see them less often. It's important, Martin. It's only reasonable. And it's in their long-term interest.'

'You have my assurance,' Hamer said.

It's Heidi's life, he thought to himself as he gained the mid-afternoon tumult of Friedrichstrasse. The pavements were teeming, and the traffic, glittering under sunlight with chrome and coach paint, a crawl. Then a swath was cut between the competing automobiles as a convoy liveried in the carrion black of a raven came by, the flutter of swastikas on the apex of each front wheel arch, the Führer, spectral in the third car of this procession of Mercedes, buried in conversation behind bulletproof glass with Speer, the architect of his Reich.

Hamer witnessed from the pavement the swift, determined stealth of this procession. His bag was in his hand. His towel and gym clothes were in the bag, with talcum powder to combat sweat from hands under stress, to give him a secure grip as he trained and limbered on the climbing wall. Why did he bother? He had not climbed, really, since the Eiger. He didn't think he had it in his heart to do it again. In the Führer's aftermath, the Friedrichstrasse traffic resumed its opulent parade.

He would like to kill Hessler, he decided then. The thought came as a surprise to him. Martin Hamer had never been a vindictive man. He would like to kill Jacob Hessler. He would like to accomplish the killing with his hands.

At this point in his life, Hamer had never come close to killing anyone. The outbreak of war was six weeks away. He went to find a tram to take him back to the Berlin barracks so that he could pack for his return the next day to Dresden.

★ ★ ★

Julia Smollen had been brought to the camp originally to be hanged. She had been arrested and taken there in the back of a lorry, her hands bound above her head to one of the frets used to frame the lorry's canvas covering. There had been no covering that day. She had been paraded in the lorry through Poznań in the rain, swaying each time the vehicle braked, the bonds cutting into her wrists with every bump when the lorry got to the outskirts of the city and took the rutted road that led to the newly constructed labour camp.

The Polish army had fought with lunatic courage to repel their invaders. But the Germans had overwhelmed the country in numbers and force. Then they had either shot or hanged what they thought of as the Polish intellectual elite. They had killed the priests and the medical doctors and the teachers and the lawyers and the accountants and anyone else they could find with a professional qualification. A slave population did not require academic credentials. After the conquest, such credentials became a crime punishable by death.

Julia had been the first person in her family ever to qualify for a university place. It was an achievement sought by poor parents ambitious for their precocious girl. Boys with results as good as hers achieved metriculation. But the times insisted they seek careers in the bustle of business or the swagger of the Polish army's officer corps. Against little local competition, she gained a Church scholarship and off to university in Warsaw Julia went.

She was good at languages. But Julia was more than simply gifted with the mathematical knack for grammar, or talent for mimicry that usually gives linguists a facility for foreign tongues. She loved language, loved its intricacy and contradictions. She loved the literature of the languages she seemed so effortlessly to master.

Librarianship was an obvious choice. Her class and gender precluded much else. She rejected teaching because she rejected the notion of teaching dullards. In her own quick and clever childhood, Julia Smollen had encountered many children she had considered dullards. Librarianship was dull enough, but it continued the access the university had given her to books. It gave her an independent wage. It was a profession. And in a world full of looming threat and chaos, it was a stable profession.

They came to the library a day after achieving the occupation of Poznań. The men in black uniforms dragged the director of the library out of his office by his hair. In the time she had known the man, Julia had judged his only crime to be the translation of classical Greek and Roman verse without proper consideration of scansion or rhyme pattern. But as she saw him put up against the library wall and shot, she knew the invaders were not killing him for this. He had been a kindly boss to her, despite the stubborn aura he'd maintained of academic vanity. They bulldozed his corpse with a dozen others into a ditch. And then they questioned her.

She'd only ever thought it a matter of time. It was a question of how much culture Poland's new German masters would wish to destroy before they decided they had done enough to eradicate the country from the collective memories of the people left alive there. Julia thought the Germans thorough and energetic. She had not believed she would survive their attentions for very long. She was glad her mother and father were dead. She had loved them. They had died worn out after sharing a lifetime struggling to make a living from the land. They had been spared the destruction of their homeland. It was some small consolation in her mind for their lives of unremitting toil. She, their daughter, had brought them pride and pleasure. They had attended her graduation, her father in his only suit. Six months later he was dead. A listless fortnight after, her mother had followed him into the burial plot. Her brother had died defending Łódź. Julia was unsentimental about this. Tomas had wanted to be a soldier since stomping up and down their yard as a boy with a pot on his head and a broom over his shoulder. Soldiers discovered death or glory. The enemy had been too formidable for the latter and so Tomas had found the former instead on a battlefield at Łódź.

There'd been a boyfriend too. After the occupation he'd constructed a hand press for the printing of leaflets in their banned language. He'd attended clandestine meetings. He'd started speaking in a confidential manner out of the side of his mouth and whispered to Julia that he owned a pistol and knew where a secretly assembled radio set was in communication with the Free Polish Movement in London. He'd taken to riding his bicycle in defiance of the curfew. And then the men in black uniforms had come for him with dogs. He'd died screaming for a priest, it was said, in a barn outside Poznań. The more Julia thought of him after his arrest and murder, the more she thought of him as a callow fool. This until she dismissed him from her mind entirely.

She was brought before a tribunal comprising Crupp and Buckner. She didn't then know their names. They were sat facing her on the same side of a table. Hans Rolfe, whose name she was soon to learn to dread, stood to the left of the table, slightly behind the two seated men. The senior officer had a boil on his cheek and lips that coloured purple. His hair was scraped in an oily hank across a bald skull. The man seated next to him was fat and had protuberant eyes. There was a stink in the room. Julia thought it came from the sergeant, who stood and stared at her from behind his colleagues like someone in search of a meal.

There was a leaflet on the table in front of Crupp. It was cheaply printed and written in Polish. He gestured at it. 'You're the author of this?'

She peered at the leaflet.

'Don't be coy,' Buckner said. 'Pick it up.'

Her fingers felt dead with numbness after having been bound for so long, bloodless above her head, in the back of the lorry. She clapped the leaflet between flat hands and looked at it.

'You're the author of this?' Crupp said again.

'No.'

'Your opinions are at odds with what it says?'

'Not really, no. But if I'd written it, it would be more clearly expressed. It would be more succinct. And the grammar would be better.'

'Your German is flawless,' Crupp said. 'Are you a spy?'

She had to laugh at that. It didn't matter, laughing. They would kill her anyway. Crupp was evidently influenced by the sort of cheap espionage fiction they had always refused to stock at the Poznań public library.

'I speak French and English too. Of course I'm a spy.'

'Take her out and hang her,' Crupp said to Rolfe. 'Leave the body on the scaffold for a week, as a lesson.'

Buckner began to rise from his chair. Rolfe went over to Crupp and whispered something. Crupp thought for a moment and then laughed.

'Remove your clothes,' he said to Julia. Her fingers were clumsy accomplishing this.

'Your underwear too.'

She stood before them, naked. Crupp turned quizzically to Buckner. Buckner merely shrugged. Rolfe licked his lips and continued to stink.

And so Julia Smollen joined the camp's small

Joy Division, reprieved by lust and expediency on the day she was due to be hanged.

* * *

Heidi came to see Hamer at the Berlin barracks as he packed the small selection of items that comprised his much-reduced life. He had been born on an estate that had been in his family for four hundred years. But his family had lost their home and land, their title deeds, to the vindictive peace that followed defeat in the war. He had shared a home in Cologne with Lillian, his wife. But she was dead now, and the house they had lived in together was long sold. He had sold or given away or burned all their shared possessions. Last had been a toy boat built for a child's bathtub and purloined from a hotel on a holiday in Scotland. He was the last of his bloodline and incapable of fathering a child. He had some money in the bank and a rank in the army and he possessed a store of memories he dared not visit because he did not wish to sit on a cot in an army barracks, unmanned by his loss, and weep with pity at his own situation.

So he was glad when an orderly knocked at his door and told him a visitor waited to see him.

She wore a blue wool coat tailored to suit her high waist. It looked expensive and smart, and Hamer thought it was probably a gift from Jacob Hessler. The weight of her hair was carried in two ornamental combs clasped to the sides of her head above her ears. She had applied lipstick to her mouth. She was beautiful, sitting there.

She smiled and stood when she saw him and then the smile disappeared and she tilted her head to one side. He took her hands in his and kissed her on the cheek.

'Martin, you've been thinking sad thoughts,' Heidi said.

He shrugged. She had known him too well for too long for him to try to lie to her. His heart wouldn't be in the lie. 'I'm happy to see you,' he said truthfully.

He took her for supper to a small restaurant recommended to him by a fellow officer as somewhere the SS and Gestapo did not really care to dine. There was a persistent rumour that the owner of the restaurant was a foreigner, a Hungarian Jew. This rumour had no effect on the quality of the service or the food. The restaurant was busy. But they were found a corner table. Behind Heidi's head, Martin could see the restaurant window start to streak and the headlights on the cars outside contort into yellow lozenge shapes that glided across the glass. It must have started to rain.

'Who's taking care of the twins?'

'They have a babysitter. I wanted to see you before you went back to Dresden.'

'Where's Jacob?'

'He's on a course in Leipzig. Something to do with codes, for a week.'

That's odd, Hamer thought. Hessler hadn't appeared to be breaking codes in Leipzig earlier in the day at the gymnasium on Friedrichstrasse.

'I think he's going to ask me to marry him. I'm going to accept.'

'I hope you'll be very happy,' Hamer said.

Heidi sipped her wine. She touched his hand on top of their table. 'On the day I introduced you to Lillian, none of us could have predicted the way that things would happen, would change in our lives.'

The mere mention of her name was painful to him. It was all Martin could do not to flinch, not to physically recoil when people spoke of Lily. But Heidi had the right. Heidi had been his wife's best friend.

'It took me a long time to reconcile myself to what Karl did,' Heidi said now. 'What he was. I still see him every time I look at the children we had together. Their appearance so much favours their father.'

This was true. The twins had their father's good looks, his robust energy and pale colouring. Poor Karl.

'Poor Karl,' Heidi said. It was evident she had long forgiven him. She still had hold of Martin's hand on the tabletop. 'I need stability in my life,' she said. 'We all crave that, don't we?'

Hamer didn't say anything.

'I believe Jacob will bring me stability. He's thoughtful and generous. He's patient with the children.' Heidi smiled. 'He seems to want me very much.'

Martin wanted to put his arms around her, then. He wanted to offer Heidi his love and protection. But only one of those things was his to give. And one without the other was of no use to her. He looked up and saw a slight movement on the other side of the street, through the rain, behind Heidi's head.

'Excuse me.' Hamer was on his feet and through the maze of tables and out of the door. There was nobody on the other side of the street now. He crossed it, oblivious to brake squeals and skidding tyres and the blared protest of car horns. There was only one side road, a single route of escape. Hamer caught him at a sprint and turned him around. He still had the marks on his face from the earlier sparring session.

'Hello, Anselm,' Hamer said. 'Finished our filing, have we?'

The Gestapo man bunched his fists but Hamer had backhanded him twice, the double blow juddering the flesh on his heavy jowl before he could raise his hands. The slow expression on his face showed his brain registering the speed at which he had been hit. His posture slumped as he thought better of continuing the fight. The rain was soaked into the shoulders of his coat and the brim of his plain-clothes man's hat. He had been outside the restaurant in the rain for a while, then. Blood started to trickle out of the corner of his mouth, fissuring through the wet bristles on his chin. He would not now look Hamer in the eye.

'If he harms a hair on her head, I will come for him,' Hamer said. 'If he hurts her, I will kill him. Make sure you tell him this.' He patted the farm boy on the shoulder.

He smiled at Heidi as he sat back down. 'Thought I recognized an old friend on the street,' he said. 'But I was mistaken.'

Heidi pouted. Nature had endowed her with

the lips for a theatrical sulk. 'And there was me,' she said, 'thinking I had your full attention.'

Anselm the farm boy would not, Hamer knew, pass on the warning to his boss. He would not confess that his surveillance had been discovered. He was frightened of his boss. Hamer thought it only sensible of him to be so.

⋆ ⋆ ⋆

Crupp insisted on a full debriefing on Hamer's return to Poznań. There was an adjutant waiting for him at the railway station. He was taken by staff car to the barracks and the waiting camp commandant. He was offered and accepted coffee and then it was down to business, Crupp demanding every significant detail of the six-week trip. He seemed particularly fascinated by the events at the Wolf's Lair.

'I don't know how Göring continues to have the Führer's ear,' he said in apparent awe at the field marshal's political skills, when told about the specially bred boars brought to East Prussia only to satisfy the occasional thrill of a hunt.

The atmosphere here is wholly different, Hamer thought. There is energy and focus where before there was only indulgence and lassitude. He felt the strong intuition that Crupp had a new sponsor. The commandant had been Heydrich's man. But Heydrich was a legend now and his name nourished no career except his own, that gathering strength still, but only in the lifeless vacuum of retrospection. It must be Goebbels, Hamer concluded. It was Joseph

Goebbels, of course. And he had been Crupp's calling card on the Reich minister.

After answering the commandant's questions, he was told about the agricultural competition and the prize-giving. The date for the event was four weeks hence. Hamer thought about the tedium of another month in the camp. He thought about the endless war being waged to the east across the Russian steppe. The thaw would have begun there now. They would be shedding their white winter uniforms, their dogskin coats and fur-lined hats and clumsy overboots. He thought about the smell and touch and texture in darkness of Julia Smollen lying with him in his quarters in his cot.

'I thought that, healed, I was to go back to the Eastern Front. There was talk of a promotion on the last occasion we spoke. The promotion, frankly, I can live without. But I'm not suited to guard duty in a labour camp, sir, with the greatest respect.'

'Of course you aren't,' Crupp said. 'It's fitting to neither your temperament nor your training. You're to return to the fight, but there's been a necessary delay. You're to lead a unit which is currently well below strength. The intention is to bring this unit up to strength prior to your departure. Selecting and equipping those men will take six weeks.'

Hamer nodded.

'You're a professional soldier. You must be used to delays.'

'Yes, sir.'

'So. You'll be here to give the prizes.'

Hamer said nothing.

Crupp sighed. 'I'll give it to you straight, Hamer, since you think I'm winging this.'

'Which you are, sir.'

'Which I am,' Crupp said behind two raised palms, impatient now. 'Goebbels was impressed by you. You look and sound the part.'

'That's gratifying to know.'

'Don't be impertinent,' Crupp said.

There was much Hamer wanted to say. He said nothing.

'You're an intelligent man. Even Ariel Buckner concedes the point. It must be demeaning to be seen simply as a symbol of fortitude on the battlefield.'

Hamer smiled to himself, thinking of the fortitude he had seen on the battlefields he had fought across.

'Well,' he said to Crupp. 'I'm a soldier, to whom delays are part and parcel of the job.'

'Exactly,' Crupp said, satisfied with his own job of soldierly diplomacy. He would have Hamer for his prize-giving. After that he thought the man perfectly entitled to go back to Russia and get himself killed.

* * *

He'd lingered in the restaurant with Heidi in Berlin. They drank coffee and sweet liqueurs as the crowd of evening diners thinned for other destinations: nightclubs, Berlin's still thriving red-light district, casinos, theatre clubs, cabarets or just their beds. Finally Hamer looked at his watch. 'Your babysitter will think you've been abducted.'

Heidi smiled and played with the liqueur glass in front of her.

This evening signified the end of something, the beginning of something. They were both aware of it. It was the reason for their reluctance to say goodbye to one another.

'At least you won't have to fear the knock at the door in the night,' Martin said. 'You'll be with the man who does the knocking.'

Her face told him it was a joke in bad taste. Maybe he'd drunk too much. He didn't think he had. Why had Hessler lied about Leipzig? Why was he having her watched?

'Did you tell him you were seeing me tonight?'

Heidi hesitated. Then she nodded. She sipped from her glass. 'He doesn't quite know what to make of you. Most people, he says, conform to a type. He says that you don't. He says that this makes you unpredictable.'

'He makes me sound like a neurotic.'

'No, Martin. He doesn't think you unstable. But he says you're a difficult person to predict. He likes things black and white, likes to know precisely where he is with everything.'

Thus the surveillance, Hamer thought. It was just Hessler playing God. It was no more sinister than that, as though Hessler playing God were not sinister enough. He'd felt a bit sorry for the farm boy, beaten twice in one day, left bloodied and solitary on a Berlin evening in his rain-soaked suit of civilian clothes. He doubted very much that Jacob Hessler ever felt sorry for anyone. To a man like him, pity was never anything other than weakness.

'I want to thank you for what you've done for my children,' Heidi said across the table, and Hamer knew that their time together was drawing to its conclusion. 'Thanks to you, they think that a dragon grows in the darkness under every fallen log. Thanks to your time with them, their imaginations are filled with mountains and magical beasts.' She smiled. 'And toffee-apples.'

Hansel and Gretel. Gone from him now.

'My time with them has been a joy,' Martin Hamer said. He asked a waiter for their bill.

* * *

'You know about the scandal of the wood?' Crupp asked him.

'I know that I have a warped floor in my quarters. I know that Ariel Buckner's quarters are warping like the fun house at an English seaside fairground. I always imagined Hans Rolfe pocketed a backhander when he turned a blind eye to immature timber during the construction of the place.'

'There's a wood a mile from the camp,' Crupp said.

Hamer knew the wood well. It was where he had gone to pick wild spring flowers for the first visit paid him by Julia Smollen. He went there sometimes for seclusion. He had been an only child and he had grown up on his family's estate. He had always enjoyed walking in woods, listening to the surreptitious music of seclusion;

the birdsong, the wind soughing through branches and leaves and whispering through ferns, against bark. He felt happiest and most secure at the heart of the older places in the world.

Crupp's proposal in the wake of the timber scandal was that the camp should become entirely self-sufficient in wood. All usable trees in the open country surrounding the camp were to be felled and stripped and cut into planks to season properly. When weathered, they would be used where necessary and the excess sold for profit.

'Who owns the wood?' Hamer asked him.

'We do, of course,' Crupp said. 'We own everything.'

Hamer would supervise the clearances. He would pick an NCO to assist him and take a labour gang from the camp in a lorry to do the work of tree felling. The gang would load the lorry with timber. Hamer would bring the laden vehicle back. The NCO would force-march the labour gang back to the camp. It was a perfect scheme. It would give Hamer something with which to occupy his time.

'What do you know about trees, Martin?'

'I grew up on my family's estate. There were trees on our land.'

'Precisely,' said Crupp, rubbing his hands together. He was a man who liked it very much when things went well.

⋆ ⋆ ⋆

'Who did this?'

'It doesn't matter.'

He reached out to touch her head and she flinched away from him. He left his hand there the way someone might trying to tame a sparrow into taking food from their fingers. She straightened her neck and was back within his reach. He extended his hand slowly and touched her scalp with his fingertips. It felt like peach fuzz, with the hair growing back, where her head was not scabbed and bumped with healing cuts and grazes.

'Why was it done?'

'Because of you.'

He caressed the side of her face with his fingertips and took her chin gently between index finger and thumb. He turned her head to the light from the single candle illuminating the room. The gash in her mouth had more or less healed. But there was a black and purple bruise under her cheekbone where she had been kicked. Hamer bent his head and kissed the bruise. His lips were a brush so light against her face that she barely felt them. His smell came back to her then, the strength of him.

'They did it thinking you were dead.'

He kissed her eyes, her mouth. 'I've missed you,' he said. He had his arms around her.

'Don't you think me ugly?'

'What was done to you was ugly, Julia. You're not ugly. You're very lovely.'

Later, as he put his clothes back on, she smoothed the sheets and blankets on the cot and then sat with her back against the wooden wall.

He had bought her tobacco in Poznań and she rolled a cigarette. He lit it for her with the candle stub. She took a long drag and then grimaced and stubbed the cigarette out on the locker by the cot.

'Is the tobacco stale?'

She shook her head. She had grown pale. She looked about to retch. 'I've just gone off the taste, I think.'

Polk salad, Hamer thought. Hillbilly genes.

'You're pregnant, aren't you, Julia?' It was not a question.

She nodded her head. 'Ten weeks, by my own calculation.'

'The father?'

'It's yours.'

'Liar.'

She laughed and looked at the ceiling. 'It's yours, Martin Hamer.'

He stared at her. 'If you were a man I would strike you.'

'No, you would not. I can see the look on your face,' she said. 'If I were a man, you would kill me. But if I were a man, we would hardly be having this conversation.'

'I'm infertile.'

She shook her head. There was a smile on her lips but her eyes were wet and angry. 'What man in this camp would touch me knowing I am where you take your pleasure? What man? I have a child inside me. And the child is yours.'

'What will you do?'

'I won't do anything. The luxury of choice was taken away from me a long time ago. When the child grows big enough, the monster called Buckner will scrape it out. If I'm very lucky, he'll give me an anaesthetic first.'

'Please leave.'

Julia Smollen got up off the bed and left. A few minutes after she had closed his door behind her, Hamer took the black dress he had bought for her in Poznań, took it outside and dropped it into the swill pit that served the kitchen block.

* * *

After his appointment with Dr Stresemann, on the summer day on which Martin Hamer encountered his first Jew, he dozed on the train on the way back to the doctor's house on the Wannsee. And so when he met Lillian there, he was refreshed, having slept off the effects of the beer consumed in the sunshine after hearing Stresemann's bleak prognosis. He sipped lemonade poured for him by Lillian in her father's kitchen. Ice clinked in the glass pitcher when she poured his drink. Late sunshine splashed yellow light, and pale blue ripples reflected from the lake outside on the kitchen's walls. The world was beautiful, Lily beautiful at the living centre of it, and Hamer sat there with a hollow heart and confirmed to his wife that because of a deficiency in him their marriage would be childless.

She sat and listened still wearing her swimming costume. It had dried on her as she reclined and sunbathed in her father's garden earlier after a long swim, Fitzgerald's *Tender Is the Night*, the book neglected, dampening in her lap. The costume was black, her hair and skin tawny and golden, her expression grave, mouth dimpled with seriousness as Martin delivered the dismaying verdict on his capacity for life. She gripped his hand while he spoke and held his eyes with hers. And when he finished speaking, she continued to look at him, unblinking.

'I married you,' she said. 'I married not to breed, but to be with the man I loved. This is a disappointment.'

'It's a tragedy,' Martin said. 'If you stay with me.'

'It's a disappointment.' There was steel in Lillian's voice. She brightened and smiled. 'The lake is warm. I'd very much like my darling husband to come and swim in the lake with me.'

They swam until Hamer's limbs were leaden with the effort. He was a muscular man who carried no fat as ballast, and the water of the lake was clear, not buoyant with salt like the sea. You had to work to float in this elusive element, he felt, never mind to travel through it. Lily was by far the stronger swimmer. She was slim, but gifted in the water. She had won prizes in swimming races. Her strokes had a clean economy that had Martin toiling like a learner in the smooth churn of her wake.

'Let's swim to the raft,' Lily said finally.

'About time,' he said, treading water. 'Another minute and I'd sink.'

'I'd dive down after you, Martin,' she said. 'I'd rescue you. I'd give you what the English call the kiss of life.' Her hair clung in wet fronds to her neck. Her breasts rose to tantalize, and then dipped beneath the water she trod, kicking. He knew that she was serious.

It was approaching dusk when they gained the raft. Martin hauled himself on to its white, cooling planks. He lay on his back and regained his breath, panting until there was air again in his blood and his lungs felt capable of filling normally. He sat up. Lillian was peeling off her wet costume. She rolled the tight black fabric down over her breasts, which swung with the motion of her continued undressing, high and golden, the nipples hard, engorged. She lifted her bottom off the raft and suddenly her body was free of her costume.

'There,' she said.

Her pubic hair had formed wet coils of gold. She took Martin's hand and put his fingers into her mouth. Then she pressed his hand against her sex. His middle finger entered her to the second knuckle, and she groaned and shuddered. She leaned forward and bit his shoulder hard enough to break the skin. His fingers were hot inside the wet warmth of her.

'I want you,' Lillian said, licking him where he bled.

When they were finished, it was fully dark. She lay, dozing he thought, his arm around her shoulder, her head on his chest, the knee of one long leg pulled up across his stomach. He looked at the night, at the stars. When they had made love like this in the past, he had sometimes hoped for some consequence beyond the act, as she had, he was sure. When two people collided with such ecstatic force, their vanity alone would compel them to believe that there were things triggered, forces set loose, beyond the immediacy of what they were doing. But there was nothing, would be nothing, for Lillian and him. Hamer looked at the stars. A man could go mad in contemplation of the stars. Their remoteness, their immensity, humbled a man and defied reasonable thought. Lights in the house across the lake signalled the good doctor's return. Lillian was his only child. Naval admirals and pugilists of world renown queued to consult him. He would be contemplating now the fact of the end of his bloodline, should his daughter remain faithful to his son-in-law. Hamer sighed and Lillian gripped him with her knee across his stomach more tightly.

'I love you, Martin.'

'And I love you,' he said. In his life, he had never spoken truer words.

* * *

In the dawn that followed the revelation of Julia Smollen's pregnancy, Hamer walked in the wood doomed now by the vain industry of Wilhelm Crupp. He could not surrender, though, to his thoughts. He could not enjoy his moment of seclusion in the wood. He had been followed there. He was aware of it from the moment he left the camp. The pursuit was skilful and discreet. But Hamer had an instinct honed by years of fieldcraft. He thought the surveillance more than just intrusive. He thought it an insult to him. And so he set a trap, in the calm and seclusion of the wood, for his sly observer.

He heard the snick of his trap as the noose closed on a snared foot and the stalker, suddenly turned prey, gasped in surprise. He heard the rattle of a rifle bolt. And then the struggling man was hauled into the air by the sprung trap and the rifle clattered to the forest floor and there was the profound report of a single rifle shot. Hamer climbed down from the branches that had concealed his hide. Landau swung by one snagged boot, his hands trailing moss and lichen on the forest floor, his head a foot and a half above the ground. Hamer picked the rifle up. He emptied its magazine, scrupulous to recover and pocket each shell from the forest floor.

'Buckner?'

Landau swung, his mouth open.

Hamer pistoned a short punch into his balls.

'Don't fuck me around. You've no idea how much pain a man can live through. Buckner or Crupp?'

Landau had vomited. It was a difficult accomplishment upside down. He gagged and spat, turning on one suspended leg, trying to clear his throat of bile and puke, trying not to drown in his breakfast. 'Buckner does nothing,' he said.

'Crupp, then,' Hamer said, nodding. It made sense. It was why Landau was still here, instead of at the Russian Front, where Hamer had recommended to Crupp he be sent, after the attempt in which Landau had colluded with Rolfe on his life. He took the knife from his belt and cut Landau down, gave him back his emptied rifle. He watched Landau gain his feet and collect himself. He was a short, thin, inconsequential man, was Landau. But he was an excellent shot, apparently. It did not take too much strength to squeeze a rifle's trigger. Landau tried to brush flecks of vomit from his face and hair.

'I come here for the solitude,' Hamer said. 'I come here for peace and seclusion. Don't follow me again, friend. I've given you your chance.'

Landau limped off, his useless rifle trailing him, one hand couched over his ruined manhood. The birds began to sing again in the aftermath of the shot. From somewhere close, there was the trickle of a stream.

To Hamer, the wood now had a fraudulent look, like stage scenery from a play. If he sniffed he would smell the season, the spring, come to the wood in warmth and life from the soil, and the faint scent of early blooms, of snowdrops, crocuses, wild daffodils. If he listened he would hear the pick of the breeze through new leaves green and urgent with life. But the wood was no longer real to him, or a comfort any longer. In a matter of days they would come with chains and saws and pulleys and render the place as flat and featureless as the rest of the Polish plain. The wood waited, water trickling in it somewhere, for the act of vandalism that had already destroyed it in Martin Hamer's mind. He thought of the Wolf's Lair then, of the blood banner brooding in the corner of the lodge, of the portrait of the Führer brooding under a blood-flecked sky, of the bleached skulls mounted as trophies and the broadswords and battle-axes on its walls. He was a man who knew his history. It was not a fact lost on him that the Vandals had been a German tribe.

⋆ ⋆ ⋆

Ariel Buckner seemed so excited that he could barely get the key into the padlock. Certainly it would make a change, Hamer thought, from treating the camp brawlers for their bruises, from checking the women for gonorrhoea and syphilis. He wondered why he had never really noticed this building before. It was made of some pressed, corrugated material the same colour as the earth that surrounded it. You descended to its door down a small set of steps. It was a building longer than it was wide, and half its height was concealed because it was half-buried in a man-made depression in the earth. It was Buckner's clinic. It was under-employed as a facility, he told Hamer, grappling with the padlock. But he had high hopes for the work he could do there in the future.

The building was served by the same generator that powered the searchlights on the camp watchtowers. Caged industrial lights were recessed in two strips on either side of the interior where the ceiling met the walls. Their bulbs, when Buckner switched them on, stripped the clinic of shadows, flooding it with a hot glare of intense white light. Hamer looked around. Organic matter floated in storage jars on shelves.

There were test-tubes, burners, a large metal sink. He saw shiny surgical tools. An industrial refrigerator with an American name occupied a corner. The place was spotless and new-looking. It had a smell of newness and mild antiseptic. Hamer had expected the stink of ether, but that was absent. This was not a place, apparently, in which Buckner indulged his personal vices.

'You have the sample?'

Hamer had the sample. He took a small glass cylinder with a rubber cap from his pocket and handed it to Buckner. The procedure had grown no less distasteful or undignified with the passage of time.

Buckner held the sample up to the light and examined it. 'Come back in an hour.'

'That's all the time it will take?'

Buckner was already busying himself with a Petri dish, a swab and a microscope slide. 'In an hour, you will know.'

It was eleven o'clock in the morning. 'Come to my quarters at twelve fifteen,' Buckner said. 'Early for a drink, but who knows? We might be celebrating.'

Hamer walked outside. He could hear the frenzied noise of Buckner's dogs, howling to be fed. The spring sunshine seemed to sulk across the land after the powerful man-made brightness and spotless walls of Buckner's clinic. He felt the way he did before battle, he realized with surprise. The same sensitivity, as though his body were bruised. The same tightness across his face, as though his skin was ill fitting over his facial bones. He felt as though he needed to pee, but was dry-mouthed at the same time. And he felt a weariness but could not still his limbs from moving him aimlessly around.

The thing was, he believed the woman. He knew that she was pregnant, could see it in the shine of her eyes and the new lustre it had brought to her badly nourished skin. He had seen this rejuvenation in other women, in Heidi and Lucy. He knew that when Julia Smollen's hair grew back it would grow back shining and strong. The other night, before he guessed, she had seemed ripe, fecund. He hadn't been able to keep his hands off her.

And he believed that she had been with no one else. He had not at first, when he had sent her away and done the spiteful thing with the dress, of which he was now ashamed, but he had come since then to believe her. Her stricken indignation had been no act. There was nothing here that she could profit from. She had only the blood and pain of Buckner's invasion of her body to look forward to. No, the woman had told him the truth. The child she carried was his. He had enjoyed the miracle Stresemann had said it would require for him to experience fatherhood. The voltage baths and massages taken in Switzerland several years ago had finally worked their expensive magic. It had to be that, didn't it? The alternative was something Martin did not have the strength to contemplate. When he tried to think about the alternative, about its abysmal implications, for the first time in his life his courage failed him.

* * *

Buckner already had the drinks on the table when Hamer knocked on his door. 'Congratulations, Martin,' he said, raising his schnapps. 'You will not be the last of your family after all.'

'No?'

'On the contrary,' Buckner said. 'You have it in you to sire a dynasty, my friend.' He clinked his glass against the lip of Hamer's, which remained untouched. Hamer could not understand why the schnapps glass was not shaking between his fingers, why he had not dropped it to the floor.

Buckner looked at him, concerned. 'You've become very pale, Martin. Your skin looks like pewter. An emotional moment, I'm sure. Here, you'd better sit down.' The doctor pulled over a chair and Hamer sat in it.

'Drink your drink,' Buckner prompted. 'Drink your schnapps.'

'I've enjoyed a reversal?'

Buckner looked at him and then looked at the pictures on his wall. They illustrated operatic themes. *Parsifal, Tannhäuser*. His voice, when he spoke, was surprisingly gentle. 'There has been no reversal. There never is, for a sterile man. Your semen is that of a man who eats properly, who takes regular exercise, who drinks only moderately. There has been no reversal, Martin, because a reversal was never necessary. Your issue is healthy. It has been so since puberty.'

Hamer drank his schnapps. 'Thank you, Herr Doctor,' he managed to say.

* * *

'I believe our Reich hero may have tupped his Polish whore.'

Crupp looked up from his food, chewing. He dropped his cutlery. 'I've read the file on him. The file is comprehensive. He's lethal in the field, but between the sheets he's firing blank ammunition. According to the file he is, at least. And this is a Gestapo file we're talking about. You'd better explain yourself, cousin.'

Buckner had a moment then to regret his revelation. He had wanted to impress the son of his mother's sister with unexpected information. But Wilhelm Crupp had become a more formidable man in the weeks since his frequent conversations on the barracks telephone with Joseph Goebbels. Buckner was nostalgic suddenly for the chessboard, where gain and disadvantage were abstracts in chequered space, merely moves of shift and sacrifice, decisions of no true consequence in the material world. He cleared his throat. 'Hamer has been the victim of a hopeless misdiagnosis.'

'Hard to believe,' Crupp said, 'given the eminence in your profession of his late father-in-law.'

'Correct, nevertheless,' Buckner said. He was a trained doctor before he was anything. He was a scientist. If he denied the proof of science, he denied himself. 'Hamer has been long and hopelessly misled. It's hard to believe, frankly, that the deception could have been anything but deliberate.'

‘How were you with Hamer, delivering him this news, cousin?’

‘Professional,’ Buckner said. ‘Solicitous. I was full of manly scruple and showed sensitivity of the stoical kind a type like Hamer would appreciate.’

Crupp laughed. ‘A perfect bedside manner, then.’

Buckner felt grateful and relieved at his cousin’s reaction. But then he felt he had read Martin Hamer pretty shrewdly.

Crupp frowned. ‘They breed with such ease, these Slavs. Like Jews and Orientals.’

‘Like rats,’ Buckner said, agreeing.

Wilhelm Crupp picked up his knife and fork and his face brightened. ‘Hamer might wish to stay with us here in the settlement now. He could find a wife easily enough, a man who looks like he does. He wouldn’t be so willing to be food for bullets with a family on the way. He’s a sentimental man, you know.’

Buckner nodded.

‘The whore?’

‘I’ll scrape her out when she’s ready,’ Buckner said.

‘We really should have hanged her,’ Crupp said.

‘We will,’ his cousin agreed. ‘After the prize-giving. After the departure of Martin Hamer for the Russian Front.’

* * *

Hamer lay on his cot. His eyes were closed but he was not sleeping. Thoughts without pattern or consequence, memories, filed in random procession through his mind. He was telemarking in an Alpine spring down an endless glacial slope with Lillian. He was rowing a boat as insects bit him, thirsty for his blood. He was listening to a lone piper play a lament as the mist of evening crept across a Scottish loch. He was suspended above a black chasm on the Eiger watching his father tamp tobacco calmly into the bowl of his favourite pipe. He was lifting a log from a forest floor as two infant children stood and waited in fascination. He was kneeling shoulder to shoulder before a charging boar with a dead soldier named Ludwig Kurtz. He was extending the butt of his pistol to Karl in a holding cell rank with the smell of terror. He was running his fingertips over the fake rivets lining the hull of a model ship as he finally found the resolve to grieve for his wife.

Jacob Hessler had asked him once whether his was a sham marriage. Lying in the darkness in a labour camp in Poland, Martin Hamer thought now that it was worse even than that. He now felt that his had been a sham life, and the fact tormented him, filled him with a pain so overwhelming that he was hardly able to breathe through the burden of it.

How tortured must his barren wife have been to engineer the deception? How hard had it been for her to persuade her father to violate the ethics of his profession and facilitate the lie? Perhaps it had been her father's idea in the first place. Martin could not see a woman possessed of her independence being cajoled into such a scheme. But he had never thought his wife capable of deceit, let alone deceit on a scale so grotesque. Their intimacy had been a cherished lie.

In the darkness, on his cot, Hamer groaned. He had thought the pain of his wound in Russia bad when a machine-gun bullet had torn a hole in him. But he had packed the wound with snow and carried on, enduring it. The pain he felt now, he felt to be unendurable. Lillian had not been taken away from him. He had never had Lillian, had never properly known his wife. He couldn't have. A secret had been locked within her heart. She had never truly opened her heart to him. His wife had been a stranger to him, careful and dishonest and alert.

He had nothing. He didn't even have his memories. The store of happy memories that had given Martin Hamer his consolation lay strewn and violated, exposed and debased by the force of Buckner's proof.

He sat up on the bed with his arms clasped around himself and rocked. His eyes were clenched and wet. The breaths he took shuddered through him in harsh gasps. His lungs would not fill. He was drowning in sorrow. He could not tolerate this pain. He could not. He did not believe that any man could. He reached for his pistol, hanging in its holster from a peg on the wall. The weapon had claimed lives before. It was an efficient killing tool. His had been a counterfeit life, but a bullet would not discriminate. He had nothing. He had come to nothing. He would go to nothing now.

He raised the barrel of the weapon to his temple and smelled pipe tobacco drift uncertainly through the darkness of the room. That wasn't right. His gun always smelled of steel and the thin lubricant he used to clean its mechanism. 'I've lost my mind,' he said out loud, heard himself say. He pulled back the hammer of the pistol with his thumb. He started to squeeze the trigger.

He heard his father's cough. It was the cough his father had sometimes used as a rebuke. He eased the pressure on the trigger of his gun.

'Papa?'

'It isn't true that you have nothing, son,' his father said. His father's voice was firm and kind. His father's voice had always been kind. 'You have responsibility and honour.'

'Duties.'

'Some duties are worth performing, Martin. Can you not think of one, solitary duty deserving of you?'

'None.'

His father tutted. 'Come, now.'

'One,' Hamer said. 'I should do all I can to protect the baby growing in the Polish woman's belly. I should do all it is in my power to do to enable my unborn child to live.'

This truth came to Hamer with the unexpected force of revelation. He was stunned by his own words, by what they would mean and by how profoundly he meant them. His father's question had triggered in him a sudden avalanche of feeling. He knew with certainty that he would happily die defending the life of his child. And his child had not yet even been born. He allowed himself to imagine for the first time in his life that he might make a good father. Certainly he would try.

'Papa?'

But he was alone again in the room. Perhaps it was just as well. Martin Hamer had lived his life principally as a man of action. And he had just given himself a great deal of thinking to do.

* * *

Heidi Jodl was married to Jacob Hessler in a civic ceremony in a smart suburb of Berlin a fortnight before the outbreak of war. The twins carried the train of their mother's dress. They wore little khaki uniforms with swastikas banded to one arm. Almost everyone at the ceremony wore a uniform of one sort or another. Heydrich and Eichmann, of the more senior ranks of the party, attended. Hamer hadn't known that Hessler was so well connected. But it made sense of his arrogant confidence and the persistent preening to which the man was so inclined.

The reception was a drunken affair. Most social rituals attended by party men turned into drunken affairs in the absence of their abstemious Führer. Drinking was a part of the German culture, after all, almost a patriotic duty in the eyes and minds of many party men. There was a double standard in a society in which a man like Reinhard Heydrich could drink himself into a stupor, while the common drunk risked sterilization and a one-way ticket to a labour camp. But the observation and enforcement of double standards were two of the chief preoccupations of an elite that ruled by fear and by force. Martin suspected that these thoughts were probably treasonable. He also knew that most of his regular army colleagues shared them.

Close to midnight he found himself briefly alone with the groom. The Gestapo man was flushed with drink, but it was more to do with his colouring and the heat in the hall than intoxication, Hamer thought. Certainly Hessler was not as drunk as his honoured guest Heydrich, who had caused a stir earlier in the evening by fondling a waitress with a little too much enthusiasm for the girl's appetite for being groped. He had been drinking, though, had Hessler. And Martin Hamer didn't know a man whose tongue was not loosened a little by a few beers.

'Anselm told me you hit him.'

Hamer wondered if the farm boy had also passed on his warning.

'How was Leipzig?'

Hessler smiled and blinked. 'You didn't let on?'

'Of course I didn't.'

'It was a necessary deception.'

'I've no doubt.'

Hessler nodded. He blinked again. 'Anselm was very impressed,' he said. 'Apparently you hit him twice. He said that he wouldn't have predicted the blows. Told me you moved the way a tiger does when it claws a morsel of food from its keeper through the bars of a cage.'

'It's a poetic way of putting it,' Hamer said. 'Educational standards must have improved since I was last in Westphalia.'

Hessler blinked again, slowly. It was an oddly girlish mannerism, something he obviously did when he was drunk. 'I'd love to fight you, Hamer. I'd really enjoy it,' he said.

'No,' Hamer said to him. 'I really don't think you would.'

Neither man got the chance to find out, because Heidi came over then to where they sat. She had been home to their new house to put the exhausted twins to bed. Hansel and Gretel living under the same roof as Hessler was something Hamer felt uneasy about. There was something about the way that violence excited the man. But the Gestapo vetted their own people pretty thoroughly. And if her new husband made their mother happy, this would surely have a beneficial effect on her children.

Heidi did look happy. And she looked beautiful.

Martin kissed her on the cheek. The Führer's taste for it had made an epidemic of the kissing of women's hands. But he didn't much care for the practice himself. They weren't living in seventeenth-century France, after all. 'I don't think I've ever seen you looking lovelier,' he said. 'If your husband doesn't mind me saying so.'

'I agree wholeheartedly with the observation,' Hessler said. 'And I hope I will always have the manners to accept a well-intended compliment with good grace.'

This was interesting. His wife's attentions had sobered him in a way that Hamer's had failed to. He underestimates me, Martin thought. Unless he just overrates himself.

Over in one corner a group had started to sing the Horst Wessel song. Hessler rolled his eyes at his two companions. 'Beers and tears,' he said. 'Always the same in the end. We're a lachrymose people. But there are worse vices.' Then he saw that Heydrich was conducting the singsong, red-faced, furiously drunk, and he went off to add his voice to those of his comrades.

'Thank you for coming.'

'Yes, well. A better day than the last time you thanked me for coming.'

'It must be hard for you,' Heidi said. 'Doing this sort of thing on your own.'

Martin smiled at her. It was a small smile, but genuine. 'You brought a lot of happiness into my life when you introduced me to Lillian,' he said. 'I'm grateful for that. And today I got to see my godchildren. It was hardly an ordeal.'

Half the room was singing now, and the singing was on the way to becoming a roar. Heidi put her mouth to Martin's ear. 'You'll meet someone some day,' she said. 'And she'll make you a happy man again.'

* * *

'You must be insane,' Julia Smollen said.

He looked at her. She looked the same. The

spread of hair growing on her shorn scalp might have thickened and darkened imperceptibly. The bruise on her cheek might have faded a touch. But the posture was the same strange mix of compliance and insubordination with which her body always struggled in his presence. The green eyes above the sculpted bones wore their familiar look of alert, untrusting intelligence. Everything was the same. And everything, Hamer thought, was different now.

'You don't think I can get you out of the camp?'

'I'm sure you can. Your problems would start when you had to swap that uniform for civilian clothes and ceased to matter to the world you've helped to make. I don't think you could cope with the indignity of that, Martin Hamer. The first dig with a Kraut rifle butt for an insolent look and you'd retaliate, because it isn't in you to do otherwise. And you'd be shot in the street like a dog.'

Hamer took this in. He nodded.

'That isn't why you're insane, though.'

'Then why am I insane?'

'In thinking that I'd wish to carry a child of yours to term. Your people, your tribe has visited evil on the earth. Why would I wish to perpetuate that by giving birth to a child of yours?'

'I'm not an evil man.'

'I don't believe you are. But you've fought with apparent distinction for an evil cause.'

They were speaking as equals for the first time. He knew she had the right to that. In a way they were naked before one another. The thing they shared demanded it. But her voice was loud in his quarters with indignation, and he sensed that Landau, or one of Crupp's other spies, could easily be listening. He was important to their imbecilic prize-giving plan, and so Crupp was apparently more or less having him chaperoned. Treason and desertion were on his mind. If necessary he would murder to protect his child. But the baby beat with new life in the belly of Julia Smollen. And she seemed to prefer Buckner's butchery to his happy plan of escape.

'Let me tell you my story,' he said.

She laughed at him. 'As if it will make any difference.'

'Let me tell it to you anyway.'

And so he told her everything. If nothing else, it would explain his apparent callousness in allowing her to conceive.

'Come over here,' she said when he had finished. He went and sat on the cot next to her. She put her hand on his head and stroked his hair.

'Your wife didn't die in an accident, Martin. Lillian killed herself.'

He felt something inside him break and detach itself. The breath whickered in him and his eyes began to splash tears on to the coarse blanket of the cot. Julia Smollen held his head against her chest and he thought to himself: Where does this woman get the strength?

'I think Lily led a life in parenthesis with the life she lived with you, Martin. When you were with her your strength nourished her lie. When you were with her the lie must have seemed to her worthwhile. When you weren't there, the lie would have withered in her. Were you often away?'

'I was a soldier.'

'You should forgive your wife.'

'I have,' Hamer said simply.

'I'll come with you, Martin Hamer,' Julia said, her voice a whisper now. 'I'll come with you because I believe that if you depart for Russia Crupp and Buckner will have me hanged, as they would have already but for Rolfe's intervention. I make no promises about carrying the child to term. The man I used to sleep with was tortured by your army until he died. The man I used to sleep with was a fool. But he didn't deserve to die, blinded, gelded, killed by jeering foreigners with bayonets in a Poznań barn. My brother is dead and my country raped and its books burned with your compliance. So I make no promises about carrying the child of a German to term.'

'Stay the night,' Hamer said.

'I'll be seen to leave here in the morning.'

'They all know about us anyway,' Hamer said. 'Stay only if you wish to.'

'You don't care what people think, do you?'

'No,' Hamer said, who never had. But he cared very much at that moment about what Julia Smollen thought.

* * *

He studied the death mask of Heydrich mounted on the wall as he waited for Wilhelm Crupp to finish his telephone call. Heydrich's face reminded him of a line Milton had used in *Paradise Lost* to describe Lucifer where he had written about the fallen archangel's sneer of cold command. Heydrich had possessed that both in life and in death. But judging by the tone of the portion of the conversation he was party to, Hamer didn't think this ghoulish memento would enjoy its current prominence for very much longer.

'Goebbels says hello,' Crupp said, after dropping the receiver on to its cradle, confirming the supposition.

Hamer smiled.

Crupp shuffled papers and made some indeterminate noises in his throat or nose. 'Why are you here, Martin?'

'The timber clearance plan is a shambles. There's no sense to it logistically. It's ill thought out. I'm here to try to make a success of the proposal.'

'My proposal,' Crupp said. 'And you're calling it a shambles. You aren't endearing yourself to me, Martin.'

Hamer thought then about the retreat over the Russian steppe to the river Dnepr. Before the counter-attack the Sixth Army had been ordered on its long retreat to live off the land. His men had spooned the brains from the heads of dead packhorses to nourish themselves. They had gone on doing this until all the horses were eaten. And they were forced further to retreat on empty bellies. Soldiers of the Reich had scavenged the land like beggars after that, rag-wrapped and shuffling through the Arctic Russian cold, ransacking the cellars and outhouses of abandoned farms and villages on the strength of rumours about hidden stores of bread and buried potato crops. None of the rumours had turned out to be true. It hadn't stopped his men digging at the frozen earth with their hands until their fingers bled. Martin Hamer looked at Wilhelm Crupp, with his sad hank of deceptive hair and his pathetic air of bustling significance. And he swallowed his anger out of expediency and need.

'It will take two trucks,' he said. 'We can't carry the cutting crew and the tools in the back of a single truck. We can't leave the tools on site because they'll have vanished by the morning. The job can't be done unless I have two trucks.'

Crupp stared at him. 'I can't believe you're bothering me with this. You could have telephoned to tell me this. You can take as many trucks as the job requires. How many do we have garaged at the camp?'

'Six.'

Crupp frowned. 'Then I really don't understand why you're here.'

'I need requisition slips for the transport. I need a requisition slip for the tools, for the fuel for the transport. Everything is under lock and key. There are procedures to follow.'

'Rolfe would have helped with this. He drank too much, but he was a very well-organized quartermaster.'

'Rolfe is the reason we need the wood in the first place.'

Crupp sighed and took a rubber-stamp and an ink pad out of a desk drawer. He wrote words on a sheet of paper and rubber-stamped the sheet and wafted it in the air for the ink to dry. He folded the paper into three and put it into an envelope and handed the envelope to Hamer. 'This will give you access to everything you need.'

'Thank you, sir.'

'Have you a speech prepared?'

'A what?'

'For the prize-giving,' Crupp said. 'We need derring-do.'

'Derring-do,' Hamer said.

'You know, something inspiring. We need something that will make the occasion memorable, make our pioneer farmers here in the General Government feel that they play a pivotal role in the struggle towards our eventual victory. You're a man of action, I know. If you like, I can write you a speech and you can memorize the words. Though I say so myself, I've a way with language.'

'That would be very kind of you, sir,' Hamer said. Derring-do, he was thinking.

'Hamer?'

He had his hand on the door knob. 'Herr Commandant?'

'If you're taking two trucks, you'll need to take two men. Take Landau for the second truck.'

So Landau was a driver as well as a shooter. It seemed there was no end to the man's talents.

'Sir.'

The plan was a very simple one. It seemed to

Hamer that the fewer complications a plan had, the less there was to go wrong with it. He went over it in his mind on the train back from Poznań. It was important not to rely on luck. Luck had kept him alive in the past, but you were dead if you factored chance as a favourable element into any strategy. The only luck you anticipated was the bad kind, the kind that made things go wrong. He looked at the flat, sandy expanse of Poland out of the train window. The glass gave on to a featureless landscape under an undistinguished sky, sunlight weary over it through a thin covering of cloud. He had read that seventy thousand Poles had died defending this unlovely land from invasion. But then you didn't defend your country with your life because you thought the place picturesque.

His plan was a simple one. He believed it would work. He would get them away. But he had no strategy for convincing Julia Smollen that it was a worthwhile thing to carry their child to term. When he opened his mouth to speak, he spoke in a language she had been given compelling reason to associate always with cruelty and oppression. Even if he had been articulate in another language, and he was not, he would not have been able to find the words to convince her. She had to reach her own conclusion. That was her right. All he had was his ardent hope and the conviction that he could get her to somewhere where she would enjoy the luxury of being able to make that choice for herself.

* * *

He had been at the barracks in Dresden when he opened the letter sent him by Bill and Lucy. They had both signed the letter, but it was written in Bill's voice. Martin recognized the voice of his friend in the words and phrases. He could not remember a time when Bill's voice had been a sound that failed to bring him comfort, pleasure or amusement. But then his friend had never had cause to speak to him in this tone before.

Dear Martin,

We are obliged to tell you that our daughter, Hannah, was taken from us a few days ago, when an attack of scarlet fever ended her short and much-cherished life.

You are no stranger to grief yourself and can perhaps imagine the sense of loss with which we are now both struggling to cope. It is too early to try to take comfort in the fact that her brief time on the earth was spent happily with people who truly loved her. But our sorrow is mitigated by the gratitude we feel for having known Hannah for the two and a bit years we were privileged to share her life.

There wasn't a moment spent with her when her company was anything but a delight to her parents and we have to be grateful for that.

Our sorrow now is insupportable. But we believe that there will come a day when we will be able to remember our daughter with warmth in our hearts and smiles on our faces.

In friendship always,

Bill & Lucy

Martin folded the letter and put it into his pocket and walked out of the barracks into Dresden and the rain. Flags and banners hung limp from poles on the old buildings of the city. Traffic was light, and rain had made the cobbles slick. Lights burned in shop windows, and there was the faint sound of accordion music. Three soldiers joking on a street corner stiffened when they saw his rank and saluted, fearful, when they saw the expression on Martin Hamer's face. He found a bar and had the barman pour him a glass of beer. He'd been on night manoeuvres for a week in the Black Forest and had only got back to the barracks late in the afternoon. He had showered off the stubborn camouflage cream from his night concealment in the forest before settling in a chair in the mess to open his mail. It was dusk now in the bar, or close to dusk, darkness descending with stealth and inevitability over the buildings of the old city. But it was still quiet. Hamer was practically the only customer.

'Two and a bit years.'

He sipped his beer and looked around. There was a portrait of the Führer on the wall. The Führer had achieved a mountain summit. He was attired in chain mail with a wolfskin thrown across his shoulders and carried a broadsword where practicality would have insisted on a climbing axe.

'Our sorrow now is insupportable.'

Hamer had thought the whole practice of mountaineering an English recreation pioneered late in the previous century in the Swiss Alps and the Italian Dolomites. Evidently this painter knew something about climbing history that Hamer didn't. Maybe the Führer's there to ambush Hannibal, he thought. The picture was mounted above a row of candles, in the manner of an icon in an orthodox Christian church. We're becoming a pagan people, Hamer thought. Perhaps we always have been. He took his eyes away from the painting and sipped his beer. He would buy stationery and write to Bill and Lucy. They had stationery at the barracks, but he thought the martial symbols with which the stuff was embossed wholly inappropriate to the subject matter. He didn't know what he would say in his letter, what could be said to his friends, but he would write. He still remembered the comforting strength of Bill's arm around his shoulder at Lillian's graveside. He could not imagine two people less deserving of such a random tragedy. In other circumstances he would have asked for leave and travelled to see them. He lived frugally enough. There was still plenty of money left from the sale of the house he had shared with Lillian in Cologne. He could more than afford the trip. But he could not go to offer condolence and support to his friends. All army leave had been cancelled. The army was on a war footing. He sipped beer in the empty bar and watched rain patter on to the cobbles outside in the yellow spread of the streetlights. He called over the proprietor of the empty bar and asked if there was a public telephone in the place. It wasn't quite their bedtime. He would telephone Heidi and speak if he could to the twins.

* * *

He had read somewhere that human beings have no memory for pain. But Landau's behaviour around Hamer seemed to confound the theory. At the very least, the man appeared keen to stay outside of punching range. And every time Hamer looked at him, Landau would hover a protective hand over his crotch.

The truck containing the twelve-strong cutting crew would travel at the head of their short convoy with a corporal at the wheel and Hamer in the passenger seat beside him. The truck had been commandeered from a Poznań coal merchant. It was a flat-bed vehicle, and the men would sit with their feet trailing its sides in plain sight of Landau, driving the rear vehicle. In the unlikely event that any of them tried to escape, Landau would have a clear view both of the attempt and of his target. The second lorry was a standard army type and contained the tools. Its canvas covering was rolled in its rear with the saws and axes and ropes and chains. The weather was fine — no wind to speak of — perfect weather for tree felling.

Both Landau and the corporal were armed with machine pistols. The men chosen to fell the trees had been selected for their relative size and strength. It was highly unlikely that any of them would turn on the men guarding them. But the Poles had proved stubborn in resistance even after their country had been conquered. A strong man with an axe between his hands might be tempted. A machine pistol was a convincing deterrent. But Hamer was relieved to see that Landau had placed his beloved sniper rifle in the cab of the second truck. He had not been counting on that, because he never trusted to luck. But he believed it would probably make things easier.

They were about to leave the camp, on the point of putting the trucks into gear and exiting the main gate, when Buckner approached their short convoy, lurching along behind two of his leashed dogs. The Dobermans were barking and snarling with feral excitement, and Hamer caught the stink of fear as bowels loosened behind him among the men on the truck's flat bed and one of them puked into his hands and started to apologize in pidgin German. He got out of the cab.

Concealed inside the rolled canvas awning of the second truck, Julia Smollen tried not to tremble and convulse with fear. She needed to be brave. She needed to be calm because if fear forced movement from her body it would be seen and she would be discovered. She had spent three nights now in the garage in the canvas. After the night sharing Hamer's cot, it was assumed in the camp that's where she had continued to sleep. Yesterday and the day before it had rained, and Hamer had successfully delayed the expedition. It was murder, he'd said, to cut down trees in the wet. The teeth of a saw wouldn't grip wet wood. Men using saws and axes could not get proper purchase for their feet on a wet forest floor. She didn't know if these claims were true. He'd been believed, apparently.

She was mere feet from escape. She could feel it. That's what she cared about. But all she could hear was the yowl and snarl of Buckner's hellhounds. Then she heard the slam of a truck door and Martin Hamer's voice. He didn't sound calm. He didn't sound fearful, either. His voice was cold with fury. She could imagine the look on his face. On one occasion, she had seen it.

'What the fuck are you doing?'

'You should take the dogs,' Buckner said. He was sweating. Hamer could smell ether oozing through his damp flesh.

Hamer walked around the dogs and approached the doctor from his flank. Buckner wound the double leash a little shorter, trying to rein in the capering animals. The attempt was unsuccessful. 'Watch yourself, Hamer.'

He was close enough now to Buckner's ear to make himself heard speaking quietly. The dogs continued to howl and slaver. 'If either of them bites me, Ariel, I'll shoot them both. And then I'll shoot you.'

'I thought they might be useful,' Buckner said.

'They'll be useful only as pig food if you don't fuck off with the pair of them, now.'

Hamer took a step away from the doctor and put his hands on his hips. Buckner blinked sweat out of his eyes and staggered away in the wake of his tethered pets.

'That man is a fucking moron,' Hamer said, back in the cab. The corporal sitting next to him didn't say anything. In titular terms, Buckner was an officer. To make a comment about the doctor or his dogs would be grossly insubordinate for a humble NCO. But his driver's grin suggested that he shared Hamer's opinion.

* * *

The wood was quiet when the trucks pulled into a clearing and Hamer handed the cutting crew their tools from the back of the second truck. It was warm work he accomplished in his shirtsleeves. He noticed how quiet the wood was. Its population of birds no longer sang. They've vacated their nests, he thought, moved on. He had enormous respect for the intelligence shown by some species of animal. The dwellers of the wood had anticipated the destruction of their home with the same instinct that guided migrating geese and saw domestic cats pick a precise path around objects human beings could not see.

He waited until the felling and stripping of trees had stopped for half an hour and the cutting crew had eaten their meagre midday ration in a cluster, taking a small, comparative enjoyment in the sunshine, in the change in their surroundings and the relative novelty of their work, before approaching Landau, who stood smoking by a pile of newly stacked lumber.

'I'm told you think you can shoot.'

Landau smiled at him. He exhaled smoke. He felt confident on his favourite subject, obviously. 'Oh, I can shoot, sir,' he said. 'I've been half-hoping one of these bastards would run. You could brew a pot of coffee, sir, and then allow me to shoot him. I'd still be good enough to pick my spot.'

Hamer looked around him, at the sky, at the branches of the trees still standing, their new leaves stirred only by the slightest of breezes. 'I think I'm probably better,' he said.

Landau's smile widened. 'I doubt that, sir,' he said. 'With respect.'

Hamer pondered. 'We've time enough,' he said. 'Let's put it to the test. Fetch your rifle, Landau. Let the two of us have a little sport.' He turned to the corporal, who was guarding their twelve tree fellers. 'Bring the Poles, corporal. Let's remind these people how well it is a German can shoot.'

Landau fell in beside Hamer, his rifle held easy at port arms, far more relaxed with the familiar weapon between his hands than he'd been on his earlier visit, hanging upside down by one boot with vomit flecking his hair.

Since there was nothing left in the wood for them to kill, it would be target practice. Hamer fished a pfennig coin from his pocket and walked through the remaining trees until he found one with a whorl in the trunk, just above head height, into which he could wedge the coin with its face flat. He turned to Landau. 'Five hundred yards?'

Landau merely shrugged.

When she heard the first rifle shot, Julia Smollen assumed it was the signal. Hamer had said to listen out for a signal. The shot sounded distant. It had to be fifteen minutes at least since she had heard the cut against tree bark of a tool, the sound of a talking voice. She rolled herself out of the canvas and blinked against pallid sunshine. She climbed off the open tailboard of the truck. She had never felt more naked, more exposed. There was a second rifle shot and she winced. He had said she would find it thirty paces from the right rear end of the truck. He had said he would mark it, make it easy to find. The forest floor rolled and undulated here. She measured thirty paces. She had covered twenty of them when she saw his sign. It had been secured, pierced twice through, folded over a thorn. It flapped slightly in the breeze. She reached it and tore it free, looked at it, read it out of nothing more than lifelong habit before folding it into four and putting it into the pocket of her new and unfamiliar coat. It was the title page from the story of Hansel and Gretel. It was Hamer's marker. It was Hamer's clue. She dropped to the forest floor and began to scrabble with her hands as rifle fire, steady and remote-sounding, punctuated the silence of the wood.

* * *

Hamer shouldered Landau's rifle for the last time. It really was a beautifully balanced tool. He could smell the oil that Landau applied to the walnut stock of the weapon. He could smell cordite from the barrel as its sharp, familiar odour rose above the bolt. He sighted the target and began gently to squeeze the trigger. The pfennig coin had gone, shot to slivers by the force and nagging accuracy of the two men's alternating fire. Hamer targeted daylight. They'd shot the tree through, punched a hole in the tree with the force of each successive round. Hamer's final shot was no different from that which had preceded it. The bullet sang cleanly through the narrow tunnel in the tree. The sound of impact would have signalled failure. There was no impact, just the final report of the rifle fading through trees and space.

The corporal whistled.

'That's it,' Landau said. 'That was my last bullet.'

'You didn't bring any more?'

'I haven't got any more, sir. I make them myself. I make the bullets in the machine shop at the camp. You can shoot, sir. There's no question of that. With respect, I still think I'm the better marksman.'

'Maybe one day we'll find out,' Hamer said. He smiled. Ordinarily target shooting bored him. But he felt that on this occasion it had been worthwhile.

Landau looked at him with an expression hard to read and held out his hand for them to shake on the tie achieved in their contest. Hamer was loath to touch the man but took his proffered hand, which was cold and small and dry.

The two lorries returned to the camp at dusk, one laden with a stack of felled tree trunks, the other with tools now sticky with sap, gritty with wood chippings and sawdust, forest scented after their day of damaging toil. The weary crew were down the road being marched back at the point of his machine pistol by the corporal who had sat next to Hamer on the outward journey. It had been a satisfactory day, Hamer thought, driving the laden lorry back through the camp gates, if you thought a couple of tons of usable timber a worthy reward for the destruction of somewhere the elements of the earth had conspired to make beautiful. Certainly it had been an unusual way for a professional soldier to spend his last day wearing the uniform of an army he had tried so hard for so long to serve with loyalty and distinction.

Backing the truck into its garage, Hamer knew that tomorrow he would begin to be judged as a man who had failed his country. He was not arrogant enough to consider that his country might have failed him. He was sure, though, that what he was doing was right. If he continued to serve, he continued to serve a power that would demand as blood sacrifice the life of his child. The life of his child was the proof of his loyalty. But all Martin Hamer's loyalty was owed to the life growing in Julia Smollen's belly. His father had asked him if there was not one living duty worth performing. And his answer had been to say yes to the single duty compelled by the love he felt for his unborn baby.

Hamer rolled under the camp fence at three o'clock in the morning at a place he breached with the bolt cutters he had taken from the tool store accessed by Crupp's omnipowerful chit. He did so secure in the knowledge that Landau would be sleeping easy in his bed after a long and vigilant day watching the woodcutters in the sunshine. He did so five minutes after cutting the throats of Buckner's sleeping dogs. He rolled under the fence with his face camouflaged and with sufficient rations in his small backpack for a week. He'd sleep in the open, but in April in Poland that wouldn't kill him. It was thoughtful of the General Government's German administrators to replace all the street signs with names he could read. He didn't understand Polish. It would make finding the rendezvous point with Julia Smollen that much easier. Hamer was well beyond the sweep of the camp's watchtower searchlights, half a mile away, when he straightened and began to walk at full pace after a quick reading of his compass. He took a swig of water. Freedom didn't feel terrifying to him. Freedom, to Hamer, felt surprisingly good.

* * *

Julia Smollen walked into a cheap restaurant in Legnica. She wore the clothes bought for her by Martin Hamer, before her escape, in Poznań. She carried money, given to her by Martin Hamer, in the pockets of her coat. She picked up the menu, written in German on cheap paper, and began to study it. She had spent the last sixteen months of her life in a labour camp. She still wore a camp pallor and her clothes hung off her frame despite her budding pregnancy. She wore a hat to cover her shorn hair. She counted to ten again and again in her mind to try to fight the panic brought by the conviction that everyone was staring at her. She wondered if there was anything on the menu she could stomach. She didn't know if it was her pregnancy or living for almost a year and a half on a diet of bread and potato soup, but the first meal of her new freedom had not stayed inside her body for very long.

She thought about the logic of her rendezvous with the German and wondered again whether there was any merit or even sense in his plan. He had said he would get her to Switzerland, which was a neutral country with no involvement in the war. In Switzerland she could have her baby or her termination at a well-equipped clinic run by expert medical staff. But to get to Switzerland they would have to travel by train through Germany. Hamer had told her he did not think he would become the subject of a general manhunt. He reasoned that he had been made too public a hero. He believed men would be sent after him to try to kill him, but felt sure the authorities would stop short of wanted posters tacked to the waiting-room walls of railway stations or the notice boards nowadays familiar in public squares. He'd been too public a hero for such a damaging propaganda reversal. They would try to kill him quietly. He had even told her the name of the man he thought they would send after him to do the job.

But Martin Hamer was an expert fighter, a man whose strength could be put to appalling use. She'd spoken to a camp inmate who had seen the body of Rolfe before it was removed from his porch. Nevertheless, the thought of travelling through Germany terrified her. Together they would be twice as conspicuous.

She could go in the other direction, to Warsaw, alone, and simply disappear for the duration. She knew the city from her student days. She knew people there she believed she could trust. She knew she was not important enough for the Germans, fighting their war on two fronts, to bother sending anyone after her. If she risked Poznań, she knew someone through her dead boyfriend who could forge a new identity for her and would take that risk in return for some of the money the German had given her. In Warsaw she would be picked up only if extremely unlucky and could easily avoid recognition once her hair grew to an acceptable length and she dyed it a lighter shade.

In Warsaw she would bleed to death after a backstreet abortion. Martin Hamer, who had saved her life and freed her, would be left alone, waiting, bereft and betrayed at their rendezvous.

A waitress came to her table. Julia Smollen tried to smile. She ordered her meal in Polish, pretending to struggle with the waitress over the pronunciation of the German names for the dishes on the modest bill of fare.

* * *

Crupp and Buckner waited for their visitor. The mood in Crupp's barracks office was morose. Reinhard Heydrich stared balefully down from the wall on to his former protégé. His new sponsor, Joseph Goebbels, had refused to return his telephone calls. He had been informed by telegram that the funding for his planned prize-giving had, in light of the new circumstances, been withdrawn. There would be no morale-boosting ceremony for the pioneer settlers of the portion of the General Government over which Wilhelm Crupp so benevolently presided. The accounts of the camp were to be scrutinized. His little empire, so carefully accrued, was in rapid decline.

'I've not even had time to properly mourn the passing of my dogs,' Buckner said.

'If the man we're expecting is anything like his reputation, you'll probably be reunited with them soon,' Crupp said. There was a silence. 'What a mess, Ariel,' Crupp said eventually.

'I want to go after him,' Buckner said. 'I want to take Landau. Landau can hold him at gunpoint while I rip his bastard out of her belly and he's forced to watch me do it.'

'He'd kill you before you saw him, Ariel,' Crupp said. 'He broke Hans Rolfe in half. He killed your dogs while they slept. Shouldn't they have awoken?'

'You sound almost as though you admire him, cousin.'

Crupp pondered on this paradox. 'I don't admire Hamer,' he said. 'I admire the strength of men like him in the field. I appreciate that their courage is winning the war for us. Hamer I think has gone mad, his reason vanquished by your diagnosis, which made a lie of his life. The man is insane and has ruined my reputation. So no, cousin, I don't admire him. I'd like to see him killed. And I'd like the killing accomplished slowly.'

‘Well, perhaps the man we’re about to meet can engineer that,’ Buckner said.

There was a double rap at the door. Before Crupp could respond to it, the door opened and Jacob Hessler entered. He carried his cap under one arm. His greatcoat was open over his immaculate black uniform and an Iron Cross, First Class, hung on a ribbon around his throat. In the four years since his conversation with Hamer at the gymnasium in Freidrichstrasse, his frame had filled and strengthened slightly. The war had evidently been good to him. He did not appear at all wearied by the ardures of his journey here from Berlin. He wore his full head of blond hair shaved to within half an inch of his skull. The style accentuated his cheekbones and the thoughtfulness in his eyes. Whether the impression was calculated or not, the effect was intimidating. Both Crupp and Buckner snapped to attention and saluted, though technically Crupp still outranked the Gestapo man. If they had expected a scowl from him, they were surprised. Hessler beamed at them. He took off his greatcoat and hung it with his cap on Crupp’s hatstand.

‘Coffee would be lovely,’ Hessler said with a clap of his hands after the introductions were complete. ‘And then I want you to tell me everything you know about the Reich traitor Martin Hamer. I do mean everything, gentlemen. Leave no thought or impression, however tentative, however speculative, out of your account.’ He smiled. ‘We’re all on the same side here. So let’s none of us be shy.’

* * *

He had done as Julia Smollen had suggested and stolen clothing from a washing line to wear at first. He had buried his uniform in the soft bank of an irrigation ditch at the edge of a cabbage field on a pioneer farm feeling none of the grief for his old life he might have anticipated. He had kept his medal, put it in his pocket. One day he hoped to tell his child about the honourable things he had done as a soldier. He knew that this was a vain and sentimental wish. But what father wouldn't have succumbed to the same temptation? So he kept his medal and he kept his father's hip flask and put it in the breast pocket of the shirt he'd freed on a Polish washing line from the grip of two wooden pegs.

The clothes felt strange on him, soft and insubstantial after so many years inside the pressed and belted stricture of a uniform. They had a saying in the army that the uniform wore you. And it had become increasingly true in the strident peace that preceded it, never mind in the war itself. Martin Hamer knew men who could not have existed without the power, privileges and licence for abuse they were given by their rank and station. The runic symbols and skull and crossed bones motif worn on the collar of an SS tunic were there by calculation and not by accident. They were designed to provoke terror in those confronted by them and to give the men who wore them a collective feeling of ruthless superiority. It was equally true of the trappings of the Gestapo. And the army was hardly immune. Men like Landau satisfied a sick pathology in uniform. Hamer had seen the happy look on his face at the fear among the Poles, sitting in their leg irons, defenceless on the back of the wagon at the approach of Buckner's dogs.

They would send Jacob Hessler after him. Hessler would insist on the assignment as soon as he heard about the disgrace of Hamer's desertion, learned of the collusive sin of his treachery. Hamer had no fear of Hessler. The burial deep in peaty soil of his uniform had not unmanned him in the way he felt it might have his adversary. He felt just as confident of his fighting skills wearing the faded chambray of a Polish peasant. He still carried his pistol, and his fighting knife lay sharpened in a sheath strapped to his calf. Deprived of weapons, he could fight with his brain and his hands. He'd fought with his hands in the rubble and darkness of ruined cellars in the permanent midnight of Stalingrad. He'd swap these clothes for less humble attire when he decided to risk a large enough town to boast a gentlemen's outfitters. He'd seek the anonymity of a sober suit and a topcoat for the travel aboard trains they had planned. Such a change would not inflict on him the fighting attributes of a clerk.

His problem in fighting Hessler, should Hessler find him, would be in killing the man. Jacob Hessler wouldn't stop unless he was killed. His intent regarding Hamer would be execution rather than capture. But widowing Heidi Jodl for a second time was something Martin Hamer did not want on his conscience. He did not know what kind of man Hessler was at home. Some men were capable of living a domestic life as cosy as their professional life was callous and brutal. What if Jacob Hessler was such a man? Heydrich apparently had been, who had been at Hessler's wedding to violate a serving girl and orchestrate the singing of the Horst Wessel song. Martin Hamer's relationship with Heidi's twins had been made remote by the war, had dwindled to one of occasional notes and cards and telephone calls during which they spoke with a tender formality to their once familiar Uncle Martin. What if Hessler was a devoted stepfather?

Wasting mental energy on speculation of this sort was futile. He needed to stay alert in his situation. He needed to stay in the moment, all his senses alert to the here and now. He probably flattered himself that they would send a man as important in Berlin as Jacob Hessler was, just to hunt down a deserting soldier. But instinct stubbornly insisted to Hamer that he had not seen the last of the man.

He had the more pressing problem of achieving their rendezvous at the time he had told Julia Smollen they would meet. And he had the more pressing worry that the Polish woman might not turn up at all. He knew that the prospect of travelling through Germany was terrifying for her. She could disappear easily, with her linguistic gift, into the General Government. She could pass as a German, with her German accent, on the strength of forged papers. Her immediate family he knew to be dead. But there had to be people in Poland who would help her. The Poles were stubborn under conquest. He remembered the gesture Julia herself had made to Rolfe, the one that provoked the dog attack on the first occasion he had laid eyes on the woman. The Poles, enough of them, were brave and defiant. She would find help, he was sure, if she looked for it. He wondered if he had perhaps seen the last of her before seeing the first of his child.

* * *

Hessler sat in Martin Hamer's vacated camp quarters and studied the inventory reluctantly surrendered by Crupp. The level of corruption in the camp did not surprise him. He knew that the General Government was corrupt. All of Greater Germany was prey to the carpetbaggers of wartime expansionism. It would require the peace that followed victory to root out these squalid profiteers and carry out the summary executions that would be their eventual fate.

He was not surprised by the venality. But he was depressed by the administrative incompetence that co-existed with it. Self-respecting embezzlers at least took the trouble to doctor the books. But the books Hans Rolfe left were a shambles. There were no accounts for the wages paid the camp for the labour borrowed from it by the pioneer farmers and workshops and factories in the district. There was no record of income derived in the camp from what its inmates manufactured and Crupp had sold in Poznań and around. There was no record of expenditure on raw materials. No proper roll call of camp inmates had ever been a part of the daily routine of the place. That was why it had been three days before they realized that Julia Smollen had probably absconded with the traitor Martin Hamer. Rolfe had lent labour to farmers on an ad hoc basis for cash payments Hessler was certain had been shared with Crupp and Buckner. No roll call had been possible, because any daily record of who was and was not inside the camp would have exposed the scam.

Hamer would never have got around it all. He had probably not even noticed it, Hessler thought. Hamer had no real interest in money. He'd had no interest whatsoever in the efficient management of the camp economy. His passion was for combat. Combat defined him and but for his skirmishes with Rolfe he had been deprived in the camp of that. So he had discovered a new passion, between the thighs of his Polish whore. And when she had fallen pregnant, his mind unbalanced by the lie exposed by Buckner at the heart of his life, he had surrendered to the sentiment that Hessler had always believed to be the man's particular flaw.

He had watched in disgust and incredulity years earlier as Hamer hugged his doomed friend before assisting him to his death. Imagine touching a man so tainted. Sentiment, he realized then, was Hamer's undoing. He well remembered on that broiling Berlin day feeling happier, more secure at having discovered such a fundamental weakness in someone whose appearance had seemed so formidable.

Now, he looked around. Faded flowers, dried and atrophied, sat in a water-stained glass as the room's only embellishment. There was a small, stickyish stain on the locker beside Hamer's cot, next to a dish containing the tamped remains of a single rolled cigarette, which had been lit but barely smoked. Despite the fastidiousness Hessler felt distinguished him, he wet his forefinger and worked the stain with its tip. He was an investigator; he was here to investigate. He tasted the residue gathered by the print of his finger. It tasted sweet and old, like cognac. He had not figured Hamer for a drinker. But it was as well to know all the weaknesses a man had, especially if from time to time you shared some of them.

The flowers would have been gathered as tribute to the Polish whore in the wood, he thought. He still could not believe the blind, corrupt stupidity of Buckner and Crupp. He had been accompanied by them to the denuded wood earlier in the day, once he had realized the number and selection of tools Hamer had taken from the camp workshop under the blanket justification of the chit signed and stamped by the camp commandant.

He found the hide Hamer had constructed for his whore fairly easily. It was, despite this, skilful work. It was spaciously dug and carefully revetted with branches pruned from strong, resilient trees. Hamer had fretted branches together for its roof and then covered them with some craft in a layer exactly convergent with the foliage of the forest floor. He'd used fibrous reeds from a stream bed to bind a makeshift hinge to his contraption. The care of the construction, its fundamental strength, spoke eloquently of Hamer's fear that it might collapse and bury and suffocate the woman and his unborn offspring. This thought made Hessler smile.

'Where would he have learned how to do this?' Buckner asked the silence that now occupied the void where Hamer's wood had been. 'It's like something a Huron might have fashioned in the American Midwest.'

They knew nothing, these ignorant, avaricious men. Their ignorance was an affront. 'He was a tank killer,' Hessler said, without looking at Buckner. 'He led an elite patrol of tank killers. His men would sometimes dig and build these hides and then let the tanks roll past them and attack the tanks from behind.'

Crupp studied the hide. 'Wouldn't the tracks of a tank crush one of these?'

'Of course,' Hessler said. 'But the tracks of a tank are comparatively narrow. It was a risk Hamer and the men he led deemed acceptable.'

He looked at the slack jaws of Crupp and Buckner. They will swallow their pistol barrels, he decided then. After the disgrace of what their greed and incompetence had permitted, they would elect to take the honourable way out.

* * *

In Hamer's spartan quarters, Hessler snapped shut the last useless, fraudulent book of figures he'd been given to study. He stretched his length on the top blanket of Hamer's cot. He had wished ardently for this resolution for a very long time. He had coveted Heidi and her twins from the moment he first saw this perfect family with the dolt of a husband who owned it on a Strength Through Joy trip in Bavaria. Heydrich himself had advised him subsequently of the suspicions concerning Karl's predilection for boys. Heydrich, a past master on the mechanics of the trap, had advised him on the methodology of the honeypot. It had been perfectly executed. Karl had taken the only way out possible. And then Heidi had flaunted her affections before the widower Martin Hamer. And Jacob Hessler had been put through the grovelling ordeal of delay.

Hessler had seen, and been profoundly impressed by, a portrait of the Führer mounted on a charger, carrying a lance, in the guise of a medieval knight. He had never read history or historic fiction. He could not follow music, was tone-deaf to it, and so did not know whether some opera or another had inspired the picture. But he did know that like the Führer he was blessed with the genes of a warrior race. He had been predestined to fight Martin Hamer, he believed. They had been fated to meet in single combat, these two formidable adversaries. Hessler believed this with the same conviction informing him that their trial by combat could have only one glorious outcome.

* * *

He waited for her in the derelict barn, breathing in the fusty odours of old straw and rabbit pellets and decay. He did not bother to conceal himself. He knew he had not been followed here. Sunlight slanted in sharp motes through dozens of places where wood was missing in the fabric of the barn. Outside its cities and towns, Poland was a flat wilderness under a broad, oppressive sky. It seemed an ominously underpopulated country. Crops grew untended in its abandoned fields. It was a place of defeat and desolation. Atrocity lay like a dark stain over many of the places Martin had passed in the night as he attempted to escape the country.

His ears were alert to any approach, and through the breached walls of the barn he would see any sign of movement over the featureless land.

This was a place she had known as a girl. She had cycled for sport, belonged to the Poznań Cycling Club, and had cycled on trips to the river Odra, stopping at this farm, which had not been derelict then, to buy apples from its orchard and lemonade with her cyclist friends. Hamer smiled. He had teased her about her choice of a sport made so easy by the absence of hills to struggle over, climbing on a bike. She'd argued that cycling was more popular still in Holland, which was even flatter. And Holland had produced its share of distinguished cycling champions.

The real point he took from the conversation

was that he knew nothing about Julia Smollen. He knew a little of the woman she had been forced to become in the camp. Their physical intimacy had been passionate, unrestrained. But before the invasion had deprived her of it, she had led a contented and successful life. She had read and listened to music and cycled and laughed. She'd had a home and a lover and ambitions. She had gone from that to enduring Hans Rolfe and his frequent, stinking violation.

What could he hope for from Julia Smollen? He'd found her irresistible from the first, the first woman so compelling after Lillian that he had not been able to ignore the attraction. When he was with her he found it hard to look away from her face. When he'd seen her shorn hair for the first time, the grazes on her scalp, the bruise darkening one cheek under its sharp shelf of bone, he had felt sympathy for her and anger over what had been done to her. But after his absence from the camp he'd been mesmerized, too, by the glitter of her eyes and the fullness of her lips and had wanted to kiss and touch and hold her. What could he hope for from Julia Smollen? That she'll turn up, he said to himself, looking at the dial of the waterproof watch he had bought with money saved for his marriage to Lillian, prior to the folly of his assault on the Eigerwand. That would at least be a start.

He caught movement then, through one of the slats missing in the wall of the barn. Then it was gone under a ripple of indisciplined corn. It had been faster than a woman walking, and he looked around, thinking hard about what cover he could find here for concealment and, if necessary, ambush. He caught sight of the movement again, this time for long enough for his mind to make sense of it. She had found a bicycle. That was all: she was riding a bicycle to the rendezvous. What could be more normal in daylight, in a land under curfew, in a land whose population had been deprived of every requisitioned automobile, than a woman riding a bicycle along a country road?

Relief and joy thrilled through Martin Hamer. He could feel the blood sing in his veins. Did he love her? Could it be that he was in love with her? She came into the barn, still aboard the bike, and braked, skidding to a halt on old straw and ancient rabbit shit. Her cheeks had coloured with the wind in her face and the exercise. Her face dappled by sunlight, she smiled at him from under her hat. It was more of a grin than a smile, and there was hope in it. It was the first time she had allowed him to see this expression on her face. Hamer had no doubt then. He was filled with a feeling he thought had long died in him. He loved Julia Smollen. He loved her. And he would save her life.

* * *

They were in Buckner's quarters. There were three of them. Anselm had grown much fatter than he had been in the days when Hamer had compromised his surveillance and hit him in a Berlin alleyway in the rain. But he was still recognizable as the same stubborn-jawed Westphalian farm boy he'd been back then. And of course he remembered Martin Hamer. His hand touched his face, instinctively now, at the mention of Hamer's name, at the recollection of the night he'd been hit by Hamer, hit harder and faster than he'd ever been hit before or, happily, since.

Buckner's quarters provided Hessler with the most comfortable makeshift office in the camp. There was a lingering medicinal smell. And there was persistent hammering today from the adjacent carpentry shop. But the chairs were leather and well upholstered and there was a coffeepot on the small, coal-fed stove. There was plenty of coal to fuel this, of course, since Germany now owned the coal mines of Poland. And there was a large jar of excellent coffee. Hessler was very partial to coffee.

'What makes you think he won't fly, sir?'

The question came from Landau, who was the third man in the room. It was a reasonable question. Hamer had been taught to fly before the war. He was not an outstanding pilot, had not put in the flying hours, but he knew how to take off and land in an aeroplane all right and was a skilled navigator.

Hessler sipped his coffee. 'If he were going to fly, he would by now have flown. There are no civilian flights currently in Greater Germany. He would have had to breach airfield security and steal an aircraft. The theft would have been quickly discovered. He would have been tracked and shot down by one of our fighters. Nothing of the kind has been reported, which means that it hasn't happened.'

They were planing now in the carpentry shop next door. A plane blade squealed in protest, stuttered over a knot in a plank of wood.

Anselm cleared his throat and said, 'Where do you think he is, Jacob?'

'In Germany by now,' Hessler said. 'Probably somewhere in the vicinity of Dresden or Leipzig. He knows Dresden, was stationed there.'

'He could be anywhere, couldn't he, sir?' This from Landau.

The planing had stopped. They were hammering again. The wood must have been sufficiently smoothed.

'He could, because we can't make him the subject of a general alert and manhunt. That doesn't mean the Gestapo aren't on the lookout for him, for them. But where they are isn't really the issue,' Hessler said.

Landau and Anselm looked at the senior man. The looks were as questioning as their fear of him would allow. The banging next door was incessant now. Hessler had to raise his voice to be heard above its industry. 'That noise bothering you, Landau?'

'Not at all, sir,' Landau said.

They were making coffins next door for the bodies of Buckner and Crupp. Both men had apparently done the honourable thing and shot themselves. The bodies were outside, uncovered, side by side on trestle tables borrowed for the purpose from the building in the camp where blankets were woven. The bodies were there as an example of the price of a failure that had been unacceptable. The reason for the level of noise from next door, for the squeals of wood worked under protest and the curses of the carpenters, was Hessler's insistence that they fashion the coffins from the unseasoned wood newly felled at Crupp's instruction. Hessler thought this a fitting fate for the corpses of the two men. The boxes would have no integrity. The wood covering Buckner and Crupp would warp quickly in the ground and surrender them to the worms. It was all they deserved.

The two suicides had not died well. Crupp had broken the top plate of his dentures biting down on the gun barrel, convulsed with terror. Neither man had died in the way that Hamer's deviant friend had died. It was Hessler's experience that you could never tell with these things.

'What matters isn't where Hamer is with the whore, but where they're going,' Hessler said. 'I believe they are headed for Switzerland. Hamer has a wealthy American friend who will probably fly them from there to the United States, where they will dream of raising their bastard in safety and, I should think, in some material comfort. Except that this isn't going to happen, because we're going to fly ourselves to the Swiss border tonight, and we're going to prevent it.'

Landau's eyes shifted between the two men. Hessler caught the expression. He was an unprepossessing little man, was Landau, but apparently an excellent shot, not really culpable for the part he had played in providing Hamer's diversion. He might use Landau to kill the woman in the last resort should she and Hamer get as far as the mountains.

'Something troubling you, Landau?'

'I don't think three of us is enough, with respect, sir. I've experienced something of what this man can accomplish.'

'We can always arrange for more assistance,' Hessler said. You're wrong, Landau, he was thinking; one of us is going to be enough.

* * *

They spent the night at an inn outside Regensburg. They made love for the first time with one another in a proper bed with a real mattress and pillows under an eiderdown filled with goose feathers. Earlier they had eaten dinner together for the first time. Now they lay listening to the silence of the night, Hamer's hand on Julia's slightly swollen belly, his palm and spread fingers feeling the beat, the pulse, the life of it.

She lay with one arm under his head and stroked his face with her other hand. 'Your touch is very gentle,' she said, 'for the man you are.'

'You haven't met the man I am,' he said.

'I have,' she said. 'I believe I'm with him now.'

He was quiet for a moment, thinking about their conversation over dinner.

'Julia, do you ever think in German?'

She laughed. 'It rather depends on what it is I'm thinking about.'

She had arranged for the papers to be forged

in Poznań. He was a chemical engineer. She was a medical secretary. They had been married for five years. They came originally from Ulm and had made their home in Biberach. Hamer thought the quality of the forgeries excellent. So far they had encountered no Gestapo on the trains. Most of the regional police they had seen — the ticket collectors and train guards and porters too — had been old men brought reluctantly out of retirement, pressed into their old routine by patriotic pressure. Judging by the cursory way in which their papers had so far been checked, these men had their minds on the comfort of home and hearth.

They had stayed away from the busier railway connections and had managed to avoid large cities. But it was still shocking how few young men there were left now in Germany. Fighting a war on two fronts was depleting the population. It occurred to Hamer that if the Führer were granted his wish of a war every twenty years they would not be the wars of rejuvenation and purification of which he had spoken. They would be wars of rapid annihilation and extinction. Shame was all Hamer felt when he recalled then the last day of his life in their flat in Berlin with Lillian, recalled his own hollow hankering after war.

'What decided you?' he asked Julia, now, in bed.

She lay quiet for a moment. He stroked her hair. It was soft and black, growing out like caterpillar fur.

'It was the story you told me about your

friends, Bill and Lucy. You called the death of their daughter a random tragedy. I thought our child deserved a random chance at life.'

Hamer swallowed. Our child. It was happening.

'There's enough death in the world, Martin.' She put her hand on top of his, over her bump. He felt the warmth of her sealing him there. He was aware of the enveloping closeness of the woman. He had never imagined he could be this happy.

'I was in this shitty restaurant in Legnica.' She laughed. 'Legnica was shitty before the Germans came. It's shittier now. Anyway, I had some tomato soup and an omelette.'

'Wise choices.' Hamer remained incredulous about Polish food.

'I couldn't keep them down. A kind waitress, a girl from Katowice, helped me to the lavatory. I knelt on the floor with my hands around the bowl and began to talk to the baby, admonish it for the lousy way I felt. And then I thought of its defencelessness, its abject innocence. And I started to love it. And I haven't stopped.'

Martin thought of Bill. He thought of Lucy, who had died of grief. The doctors had called it heart failure. Her heart failed because it was broken, Bill said in his letter afterwards. Bill had married again. He had married an actress from Milwaukee and they'd had a boy together. You have to try, Bill had written him. Don't try, kid, and you don't fail.

'I hope that nice girl gets back to Katowice

one day,' Julia said. 'Nobody should have to live in Legnica.'

* * *

For the entire duration of the flight personally sanctioned by Joseph Goebbels, Hessler studied the thick file detailing the life and career of Martin Hamer. He was familiar with the file, had read it a number of times and was reading it again now to reassure himself that his instinct about what Hamer would do, where he would go, was the best possible projection.

Goebbels had sounded on the telephone as passionate as Hessler was himself about resolving this squalid business with as much honour as possible. Hamer was to be dispatched with the minimum of fuss and not one shred of attendant publicity. Goebbels had confided to Hessler that the actions of the traitor had been kept and would continue to be kept from the Führer. Things were not going well now, either in the east or in Italy. These were temporary setbacks. But the Führer didn't need to hear about the treachery of a man he had with his own hands honoured with the highest accolade for gallantry bestowed by the Reich. Ever courteous, Goebbels had concluded their conversation by congratulating the Gestapo man on his successful resolution of the awkward dilemma concerning Buckner and Crupp.

Hessler studied Hamer's file. The man had spent far too much time away from the Fatherland. It was obvious that the seeds of disloyalty had been sown in him in the previous decades, in his trips to Britain, to France and, critically, to America. He read about Bill. Bill had played something called nose tackle on the Yale football team and been regarded as the most ferocious blocker in collegiate football. At Fort Bragg, after volunteering to fight when America entered the war in 1917, he had competed as a heavyweight and become an army divisional boxing champion. He had qualified as a lawyer, married a Jewess called Lucy and settled to a degenerate life in the world of Hollywood films. It was at the least inappropriate for a good German to have such a man as a friend, Hessler believed. He wondered, uncomfortably, had Heidi ever had any social dealings with this decadent couple.

He read about the attempt on the Eigerwand. Hamer's father, a suicide, had taken the boy to England to learn to rock-climb in the manner of the English climber Mallory. Hamer had been exposed to the taint of foreign cultures from an early age. He had been only eight when his father first took him to the English Lake District. Hessler didn't see this as mitigation for what he'd done, but he wondered if the man he was hunting had ever really been given the chance to become a pure German, as he had. Hamer's courage in the field had been real enough. But something had been susceptible in his character to corruption. Hessler had never been to a country that Germany had not conquered. He was so proud of the fact that he would relate it, fondly and often, to Gestapo colleagues.

The climbing was really the key to Hessler's theory about Hamer's flight. He believed that the fugitive would try to take the Polish whore over the Alps into Switzerland. The German-Swiss border was too heavily guarded, the terrain too flat and exposed, for them to smuggle themselves over it successfully. They would ascend into Austria, travel by train to Innsbruck and then get to Landeck, from where they would make their attempt. His file confirmed that Hamer knew the area well. He had skied in the region often with his dead, deceiving wife. He had climbed there. The spring weather meant that there was an avalanche risk in the heavy snow on the high Alpine passes. But Hessler thought that they would risk it. Hamer's attempt on the Eigerwand was conclusive proof of the fugitive's vanity concerning his skill in the mountains. He would attempt to take the girl over the Alps and into the moneyed passage provided by his American friend.

At Innsbruck, every train arriving from the north was already being exhaustively searched. They might even now have the two of them in custody. If they did, the railway police were under strict instructions to do nothing but confine the pair until his arrival. He didn't think that Hamer and the girl had got there yet, though. He felt none of his usual impatience. He felt that he himself would confront the escapees in their train carriage, surprise them at the point of his pistol — and then what? He'd blow the whore's brains out. He'd have a good look at the girl before his gun destroyed her face, though.

He was curious to see what sort of woman it was who had tempted Martin Hamer into this insane, treasonous adventure. The fate he planned for Hamer did not involve a gun.

There was a Perspex window in the fuselage of the aeroplane next to where Jacob Hessler sat. Through it he could see the shadow of their aircraft undulate like a black phantom over the fields and forests. Anselm sat beside him, dozing. Landau sat in front of them, nursing his sniper rifle between his knees. Hessler was absolutely certain that his theory concerning the flight of Martin Hamer was correct. Indeed, he would have bet his life on it.

* * *

They disembarked at the last station prior to Innsbruck. Hamer's intuition about the involvement of Jacob Hessler in the hunt for them had grown stronger with every southbound mile consumed by the locomotive pulling their train. It was not lost on him that they were headed for the land of Tyrolean hats and lederhosen. He thought of Ludwig Kurtz. He thought of Karl. If it ended now, it would have been an eventful life, he thought. He looked at Julia, who smiled at him, and knew that this was not the time for his eventful life to end.

They hired bicycles, paying a deposit, paying rental for a week, by which time Hamer believed they would be safely over the high pass above Landeck and into Switzerland. He had not ridden a bike since he'd rented them with Lillian on the Côte d'Azur during their honeymoon. He had not been on a mountain since he'd obliged Lillian to confront the dead man she thought he'd become after his descent from the Eiger.

'Are you afraid of heights?' he asked Julia when they stopped for a drink and an apple each on an old road that wound towards Innsbruck.

She shook her head. 'I don't know. I'm from Poznań. I've never been anywhere high.'

'Where you're going is high,' he told her. 'You'll know soon enough.'

Julia smiled. There was trust in her face when she looked at him now. It was an expression he had never hoped to see. He had thought her attractive from the first. When she allowed her face to open like this, she was beautiful.

He knew that he would have to leave her once they reached Innsbruck. He needed to calculate the strength of the force sent to bring him back. He was quite certain now that they were being pursued. He had always trusted to his intuition as a soldier. In the past, the pure air that descended from the mountains had usually filled him with a sense of happy exhilaration. Now his skin crawled with foreboding. If they went into the mountains pursued, they were dead. Julia had never climbed, so their progress would be at best a slow and deliberate upward plod. In the mountains they would be isolated, fatally exposed. It was possible that his pursuers had guessed wrongly about his intentions. But his intuition told him otherwise. Either way, he needed to know as much as he could learn before risking their escape over the Alps.

He was loath to leave Julia even for a few minutes once they reached the outskirts of the city. He had promised to save her, and it was a promise he intended to keep. He was aware of her horrible vulnerability, the summary execution she faced should she be identified and caught. The life of their baby beat inside her. He would have to leave them, briefly, both alone. She stood there beside her bicycle with her forged papers in the pocket of her coat and a cloche hat covering her mending scalp. Her wrists were thin extending from her coatsleeves and her small fists bunched, the bicycle leaning by its saddle against her hip. He wondered if this was going to be the last sight he ever had of her.

'Follow the signs for the Crystal Museum. They won't expect us to be looking at the sights.' He handed her a piece of paper with an address written on it. 'This is an inn I used to stay at sometimes. The proprietress is still there. I still get postcards from her from time to time. She's old and half-blind and wouldn't scrutinize your papers too carefully anyway. She's no fonder of the party than I am.' He sat astride his bicycle.

'Martin?'

He paused.

'You have our luck. And our love.'

He took a hand off the handlebars and felt the flask, familiar, over his heart in the pocket of his suit. He nodded to her and pedalled his bike away.

His plan had been to buy a pair of field glasses and climb one of the hills that sloped down to Innsbruck and watch what happened when trains from the north arrived on the station platform. In the event he didn't have to do that. There must have been a fair wait between trains, because he recognized the swollen features of a Westphalian farm boy, Anselm occupying a table under an umbrella outside a coffee house, no more than half a block from the station approach.

Hamer resisted the temptation to apply the brakes, stop dead on the bike and turn it around. The absence of movement when he braked, the unexpected halting of motion might attract a trained eye. And so he pedalled smoothly by as the big Gestapo man wrestled his lips around bread and bratwurst, his heart thudding, the blood thick now in his brain, his progress along the street on the bike impossibly serene.

He stowed the bike in a side street and found a bar with separate entrance and exit doors through the windows of which he could observe the Gestapo man. He was approached by a waitress and ordered a beer.

'Is there a public telephone in here?'

She scowled and gestured with a nod of her head. She had never seen him before, of course. Public telephones were a frowned upon tool. He dialled the number and fed change into the coin box. He heard the connection take and start to ring. The twins would be at school. Heidi might be at home.

'Hello?'

He hardly recognized her voice.

'Hello? Who's there?'

She sounded terrified.

Hamer closed his eyes. 'My name is Arthur Boscombe,' he said.

There was a silence. He fed more coins into the slot that ate them. Remember, Heidi, he pleaded in his mind.

'You must be the man who's been sending the letters,' Heidi said. 'You should know that I've burned them all. I would not bother a man so busy as my husband with such filth. It's a lie to suggest that my husband brings violence into our home. It's a vile suggestion. Vile, vile, vile.' A sob caught in her throat. She hung up.

Hamer replaced the receiver. 'God help you, Heidi,' he said. Violence, he thought. Violence delivered to their home.

* * *

The farm boy drank steadily until darkness fell, but his superior did not join him. Hamer thought this odd. He knew that Jacob Hessler liked to drink. When Anselm left the café near the station it was to tour a series of bars. Whatever alertness the Gestapo man possessed diminished visibly with each drink. Hamer followed his beery progress back to a hotel at which he assumed they must be staying. It was not difficult to follow him up the stairs as he fumbled with the key to his room.

Hamer patted Anselm on the shoulder and he turned around and Hamer softened his knees and drove a left hook-cum-uppercut into his lower ribcage that snapped bone audibly and sank the farm boy with a sad groan into the chair behind him.

'Where is he, Anselm?'

The Gestapo man coughed. Blood bubbled and pinked his chin. The force of Hamer's punch had sent two of his ribs into his spleen with piercing force. Hamer resisted, for the moment, the temptation to punish Hessler's willing acolyte any further than he had. He needed information, had to wait until the farm boy had regained sufficient breath to deliver it.

'I'm a dead man, aren't I?'

'Either way,' Hamer said.

'We've been here for two days,' Anselm said. 'Jacob now thinks you may have slipped the searching of the trains. He has another lead, a place you and your dead wife used to stay. He went there tonight.'

'Did he?'

Anselm breathed and leaked blood.

'Mountain troops?'

'Just us.'

Hamer had been crouching at the level at which Anselm sat. It was how he had been taught to question prisoners in the field. You descended to their eye level, the theory ran, and they saw you less as an enemy. They saw you instead simply as a man doing the same job as they were who had been more successful at it eventually than them.

Now he stood. He heard a glassy crack. The Gestapo man's tongue unfurled, fat as an earthworm, from his mouth and rolled, green, while his eyes widened and a gassy sound escaped him. His teeth clamped down on his tongue, biting the large part that protruded of it off. This leathery offering landed in his lap. But he was dead by then, his cyanide pill having fulfilled its basic task.

Hamer didn't wait to witness any of this. He was on his way to the inn he had recommended as a refuge for Julia and at which he now knew she was held by Jacob Hessler.

* * *

Julia did as Martin had instructed and went to the Crystal Museum. She thought Innsbruck beautiful and the upward slope of the Alps behind the city staggering. She had seen mountains only in books and in films, where they were largely clumsy paste constructions or painted backdrops tame with picturesque detail. To her eyes, the brilliant white enormity of the peaks defied perspective. The very notion that Martin had climbed these things filled her with a sort of incredulous dread. They were dreadful things, the mountains, monuments to the callous, impassive authority of the earth over men. She knew that she could never climb to the summit of one of these colossal, inhuman monuments. She was a strong woman. She believed herself to be resourceful and sometimes even brave. But the sight of the impossible peaks between Julia Smollen and freedom brought her a clumsy kind of fear.

She would fall. Her nerve would fail her and she would fall, flail into the abysmal depths of some crevasse, as Martin watched and the look on his face was transformed from disappointment into dismay.

The exhibits in the Crystal Museum were impressive in their cold and brilliant way. She felt they were the outcome of a cold and brilliant culture. She had been too poor to travel beyond the borders of Poland in her pre-war life. The inclination for travel had not been bred in her. Peasants stayed on the land with the stubborn wish of owning one day what they tilled and cultivated. Her intelligence had got her to the university in Warsaw. She had read novels written in Paris and Spain by the voguish American and English expatriates. She had read Conrad, the Polish mariner who wrote stories in English set in London and the Belgian Congo. But she had never travelled really except in her imagination. And she would never have thought of Germany, Poland's bristling, fractious neighbour as a destination to enjoy. But she now knew Germany to be more beautiful than Poland. She now knew Austria to be more beautiful still than Germany was. She had journeyed here with the German Martin Hamer unable to understand why the Germans had hankered for their living room in the east when they occupied land like this by right.

She looked at the glass, cut and glittering in its display cases. Every exhibit was a small monument to craft and precision. If actuaries made art, she thought, this is the art they would make. This is the art of infinite precision. This is the logical art of a people who have tried to eliminate chance from nature. Julia looked at the cold and brittle pieces boasted by the Crystal Museum of Innsbruck. She looked at the shards of brightness gleaming acutely from bowls and bowers and vases and goblets refracting increments of chiselled light. And she shivered and she wished as she did so for the warmth of Martin Hamer's safe embrace.

* * *

Hamer found Hessler in the cellar of the inn. He was seated and lit from his rear by an oil lamp and held his Luger pistol trained on Hamer in his hand. There had been no time for fieldcraft, no gainful point in it. Hessler's position had been unassailable. All that Hamer felt he had was the remote hope that Julia still lived and his prayer that his surrender could save her life. It was thin stuff. It was the gruel of hopeless optimism. It was all he now possessed.

'Is she dead?'

'You found me down here quickly. I heard you come through the door. Why did you come down here first?'

'Is she dead?'

'Answer the question.'

'You wear a tonic on your scalp. You wore it when we met at the Friedrichstrasse gym. Bay rum, I think. I followed its odour.'

Hessler chuckled. 'She's alive. I've had to punch and slap her a couple of times. She's spirited, your whore. I've cut one of her ear lobes off, only to concentrate her attention with pain.

I'll finish her when I take her your head as a trophy.'

Hamer disciplined himself not to rush at the madman. He needed Julia and his child to live. He had to think of that. It seemed now an accomplishment beyond him.

'Take out your pistol, Hamer, and kick it across the floor towards me.'

Hamer did as he was bid.

'Your fighting knife?'

He took the weapon from its scabbard buckled to his calf. He was finished. His nascent family was destroyed. He kicked his knife towards Hessler across the cellar floor.

'Now,' Hessler said. He gathered Hamer's weapons and opened a drawer in a bureau against one wall. It was only then that Hamer realized that the cellar had been a working space, a study perhaps. It was this no longer. All its furniture had been backed by Hessler against its walls in the search for space in which to fight. Hessler locked the bureau on Hamer's weaponry and his own and put its small key into a pocket.

'Hand to hand,' the madman said, turning to face his adversary. 'Man to man.'

The light in the cellar was poor. But it was adequate. Hamer had fought in worse. He didn't wonder if his opponent had too. He was thinking of Julia, punched and bound and mutilated in a place of apparent safety he had sent her to.

Hessler had closed the distance between them and now he kicked Martin Hamer hard. The kick landed above his left hip and its weight and pain concentrated his mind as it reduced the movement of which he was subsequently capable. If he didn't focus his thinking, Hessler would disable and happily kill him.

Hessler threw a follow-up punch. It was a confident shot based on the success of the preceding kick and he committed his weight to the blow. It was a right hand. Hamer stepped outside it and broke Hessler's nose with a head butt as his opponent followed through.

Hessler recoiled. He sniffed blood and cartilage and gathered himself. He looked at Hamer curiously. He feinted with a left jab and then committed the whole of his weight to a left hook aimed at his opponent's jaw. Hamer blocked the punch with his right, stepped inside it and smashed Hessler's cheekbone with another heavy collision from his head. There'd been pain from his nose on Hessler's face after the first conceded blow. Now there was something else. Hessler was in a place he'd never explored before. He was lost in the landscape of fear. He threw a short right, which Hamer blocked with his palm, curling his fingers around his opponent's fist and twisting it so that the tendons cracked and ground and then the bones snapped in Hessler's wrist.

'You're going to hell,' Hamer whispered into Hessler's ear. 'I'm taking you there.'

Jacob Hessler was an expert at close-quarters combat. He had studied French foot-fighting. He was accomplished at Chinese boxing. He was formidable on the wrestling and the judo mat. He had learned the dark arts of the killing school run at Lübeck by the SS. He had war stories from the gymnasium and certificates framed on his office wall.

In an Innsbruck cellar, Martin Hamer broke and gutted him.

* * *

Landau saw them first in the mirror as he shaved in his room in the lodge above Landeck the Gestapo man had put him in. They were a small black shape ascending steadily through the blank whiteness of snow on the mountain through the window behind his head.

He recognized the strength of the man. He knew the steady strength of him as Hamer carried his human burden up the mountain on his back. He was carrying his whore.

Jesus, Landau thought, he's strong, before wiping soap and shaved bristles from his face and going to fetch the telescopic sight to attach to his rifle.

Landau was fastidious about his art. He had no interest in killing the Polish woman. He felt he owed Hamer a death for the insult to his manhood inflicted in the forest and for the way his skills had been abused in providing a sideshow to allow the woman to escape. But he set himself the highest standards as a marksman. If the Gestapo man arrived now, he would be obliged to do as he was told. Left to himself, he would take one shot at Martin Hamer. One clean shot at the target was all he asked of himself. He fetched his box of hand-fashioned bullets and tipped them carefully on to a tabletop to select his projectile of choice.

* * *

Hamer climbed. She was light on his back, her breath warm and welcome on his neck, her weight the proof that they were together, her bump pressed against his spine the happy blossoming of their child. The snow was heavy and soft under the spring sun. She'd had no technique for walking upwards in it and so he carried her on his back. He'd carried heavier burdens. He'd never carried one so welcome. It was quicker this way.

There was no great urgency now. The Gestapo men were dead and he had believed the farm boy's dying promise. There were no mountain troops on their way, dispatched to hunt them down and kill them with freedom so tantalizingly close. The life would not be bled out of them in the snow. They would live. His child would be born and he would have a chance to be a good father to his daughter or his son. It was more than he could have prayed for. It was a greater fulfilment for him than the world had ever promised. He would do the best he could to be deserving of it.

He climbed. It was not climbing really, not technical climbing, not as tricky as he knew their descent would be. That would be when he would need his strength and balance, on their descent. Most men who died on mountains died in the descending. You could lose your concentration, gain momentum and slip and fall. Your careless, heavy feet could trigger an avalanche to consume you. In a few minutes they would achieve the high pass and be on their way down into Switzerland. He breathed mountain air and listened to the silence and felt the breath of Julia Smollen caressing his neck.

* * *

He'd found her in a small room under the eaves at the inn. Somehow he had known that she would be there, bound and bloody on the bed in which he had first made love to Lillian, his dead wife. Blood congealed on her ear at the edge of the wound where her lobe had been. Hessler had tied her cruelly, and her fingers and feet were blue with the gleeful tension of his knots.

'The Gestapo man?'

'Dead,' he told her, trying to knead life back into her hands and toes.

'He told me he'd come back with a trophy for me,' Julia said. 'He told me he'd come back to me with your head.'

'He was being optimistic,' Hamer said.

'How did he die?'

'Badly,' Hamer said.

Julia was silent. 'I don't know where your people get the cruelty.'

'Shush,' Hamer said. His mind, against his conscious wishes, had pictured two small children, eating toffee-apples, seated on a wooden bench during a Sunday visit to a zoo.

* * *

Landau watched them through the cross hairs of his rifle sight. It was odd, watching them. They were wearing the wrong clothes for the mountains. They looked like a pair of refugees progressing through the snow. You could tell that Hamer knew what he was doing, though. His pace was steady and his movement confident, fluent, without pause. Another hundred feet and they would achieve the pass and descend from sight.

'Put her down,' Landau said, out loud. 'Put her down just for a moment. Please.'

He had climbed a tree at the bottom of the slope. The angle would be acute and he would have to remember to aim to hit Hamer low. The bullet would have an acute-angle trajectory through the man's body. It would be necessary to take him low to do real damage. Landau feared him greatly. He would stay in concealment, risk going no closer and flee after his one shot. A gust of wind awoke the foliage in his tree and freshened the skin of his face, still raw from his recent shave. It was a beautiful day in the mountains.

'Put her down,' Landau said, pleaded.

* * *

'You'll have to put me down, Martin,' Julia Smollen said. 'It's the altitude, or the baby, but I feel dizzy with it. Put me down, just for a moment, please.'

The bullet took Martin Hamer under the right shoulder blade and came out of him above his collarbone. He knew it was bad because there was no pain. He missed a breath and knew that the wound had damaged one of his lungs. Julia screamed, and the sound echoed, tormented, around the valleys and peaks. He picked her up in his arms and shushed and consoled and carried her. He had always been strong. He had carried his father once, like this, in his arms. He had always been possessed of strength and fortitude. Now he carried Julia Smollen and their baby, whom he loved. He could feel himself bleeding inside. The two holes in him made by the bullet bled, and there was blood in his mouth. Julia Smollen shuddered in his arms. She was weeping. But he was strong, had always been strong. He would get her over the mountain.

At the times of greatest crisis in the life of Martin Hamer, his father had come to him and offered him kindness and hope. He had been the beneficiary of much kindness in his life, he believed. He'd had good friends in Heidi and Bill. He'd known brave comrades in men like Otto Fromm and Ludwig Kurtz. He'd seen Hansel and Gretel sparkle and grow in the precious, early part of their journey through life. He had loved his poor wife, Lillian. He had come to love Julia Smollen, whose child he had fathered. He didn't need his father now, in his time of greatest crisis, as the life leaked out of him and Julia grew heavy for the first time in his arms. He was a father himself, after all. He was a man of thirty-four. He knew what he needed to do.

It was a difficult descent. She had been a burden far better balanced on his back. But he had the dim instinct that something would rupture and flood in him if he tried now to shift again her weight. He would falter in the soft spring snow and fail her in a fall that would probably kill them both if he shifted her now. So he pressed on, the strength seeming to seep from him even as the air thickened to nourish his one good lung, his strength the price apparently paid in increments for each slithering step on the downward slope to freedom.

In his mind, toy screws churned a tin boat across a Scottish loch, trailed by a dark procession of midges. The loch was black with peat, and bottomless. Coke embers burned in the tiny boiler of the craft. A piped lament loured across the water and drowned the chugging beat of the little engine powering the toy. The tin boat was going nowhere. It described the diminishing, circular path of a rudder set hard to port. A child must have plotted this pointless voyage with a twist of vindictive fingers. Smudges of smoke rose from the funnels of the boat and dissipated in the thick trail of tiny insects following it. The music of the pipes became discordant, wailed with dissonance, empty and shrill. The air above the black water thrilled with foreboding as its music described chaos and loss. The small boat listed, shipping water on its futile course.

It had been Landau's bullet. It was a conceit to think so, but Hamer knew it to be the truth.

Another marksman would have pursued and killed them both. Landau, though, was a proud and fastidious coward capable of damage only under the guarantee of his own remoteness from danger. But he could shoot, could Landau. With a hand-fashioned bullet in the breech of his rifle, a fatal economy characterized the little sniper.

Martin Hamer stumbled on a rock and almost slipped, then. Julia Smollen heaved in his arms, and he was aware of the recumbent, deadly weight of her. He carried her. She carried their child. He looked down, a weakness that, when climbing for challenge and achievement, he had long disciplined himself never to indulge. But that had been before, hadn't it? That had been one of the tenets of his former life, the life he had now so completely rejected. In the abandonment of duty, he would have to discover who he was. He still carried his father's hip flask, his medal, his recovered pistol; the obdurate proofs of the life he was leaving. Had his hands been free to do so, he would have buried these artefacts, burrowed a tomb for them with his fingers in the high Alpine snow without regret. He was happy at the leaving of his life.

The snow was softening as the day matured and their descent warmed through the lessening altitude. The risk now was more of avalanche than of a perilous fall. Blood bubbled on his lips and dripped from his nose, and Martin Hamer felt betrayal shudder through the strength of his arms.

'You're bleeding so much,' Julia said to him. 'Oh, God. God help you, Martin. You're bleeding so badly.' She held tight on to him, as if to stanch the wound. He could feel a tremble through her.

'I can manage,' he told her. He was confident that he could.

He heard the wail of the pipes again. He smelled sweet heather and the air grew grainy and soft. Dusk was on the Scottish loch. Brightness burned in the toy portholes of the boat. They were pinpricks of light extinguishing one by one as the craft canted further and water lapped at the port rail of its deck. His legs were numb, he realized. The water was cold. He trailed his bare feet in the water, watching seated at the end of the hotel jetty as the little steamer wound and diminished through its final voyage. He had the hotel guest book open on his lap. The name of Arthur Boscombe had been written there in perfect copperplate, legible still in the half-remembered light of the last of the day. When he looked up from the page, he could no longer see the boat on the loch. The surface of the water was unruffled and serene. It must have just sunk, must still be sinking, he thought. He could imagine it sinking for ever through a peaty vastness.

'Concentrate,' Julia Smollen whispered urgently into his ear. The accent of her speech, the growingly familiar pitch of her voice, the press of her fingers on his shoulders, on the top of his arms, the scent of her breath and flesh, sank suddenly into what remained of Martin Hamer's strength and consciousness with the depth of impossible loss. My child, he thought, believed, skidding with forgotten skill and strength towards freedom. My child, my love. He coughed and began to drown then in his wound.

Blood broke out of him. His mind could not sustain thought. Blackness daubed a dogged path towards him. But he carried on. He was strong, after all. He had always been strong.

They were beyond the snowfield, had gained the Swiss meadow at the bottom of the mountain before he put Julia gently on her feet amid the grass and flowers, amid the warm scents of spring.

'You didn't need to carry me this far.'

'I wanted to. I won't carry you again.'

His legs buckled under him then, and he fell, found himself sitting on the ground in the sunshine. The strength and grace that had always possessed Martin Hamer had abandoned him now.

'I'm dying,' he said, surprised.

Julia Smollen knew. She stood in front of him with her hand over her mouth and her shoulders shuddered with grief.

He smiled at her. 'Don't cry,' he said.

'Don't go,' she said. 'Please, please, don't go, Martin.'

He reached out his hand, which was bloody. She unfastened her coat and dropped it on to the grass. She unbuttoned the cardigan she wore and lifted the singlet worn underneath it. She took his hand and pressed it to her belly.

'I'm finished, Julia,' he said.

She looked at the sky, as though pleading with its vacant enormity. She wiped her eyes with the back of her hand and bit her hand and sniffed. She looked at him and the look was fierce with pride.

'I will tell our child about you,' she said. 'Our child would have loved you, as I do. You are a father any child of yours would love. Would be proud of.'

Martin Hamer smiled up at Julia Smollen. He closed his eyes in the meadow and died.

* * *

The house had been built high on the beach, and sand sloped almost as white as snow crystals, but warm under the sun, to the edge of the sea. Tiny particles of sand were smooth and warm under their bare feet. They sat next to one another in wood and canvas beach chairs facing the water. Waves boomed in an insistent, soothing rhythm. A girl flickered in and out of heat ripple at the margin of land and sea. The girl had her hair tied in a ponytail that dripped when the view of her clarified with an ochre richness and weight in the afternoon light.

'She swims well.'

'She does everything well.'

They watched the girl gaining her breath, after her swim, at the limit of water and land. The man reached and took the woman's hand in his and squeezed. From behind his sunglasses, he smiled.

'Happy?'

'Most of the time.'

But the words sounded hollow and counterfeit

to her own ears, let alone his, in the wide perfection of the day. It's well named, Julia Smollen thought, the Pacific Ocean. The unsullied vastness of its warmth and colour were inviting, even seductive. But it was a wilderness, a waste beyond this manicured beach, of storms and toiling depths.

'I had dinner with Max Schmeling the other night,' Bill said. 'You've heard of Schmeling?'

Julia's eyes were on the edge of the water, watching the reaching limbs of the figure there as her daughter stooped and gathered, collecting shells. 'A boxer, wasn't he?' Her Polish lover had been a boxing fan. He'd owned a signed photograph of Jack Dempsey, the American Pole given an Irish name. The picture had hung in his bedroom, Dempsey's fraudulent signature faded to bronze on the lower edge of the print.

'German heavyweight champion, Schmeling,' Bill said. 'Knocked out Joe Louis in '36 at Madison Square Garden. Served as a paratrooper during the war. Dropped into Crete, fought the Brits in Greece, fought in Yugoslavia. Has the German franchise for Coca-Cola now.'

'Sounds like a colourful life. And a profitable one.' Julia watched her daughter untie her hair and shake it out in a heavy fan across her back and shoulders.

'Schmeling was very badly beaten in his rematch with Joe Louis,' Bill said. 'Four of his ribs and two of his spinal discs were broken. Louis hasn't prospered in retirement the way his old adversary has. But when Joe Louis needed hospital treatment recently, it was Max Schmeling who paid the medical bills.'

'So,' Julia said, 'he's discovered a conscience.' Her daughter bent and brushed sand from her knees and shins and then rose to her full height with the sun behind her. Her hair, drying, gathered life and lifted in the wind, and Julia Smollen's heart lurched with untethered love.

'I asked him, Julia,' Bill said. 'I had one martini too many and confronted the guy.'

'You drink too much, Bill,' she said. 'You have ever since the divorce.' But what he was saying was being said for her benefit. Bill was a man with a good heart. She would play along, as they were fond of saying in this country. 'And what did Schmeling say?'

'That he never shot at a man who wasn't armed. That he was a soldier. That the crimes his country committed were committed in secrecy. That he fought honourably. And that he's sorry, as all good Germans are.'

Julia laughed. 'Is there any such thing as a good German?'

Bill shifted in his chair. 'I believe so. I believe I met one, once.'

Julia did not need a parable about Max Schmeling to make her aware of the paradoxes of recent history. She knew that Martin Hamer had fought without mercy against the Russians, an enemy America now engaged in a war of ideology and atomic stockpiles that could yet claim the world. In what the newspapers called the space race, the German rocket engineers abducted by Russia competed against those snatched by America to send men into orbit for the glory of their pragmatic new homelands. The Americanized rocket genius was Wernher von Braun. Developing for Hitler the V-2 missile to devastate London, he had strolled daily past the heaped corpses of spent slave labourers with all the compunction of a man passing piles of machine-shop spoil. Now, von Braun was lionized by his enthusiastic new sponsors at Cape Canaveral.

There was talk in America of John Kennedy, the young senator from Massachusetts, running for the presidency. His father Joseph had been the American ambassador to Britain whose support for Germany had only lost its vocal enthusiasm with the bombing of Pearl Harbor. Joseph's senator son had become a hero in the war. The ambassador's eldest son had lost his life on an Allied bombing mission.

Much was made of Jack Kennedy's Irish roots. Julia was a Pole, familiar with the underdog affinity her people shared for the abused small nations of the world. She remembered how she had felt reading of the congratulatory telegram sent by Irish President Eamon de Valera to Adolph Hitler on his assumption of power. She knew that German U-boats had shipped rifles and machine guns during the war to a grateful Irish Republican Army.

The camp from which Julia had escaped resembled most closely what the free world now knew of as a Gulag. Her Polish lover had been fatally inspired by the example of the Free French. Many of the heroes of the French

Resistance, men and woman who had opposed Nazism with appalling courage, were now the most articulate and influential apologists for the excesses of Stalinism. Her own country existed only under Russian subjugation. The world moved on and it didn't. Julia did not need to hear the story of Max Schmeling, the saintly paratrooper and purveyor of carbonated drinks, to make her aware of that fact.

'Do you think of him?'

Bill had on his sunglasses. She could not see his eyes through the darkness and reflection of their lenses. He coughed. 'Often. You?'

'Every waking day,' Julia said. She looked at Bill. He nodded. But he still had on his sunglasses. She wished he would take them off.

'He was the best man I ever met,' Bill said. 'And he fought for the most ignoble cause.'

'How could I not think of him?' Julia said. She nodded towards her daughter, distant, caught in a reverie of light and spray at the edge of the sea. 'Every time she looks at me. Every time she holds me. Christ, she even smells of him.'

Bill said nothing. He looked kind and serious, which she knew him to be.

'You loved him, didn't you?'

'Love is for the living, kid,' Bill said. He took off his sunglasses and blinked against the bright glare of afternoon light. He gestured towards the girl approaching them, now, her toes trailing through hot sand and her hair pendulous behind her neck with the salt weight of the sea. 'I love her. I love my goddaughter.'

'You spoil her.'

'I try my best,' Bill said seriously. He reached for Julia's hand again and pressed it into his. 'You have to try. You don't try, kid, you don't fail.'

THE END

Other titles published by The House of Ulverscroft:

THOSE IN PERIL

Margaret Mayhew

In 1940, free-living artist Louis Duval decides to leave his studio in Brittany and, in his small motor boat, make the perilous journey to England. His aim is to offer his services in the continuing fight, and to help liberate his beloved France from the enemy. He reaches Dartmouth, where he finds lodgings with a young widow, Barbara Hillyard. Lieutenant Commander Alan Powell of the Royal Navy has been assigned the task of forming an undercover organisation to make clandestine boat trips across the channel to gather vital information. He enlists Louis Duval, who agrees to return to France to establish a Resistance network there. Alan falls deeply in love with Barbara, but she seems to have eyes only for the attractive Frenchman . . .

THE HOTEL RIVIERA

Elizabeth Adler

'Imagine a sunny, sea-lapped cove, gift wrapped in blue and tied with a bow like a Tiffany box, and you'll get the feel of my little hotel. It's a place made for Romance with a capital R. Except for me, its creator.' Lola Laforet doesn't have time for love. Her disreputable husband has disappeared, the police consider her a prime suspect and her beautiful home and business seems to belong to an ex-arms dealer. Lola doesn't go looking for danger, it just seems to walk through the door. And when it walks through the door in the form of the delectable Jack Farrar she knows she's in real trouble.